The Flies Of August

by P. J. Lee

First published: February 2013
This edition May 2013
Print edition ISBN: 978-0-9894588-0-1

The Flies of August is a work of fiction. Characters, places, organizations and incidents are the products of the writer's imagination and any resemblance to real persons, living or dead, is entirely coincidental. Real names or locales used in the book are used fictitiously.

Saltwater Publishing is registered in North Carolina.
Contact: publisher@saltwaterpublishing.com

The Flies of August

Miller

He likes to be first out in the morning while the day is still pristine. Bella lopes ahead down the bank to the tall trees near the playground. She's a Weimaraner, gray ghost of a hunting dog, nose to the scent trail at a fast trot, freezing if she sees squirrels on the ground. Miller never tires of watching her patient stalking approach to the squirrels—head, body and tail making a perfect horizontal line. The soft sides of her mouth billow slightly as she blows air across her tongue to taste it.

They cut across the springy surface of the kids' playground near the school buildings to the third field. At the furthest perimeter is a dense barrier of trees, shrubbery and shabby fencing that separates the public grounds from surrounding housing. In the summer months teenagers use the grounds after dark, producing a jetsam of shot-gunned Keystone beer cans, smoking paraphernalia, condom wrappers, even female underwear misplaced in haste.

Other dog walkers arrive soon after, but Miller and Bella are always the earliest in the morning. First to press a boot onto the tender ice forming on the puddles under the trees when November's winds freeze them, first footprints in a fresh overnight snowfall, first to see the spring sunrise streaked with jet-trails out.

Starting each day in Bella's world is one of the survival techniques he has developed, small schemes to get through the days. He has learned to be functional—to continue to eat and work and

1

pay his bills. But there's no hiding. He can be anywhere—walking here at the park, or sliding his credit card at the supermarket till, or lost in a television program, and suddenly everything in his world will be abruptly displaced by the vivid, recurring images in his memory. He thought they would fade, but they haven't. The stillness of her body on the ground. The brief, small sound, like her last breath passing through her lips, which he now thinks of as the moment her soul left her body, even though he has no religion. Because after that moment there seems to be a loss of tension in her body that conveys to him the absence of life. Rationally, he knows it couldn't have been that way, but that's what he remembers. That's what he carries with him.

DAY ONE

Tuesday. 8 a.m.

A senior law enforcement officer should not color his hair. That should be a rule. It undermines the whole command structure. My opinion. But the chief of the Webster Police Department is big on appearances and leadership buzzwords and public relations. I'm looking at his desk and it is clean of anything that looks like police work. This is my first time ever in his office, and it's just me, the Chief, and Captain Donald, head of detectives. That means something's up.

"Donna, you know about this missing teenager?" asks Captain Donald. He's a lean man with hooded eyes and a permanently skeptical expression. I always feel like anything he asks me is going to be a trick question.

"Yes, sir. I saw it on the car computer coming in."

"You're going to take a look at it."

"Yes, sir."

The chief is looking on with a benign, chiefly smile on that scrubbed schoolboy complexion that makes him look younger than he is. He remains seated behind his desk, possibly because he knows I'm taller than he is.

"Get over and talk to the parents right away," Captain Donald continues. "Let's be seen as proactive."

"Yes, sir."

"I've teamed you with di Giorgio. He's got more years than you but he's still on probation in this department, so you're the lead."

I can't go on saying "yes, sir," so I just nod.

"Donna," the chief chimes in, "extra credit if it's all sorted out without the media ever hearing about it." He smiles at me. "Under the circumstances."

The whole thing might be taking place in a high school principal's office. I give him the smile he requires and I'm out of there.

My first time in charge of a case. It's true that I have been waiting too long for this. It's also true that I am the only female detective in the department. I couldn't go to a jury with proof these two facts are connected, but I'm not looking for other suspects. Call me cynical, but I know I've only caught this case because the chief needs everyone he trusts to be working on the other case—the one that has become the most public murder case here in twenty years.

Until last week, Webster, Connecticut, was a little sanctuary, a regular on those internet charts of the best towns to live in America. That's Noah Webster of the Webster's dictionary everyone used in school—distinguished early resident of these parts.

Saturday afternoon last week, a Webster taxpayer was killed in his own back yard. Not just any taxpayer. Nathan Weisz was chairman and CEO of ConCare, one of the largest medical insurance companies in the United States. An extremely wealthy man and, by all accounts, a model citizen. Three hundred people attended his funeral and the *Hartford Courant* devoted a memorial page to his many charitable activities.

That alone is enough to make it big. But the wildfire of curiosity and speculation was lit when we declined to give details about how he died. In my view that was a blunder—there is nothing like an evasive press conference for making things worse than they seem—but I can understand why the chief made that call. Mr. Weisz was in the landscaped garden of his McMansion on this hot afternoon, clearing the crabgrass from around his rhododendrons. He was using one of those tools designed for senior gardeners with back problems, with a long handle so you don't have to bend down; four angled steel spikes in a circle at the end, and something like bicycle handlebars at the top. You rotate the handlebars and the spikes at the bottom turn in a circle and rip up weeds and roots. You can really get some torque into that rotation with your shoulders. The killer was able to remove most of Nathan Weisz's small bowel with a couple of twists. In the opinion of the Chief Medical Officer, Mr. Weisz was alive when this happened.

The Webster Police Department was mobilized like never before, but so far we do not have an arrest. Every morning, the tension in the department is pitched a little higher. Out-of-state media are sniffing around. It can't be long before the murmurs start that the Webster PD isn't up to this one. It's not that we're short of resources. On the contrary, you dial 911 in Webster for a robbery in progress, you'll get four squad cars in six minutes. When it comes to pouncing on skateboarders and joyriders, Webster PD has no equal. But this is a soft town of middle-class obedience with a thick topping of well-paid executives, families who don't need loans for college, divorced spouses living comfortably on alimony, retirees who planned well. Lawn care is probably bigger business than law enforcement in Webster. We get maybe ten suspicious deaths a year and those are mostly alcohol-related and domestics in the southeast fringes of the town.

Suspect number one for the murder of citizen Weisz is an undocumented named Jorge, no known last name, mid-20s, who was working for the landscaping service that regularly tended the

Weisz property. A week prior, Jorge was blowing off the deck around the pool when Weisz's fourteen-year-old daughter Abby stepped out of the French doors in a bikini. That evening, Mr. Weisz phoned Luis Hernandez, owner of the landscaping firm, and told him that his contract was terminated because Jorge had made indecent propositions to Abby. Which is how come Mr. Weisz was obliged to be rooting out his own crabgrass on a Saturday afternoon. Hernandez told the detectives that he had fired Jorge immediately after receiving Weisz's call. He had no records for Jorge, not even an address. Hernandez had found Jorge outside the bus station, where casual laborers meet casual employers. Hernandez himself proved to have an air-tight alibi, a green card, a current mortgage on a well-kept little house and a cooperative demeanor which survived a five-hour interrogation.

Jorge as the doer is such a neat outcome for the department and the town that he has basically been tried and found guilty in absentia, all we have to do is find the bastard. It's so thick-headed.

First off, I don't like that our entire theory of the case hinges on the testimony of the fourteen-year-old daughter and I'm furious that they didn't give me the job of interviewing her. I'm the female detective, right? I could have got inside her head. But in their wisdom they sent Ralph Generis and Sam "Beanbag" Paterniakis. The former is a competent investigator but no Sigmund Freud, and the latter got his nickname from twice using a beanbag round to bring down citizens he deemed to be a threat to themselves or others. Making him detective was a public safety measure. These two guys came away from interviewing the daughter repeating exactly what she had originally told her father. Lovely girl, they said. So we believe that a young man struggles his way illegally from Mexico to Connecticut, gets a job in the middle of a recession, and then throws it all away by offering to rub suntan

6

lotion on a fourteen-year-old? I don't think so.

On the way to find Tony di Giorgio I stop at the ladies' room, at the same time reprimanding myself for doing so. It's a professional relationship, how I look shouldn't have anything to do with it. Anyway, what's there in the mirror is what's always there: a five-foot-ten woman with strong shoulders and a nose that polite people call generous. Auburn hair cropped short and, in the summer, too many freckles. Drunks have told me my breasts are my best asset. Some of them have slept in the holding cell overnight as a consequence. I run my hands through my hair. This is not going to be easy. I've had nothing to do with Tony before, he only moved here last year from Kentucky. He's at least ten years older than I am and an experienced homicide detective. In business, you can move from company to company and your resume proves that you can do the job here that you did there. But police departments don't work like that. In a new place, you have to prove yourself all over again. So, despite his record, Tony started here driving a patrol car with a field trainer. He was a uniform on the street through last winter. He sucked it up, never complained, good for him. Now, I'm supposed to buy that he's just coincidentally being elevated to detective? Suddenly? I don't think so. He's on the case to baby-sit me. I can see it, and everyone else in the department will see it.

"Hey, Tony," I say when I find him in the squad room, "Captain's teamed us." Notice how I avoid implying my seniority; if I could work out why I do things like that, I could take a step forward in my life.

He stands up and extends his hand. "I'm looking forward to working with you." His voice and his eyes are soft and un-coplike. No taller than me. Wiry, like a long-distance runner. Prominent veins snaking across the back of his very tan hands.

I'm flustered as to how to start out with him, so I duck it.

"Let's begin by talking to the officer who took the report last night."

Patrolman Ronnie Perez is not happy about having to wait for us since shift change.

"The guy comes in at one-thirty," he says. "I thought he was a drunk at first. Very agitated."

He shows us a copy of the report he took. "He is Stanislaw Zajac. His daughter is Amber Zajac. Sixteen. She walked out of their house on Wilton Lane at around seven p.m. Not answering her cell phone. She doesn't have a car or a bicycle, she must have walked or been picked up. That's all he had."

"Did they have a fight, anything like that?" I ask.

"I asked him that, he started to shout at me, so I took that as a yes. Genius didn't even have a photo of her."

"Friends' phone numbers, that sort of stuff?" asks Tony.

"All he brought was an attitude. I told him someone would come see him in the morning. My opinion? They had a fight, she's gone to stay with a buddy, she'll be back today when she thinks she's scared them enough. If that was my old man, I'd be out of there too. Can I go home to bed now?"

We walk out of the building into the lot behind the station. Mid-nineties and a cloud cover that feels like it's compressing the humid air. Some people handle this weather better than I do. Tony, for example, is wearing a sport coat to cover his weapon and seems completely comfortable. I always go for the golf shirt and lightweight khakis—disposable stuff—you never know what you can end up wading into before the day is over.

"Should I call you Donna?" he asks.

Momentary brain-mouth lapse. "I prefer Bradley with my co-workers. It eliminates the inferior female connotation..." Listen to me babbling. I should have thought about this beforehand, now I'm stuck here, fussing with my shield on my belt.

"Bradley's good," he says. "You want me to drive?" Holding out his hands for the keys.

"You uncomfortable with female drivers?"

"Nope. Just that the junior partner usually drives where I was before. Whatever suits you."

I toss him the keys. "Actually I'll probably scare you. I follow too close."

"That's normal for a woman." This time he does smile. Which reminds me that the rumor is his wife took a walk. She must have had good reason, because it's a killer smile.

11:30 a.m.

Amber Zajac lives on Wilton Lane on the east side of town, ten blocks from the Hartford line. The houses are all pretty uniform here, on standard plots, mid-price range, nothing special. There's a For Sale By Owner sign outside the Zajacs' house, but it's not going to happen until they jack up the curb appeal. The house is overdue for a paint job and there's a broken gutter. Rainwater from last night's storm has washed dirt and mulch across the driveway where it's now baking to a crust. There's a battered truck with a contractor's lockbox bolted into the back.

As we knock, the door is snatched open by a tall, wiry guy with sharp facial angles and stooped shoulders. Stanislaw Zajac introduces himself as "Stan" and leads us into a gloomy living room. They have the blinds pulled down on the east side of the house to keep out the morning sun, but the A/C unit in the window is not running. The room is pungent with air freshener and whatever odor it's fighting.

"My wife's coming," he says, looking over his shoulder. "Rosemary!" He turns back to me. "Where have you been all morning, it's nearly noon?"

"I understand your distress, Mr. Zajac," I say. "I take it there's been no contact from your daughter since last night?"

"No, of course not. We would have told you."

"She has a cell phone?"

"Yes. It goes straight to voice mail."

"Have you called everyone in the family?"

"Yes—and her friends."

I'm seeing more of Zajac now. He has a long neck and his head is permanently shoved forward by his poor posture. It all gives him a look of a lanky bird looking for stuff to peck at. There's a small smudge of dried blood or something at the corner of his thin mouth. A black dog wiggles into the room, dying to fling itself on us, but Zajac intercepts it and ushers it out; I get a clear image of it returning in the night to furtively pee on the carpet.

Rosemary Zajac comes into the room. She looks older than he does. Her hair is white and she's pale-skinned and thin. No Botox in this Webster wife.

"Are you the ones looking for Amber?" No preliminaries.

"Yes, Mrs. Zajac. I'm Detective Bradley. This is Detective di Giorgio. Last night, after your report, the department issued a BOLO on Amber—"

"Be on the lookout for," Tony chips in.

"—which went to the computer in every car in the department, and on the National Crime Information Computer. That means if any law enforcement agency or hospital logs her, we'll immediately get an alert. We need a recent photo to add to that profile. We often get results from these." Fluent lying is part of victim liaison. "Now we get some more detailed information from you, and on the basis of that we decide how to proceed."

I pull out my notebook.

"You told the officer at the station that she left at seven last night?" Tony asks. They don't answer immediately, which I first think is because Tony speaks so softly, but when I glance up from my notepad I catch them exchanging glances.

"Was there a disagreement or fight with Amber yesterday?" I look directly at the father.

Again there's a hesitation, and now rising color in his cheeks. His wife steps in for him, "She wanted to stay at a friend's house for a few days and we said no."

"Why?" I ask.

"It's not a friend we know."

"I told her we would have to speak to the parents," says the father. "But she said that would embarrass her. So we were worried there would be no adult supervision."

"Some of the kids at that school, their parents have a lot of money and they give their children too much freedom," Mrs. Zajac says.

"What school?" I ask.

"Wycroft. Out in Simsbury."

Really? I can't see these two having cocktails with the typical parents of a thirty grand a year prep school.

"So it was a big argument? Was there shouting or anything like that?"

"How does that matter?" snaps the father. Very reactive individual.

"I'm trying to establish, sir, Amber's state of mind when she left here." I switch my attention to the mother. "Have you got the name of this friend she wanted to stay with?"

She shakes her head. "We never got that far."

"Are you certain Amber didn't take anything that might indicate she expected to be away for a while? Clothes, money, laptop?"

"I assume she took her phone and purse because they're not in her room. I can't see anything missing from her closet. She doesn't have a laptop. She uses the family computer in the study."

"Does she have a credit card, ATM card?"

"Nothing like that."

"Cash?"

"She gets money for waitressing at Hendricksen's, the dairy bar place on Parkside Avenue. Two or three shifts a week usually."

"When was she last there?"

"Saturday night till they closed at eleven."

"Sunday night?"

"She was home," Mr. Zajac answers.

"So, it's possible that she could have just defied you and gone to stay at the friend's house anyway?"

"Yes, it's possible," says the mother.

"Does Amber have any brothers or sisters?"

"An older brother, Kris. He's working in California."

"Any chance she would head out there to him? Did you call him?"

"She would not go to Kris," the father says.

"We saw the For Sale sign outside," says Tony. "Could Amber be upset about that? Moving the family can be stressful."

"I just keep the sign out there in case someone comes with a good price," Mr. Zajac says. "We're not actively marketing it."

The house phone rings and Stan Zajac spins around and snatches it off the wall.

"Hello!"

We all watch him in silence for a moment as he listens. Then he says "no" sharply and whacks the receiver back on the hook.

"Anything about Amber?" I ask.

"No."

I keep looking at him.

"It's not her!"

Tony deploys his quiet voice again, this time on me. "Why

don't you and Mrs. Zajac go and check Amber's room? I'll carry on here." It's standard practice to split up witnesses to prevent them from blending their recollections, but just for a moment I wonder if he's coaching me.

On the way to Amber's room I ask for a glass of water so that we route through more of the house. The kitchen is long overdue for a refresh. The dining room table is covered with papers and bills and a calculator. The house is more than big enough for three, but all the surfaces are cluttered with mail and magazines and knickknacks they regret bringing home but can't toss out. There's no A/C running anywhere and the humidity makes the handrail on the staircase feel sticky and grubby.

Amber's room, by contrast, is too neat.

"Did you tidy this room, Mrs. Zajac? After she left? My room wasn't like this when I was a teenager."

"No. That's how she keeps it."

Bordering on unbelievable.

"Does Amber bring friends up here?"

Shake of the head. "When she was younger, yes. Before Wycroft. Not now. The school is quite a ride from here. She doesn't really bring friends home."

"Does she have a regular hangout?"

She's lapsed into just staring at me, and suddenly I'm taking my first real inventory of her and realizing there may be more than anxiety going on here. She's too thin—gaunt, even. The knuckles on her slim fingers are swollen and the skin on her elbows is dry and flaky. She might even smell a bit off, although the air in this house is so funky I can't tell.

"Mrs. Zajac?"

"I don't know. When she was younger she used to spend a lot of time at the library in Webster center. But everything's changed since she went to high school."

On the wall above Amber's desk is a display board with ribbon crisscrossed on it so you can slip photos and old concert tickets and last year's Valentine's card in there. Just about every female American teenager has something like it.

"Is this Amber?" I'm looking at a snapshot of two kids, around twelve years old, arms entwined, hamming it up for the camera.

"Yes, but that was a few years ago."

"Who's this with her?"

"Catriona, her best friend. They met in elementary school."

"You called her?"

"Of course. She said she hasn't seen Amber for a few weeks."

"Best friends, haven't seen each other in the middle of summer? Where does she live?"

"Half a mile down the road."

She sees I've written Katrina in my notebook and corrects me.

"The Irish spelling. Her father was Irish. He left. Her mother's Hispanic, Riaz. She uses that name now. They're good people."

"Have you got a more recent photo of Amber we can use for the ID kit and posters?"

"Are you going to put posters up around town?"

"It's one method we might use."

She looks unhappy. "That's so ... public."

"I understand, but we might need the public, Mrs. Zajac. May I ask, do you know if your daughter is sexually active?"

She actually blushes. "No, of course not."

"No, you don't know, or no, she isn't?"

"I'm sure she isn't. She's only sixteen."

"That makes her a legally consenting adult. Have you had those sorts of discussions with her? Contraception, safe sex, things like that?"

"We're Catholic. And anyway ... you're here to find her, not to ask about her sex life."

"It's not a moral judgment, Mrs. Zajac. It's just an investigative inquiry."

"I can't see how it's relevant."

"If she's taken that step in the world, it means her boundaries are further out. The radius of things she might have gotten involved in."

"That's nonsense," she snaps and walks out. Three seconds later, she's back, her swollen fingers plucking at the flaky skin on her elbows. "I'm sorry! I'm just scared."

"It's okay, Mrs. Zajac. It's natural for you to defend her."

"Yes, but now I've behaved badly and I know that Stan lost control when he went up to the station last night. He's very stressed—not just about Amber. His business is struggling since the recession. Please don't let this affect what you do."

"It's okay, don't worry."

She sees my eyes on her hands and immediately stops picking at her elbows. "I'll go and get that photo for you."

I close the door behind her and conduct a swift search in all the usual places: under the mattress, under and behind drawers in the desk, under the clothes in her closet, in the pockets of the hoodies on hangers. Absolutely nothing. Teenage girls are like squirrels, there's almost always stuff tucked away somewhere, but either Amber is the exception or she's semi-pro grade. I always carry a pocket camera with me. Other detectives have laughed at me for it, but sometimes I find it hard to remember simple things—was there a phone on the table or not, stuff like that. I take a series of shots of the room with the closet doors open. I shoot the pencil holder on her desk, the colorful cheap jewelry draped over the framed photo of Amber with a group of friends, the Starbucks mug. I shoot the tampons and hair-ties in her bedside drawer. I shoot the wall where the display board is. Then I lift the board off the wall and take it downstairs with me.

In the kitchen, Zajac is shouting at Tony.

"Why? I need it all the time! Everything is on it."

Tony is completely unfazed; his voice stays right in that temperate zone.

"Mr. Zajac, I understand your concern. But the computer is one of our best sources of information on your daughter."

"Can't your person come and look at it here?"

"That's not how we work. But it won't be gone long. She'll take an image of the hard drive and work with that."

"That's worse!" he flaps his long skinny arms. "Then you have a copy of my whole computer forever. How do I know you won't go looking through all our personal files? Come back in half an hour. I will download our passwords and financial records—"

I'm about to step in when his wife does it for me—

"Stan! For God's sake! Let them take whatever they want! They don't care about our personal stuff!"

So we drive away with the computer and the display board of Amber's little keepsakes in the back seat. While Tony drives, I remove a photo of Amber from the cheap frame that her mother handed to me.

"What about that phone call?" I ask.

"Probably a debt collector," he says.

"That would fit. But the father's aggressive all round. It makes me wonder if we should look at him?"

"It can also just be the stress," Tony says. "He may have feelings of guilt, not because he's involved in any way in her disappearance, but just because she's run off. He's distraught about the argument, about not patching it up."

"So the kid's just taken off to stay with the friend, right? She's got her phone off to drive them crazy. She'll be back when she's happy she's tortured them enough."

"Perez was right," he says, "the old man is enough to drive any kid out of the house."

"So we've got time for coffee. Head for the Dunkin' Donuts there." This seems to be a good time to work on the relationship building that the chief talks about in his helpful monthly newsletter.

When he's parked I hand Tony a ten before he can offer to pay. "I'll have a Diet Pepsi. Diet, not regular. Meet you in there."

There's a CVS pharmacy and a Buffalo wings place in the same row of shops. I show the staff Amber's photo. Some of them recognize her as a customer, but no one has a specific recollection from yesterday. I join Tony at the table.

He raises his coffee. "Thanks for this."

He has made a neat pile of my change, bills and coins, along with the receipt on the table. He's very minimalist in his movements, efficient. Good hands. Bony. I've got a thing about fatty hands.

"You realize we've only got this case because they think we're the ones least needed on the murder, right?" I say to him.

"I don't see it like that. I think you're on it because it's a teenage female. You'll be able to empathize. If she really turns out to be missing there'll be tricky interviews about her state of mind and sexual activity. They think you'll have more traction than a guy. You're a good fit for the case."

"Yeah? Then how come they didn't send me to interview Weisz's daughter who fingered the undocumented?"

"Because they couldn't be seen to send a detective who's never had a murder case."

I look him over. "Maybe," I say. "But that doesn't explain you."

"Oh, I'm the one they're keeping away from the big case." He doesn't smile but his eyes crinkle a bit more. And I suddenly realize that this is probably true. Imagine if Webster's biggest case in twenty years was cracked by the new guy from Kentucky?

"Can I ask you something?" he says.

"Go."

"I hear some officers refer to you as the English teacher. What's that about?"

"Christ, is that still going around? When I went to college—U Conn—I had a vague idea of being a teacher. I started a liberal arts degree. Halfway through the second year, my dad said he couldn't help any more and I needed to apply for more loans. I did the math. A loan is fine if you're studying to be an engineer or a Wall Street crook, but it's scary for an English major who doesn't have many money-making options. So I bailed out and went to the police academy. But I stupidly told people about studying English. Next thing they were calling me the English teacher. It was just a way for the tough guys to make me look soft. I speak in complete sentences, so shoot me."

"Do you regret not finishing college?"

"I didn't miss sharing a bathroom with sorority girls painting their lips and adjusting their Victoria's Secret bras. Tell you the truth, I still don't know what you get from a liberal arts degree but I reckon it lacks what anyone can get by spending a day in their local criminal court watching a judge process the plea bargains. Maybe I just wanted to be in a club that would have me."

He stands up, wipes the table surface clean with a napkin and takes it with his coffee cup to the trash.

In the car, "My turn," I say. "What made you come here and go through all the re-training bullshit?"

"Actually, I'm a local. I grew up just the other side of the river in Glastonbury. But I wanted to get away from here after school, ended up in Kentucky. I came back now because of my mom. She has cancer, she needs someone nearby."

"Oh, I'm sorry."

"Thanks. Way it is."

"You married?"

He knows I know.

"Used to be. She met a race horse owner."

Doesn't seem right to say sorry again. I take a look at him while he's driving. He is without a mustache, beard or even stubble, which is pretty rare among cops. He has displayed absolutely no need to impress his peers, which impresses me. Law enforcement officers wear their testosterone on their sleeves and it would have been easy for this guy to be pissed that he was playing second banana to the younger female. But he seems completely cool with it.

"So what do we do, Detective?" I ask, "do we waste department resources mounting a search for this kid, or do we just wait for her to come home tonight with a hangover and a new tattoo?"

"You've got to pull the trigger. You got no choice."

Pulling the trigger means setting in motion as many channels of investigation as possible. Number one is the neighborhood canvass. Patrol reluctantly gives up six officers who are not impressed to be being taken out of their air-conditioned cars to go door to door in the heat. I give them a ten by ten block grid around Amber's house to work with copies of the photograph.

Enlisting our tame techie is number two. I walk into her office with Tony behind me, hefting the Zajac's dusty desktop computer. Cynthia is a plump citizen who looks like she should be busy with baked goods. She is not a police officer but gets a salary from the town of Webster to invade other people's privacy digitally, something at which she is joyously effective.

"Jesus," she says, "Do people still have those things?"

"Family of a missing girl," I say. "Or probably not missing, just being a brat."

"That piece of junk isn't your quickest route. You got a cell number for her?"

"Yep."

She shoves a wad of forms at me.

"I'm sure you know the drill—we fax the application to the cell company's police liaison team. Leave the computer. I'll get my hairy intern onto it. If her passwords are memorized in the browser, I'll get you her email and Facebook. If they're not, you'll have to do an application to Google and Microsoft, just like you do for cell phone records, but they're not as responsive."

"Couldn't you get in without the formal requests?" asks Tony.

She gives him a radiant smile. "That would be illegal, detective. It's one thing if I crack this computer, which is just between the owner and us. But with those online services, you've got a third party that's a massive corporation with lawyers. Better to have them onside. They're west coast, it's not even lunchtime there, you might get something back today. Leave me the parents' phone number in case I need to talk to them. You going to the media? Need a tip-line set up?"

"Not yet."

She shrugs. "Okay. I'll call you when I get anything."

Walking to the detectives' room I try Amber's cell again. Voicemail.

"It's a bitch that it's summer vacation," I say. "Would be great to corral and interview all her classmates in one hit."

"Why don't we split," Tony says. "I'll take a ride out to the school and see if I can get contact details on her friends there. You go see this girl her mother says is the best friend. She might open up better if I'm not around."

"Sounds good."

I watch him walk out the room. He's made it easy for me to offload the routine stuff on him, which is deft of him, relationship-wise. He's an evolved cop, but there's something that stops me from feeling quite at home with him. I stop by the dispatchers to get Amber's photo broadcast out to all the cars, then I head out into the heat again.

Catriona Riaz lives to the east of Amber, where Webster loses its sheen. But the house has clean, pale green siding and a purple door and shutters, which make it stand out perkily on the street. On the porch there's a set of wind chimes and on the wall, a ceramic plate with "welcome" written in happy flowers. A lively spirit runs this home. The frame around the front door is buzzing slightly with resonance from the deep bass of the music playing inside. I have to ring twice.

The teenager who opens the door is not much like the grinning twelve-year-old I saw on Amber's display board. Her hips are encased in a pair of tight denim shorts. The tupelo honey color of her legs is consistent all the way to the painted toenails. The blue straps of the push-up bra are arranged to be visible and there's an artfully located tattoo of a miniature dolphin on the swell of her left breast. There's a silver stud in the side of her nose. This comprehensive presentation of man-bait gives me a brief impulse to slap the child right out of her flip-flops.

"Catriona?" I say.

She nods. Before I can introduce myself, a gangling, bare-chested African-American kid comes up behind her, places abnormally large hands on those hips and says to me from under his Yankees cap, "'Sup, Lady?"

I let a beat go by. Then I hold out my shield. The big hands disappear off her hips and he hitches his shorts up to cover the plaid boxers and ghosts right by us like a good point guard. His departure is so urgent he's leaving without his shirt. Or perhaps he arrived without it. "Catch you later," he calls over his shoulder, wiggling his thumbs at Catriona to indicate that he expects to be texted.

"Amber hasn't been in touch with her parents since yesterday," I say to her. "You know where she is?"

"No," Catriona says. "Her mom phoned me last night. I told her then, I don't know where she is."

"Can we go inside?"

The kitchen is spotless. She offers me iced water from the refrigerator. Presumably in deference to my authority status, she removes the gum from her mouth and rolls it up in the original wrapper, which she is surprisingly able to liberate from the pocket of her shorts. When I was her age I hid inside the same baggy sweats for months. We sit at the kitchen table, which is clear except for three flowers, real ones, in a small vase.

I believe Catriona when she says that she and Amber are not as friendly now that Amber goes to private school. I believe she doesn't know of any intent on Amber's part to run away. I believe that she hasn't seen or spoken to Amber in a couple of weeks. They don't see each other as much—teenage life is all about the daily tribal business. But Catriona knows something. I can't tell if it's relevant. She probably can't either. But there's something about what these girls do or have done together, or some knowledge they share which she does not want known to the world.

The default setting for teenagers is liar. They lie about everything for every kind of reason. Not just to hide the pot smoking and the secret boyfriend. They lie to maintain appearances, protect friends, be cool, avoid unpleasantness, cause unpleasantness, avoid commitment, knife enemies. They lie like they French kiss— to see how it feels in the mouth. But principally, they lie because to them the untruth is of the same cloth as the truth; they have no ability whatsoever to rank moral priorities. Teenagers are just rehearsing being civilized. No different now than when I was in school.

"What about your friend that was here?"

"You mean Darrell?"

"Was he friendly with Amber?"

"Maybe. But you don't have to worry about Darrell. He's just a wannabe. His mother is stricter even than mine. She'd kick his butt if he did anything wrong."

"So you know the difference between a wannabe and the real thing, huh?"

She drops her eyes.

"Catriona, you seem to be level-headed to me. I just want to make sure you understand the gravity of the situation. When young girls go missing, those that aren't found in the first few days ... often it's a bad outcome."

I can see her waver. Her eyes come at me and then flick away. She nods.

"Anything you say to me, it goes no further, I promise you."

"Amber's a really nice person, honestly," she says, looking at the pale blue varnish on her fingernails. "But she changed a lot from when we were kids."

"Do you know her friends now?"

She shrugs. "Guys from that school. Guys with expensive cars."

"Any names?"

"I only met two of them once. I don't remember."

She's closing down again. I need to give her some time before I come back at her. I take out a card.

"Phone me if you think of anything."

She walks with me to the door. She's so petite next to me, it's like we're a different breed.

"Amber's really, really smart, you know? Sometimes I think that's like a problem for her, because she's embarrassed by her

23

parents. She wants to be cool, but her mom and dad are kind of old-fashioned. She started being horrible about them. And then she started being horrible about anyone, like she needed to put people down to feel good. After she went to that other school, she was up and down. First she hated it, then she was full of it. And then when her mom got so sick, she didn't know how to feel, like she was guilty."

"What was wrong with her mom?"

"I'm not sure, but she nearly died, she was in the intensive care for weeks." Catriona passes her hand vaguely over her torso. "Something with her insides. I'm not sure."

"When was that?"

"Maybe February or March? I was so happy when I saw she was driving again."

"I'll call you later, Catriona," I say, just to remind her it's not over.

On the street, someone has slipped a flyer for a tanning salon under my wiper. I just got tanned walking from the house. When I'm in the car I glance back at her. She's standing in the doorway, hips canted, phone in hand, fingers flashing. The tribal drums will carry the news of Amber's disappearance to every corner by night-fall.

3 p.m.

The Connecticut Sex Offenders registry is on my screen. Six hits within a ten mile radius of Amber's house, which seems a lot, but it's not, in my opinion, a true reflection of the potential threat. There are teens on this register who were merely sexting kids their own age.

I try Amber's cell. Voicemail. I call up Patrolman Hendry, who's coordinating the neighborhood canvass.

24

"Nothing about the girl," he says. "Some of them recognize her, but that's it. A lot of empty houses. Summer holidays."

"Anything unusual about the neighborhood?"

He scoffs. "Complaints about speeding on Wilton, seems like it's a cut through from Parkside Road to Farmington. Complaints about teenagers playing soccer on the tennis courts. Complaints about neighbors' dogs. This is why I hate door-to-doors."

I ask him to reassign three of the patrolmen: two to go visit the six sex offenders and the third to hit all the emergency rooms in the area with Amber's photo. They should have got her off the NCIC alert if she was brought in, but sometimes the system breaks down.

Tony walks into the squad room. "The school's virtually deserted. No one to authorize access to student records. They're trying to contact Amber's advisor to call me. He's the one who will know about any discipline or social issues."

"List of phone numbers of her classmates?"

He shakes his head. "The usual privacy bullshit. I don't see us getting a lot of help from them. Expensive private school, they're always thinking first about how it will affect them."

Over the top of my screen I see Webster's Animal Control Officer approaching. Theresa is a mid-20s blond with a cheerleader's body and a relentlessly sunny outlook. I bet there's not a guy in the squad room who hasn't asked her out at one time or another, but I have not personally exchanged two sentences with her.

As she says, "Hi, Tony," she gives a brief touch of fingertips to his arm.

"Hi, Theresa, what's up?"

"I just came on duty and saw that profile on the computer. The missing girl? I know her."

"Personally?" asks Tony, glancing at me.

"No. I gave her a ticket for an unleashed dog. About three

25

months ago, at the Wilton Lane sports fields. There's a bunch of residents who walk their dogs there and it can be an issue. You know, most of them are very good about cleaning up after their dogs, but it only takes one to leave poop on the playing field and then a kid slides in it and the school is calling up again and Sergeant Delvers is on my case. So often it's the good guys who end up with a ticket."

This is why they call them blonds—she might give us the entire operating manual of the Animal Control division if we let her keep going.

"Know anything else about her?" I ask.

She turns to face me and all the flirtation goes out of her face. She has that very straight blond hair I used to be so envious of in high school.

"That time I ticketed her, she was with an older guy. I assumed it was her father, but when it came to writing out the tickets he gave a different address and name than her. I've seen them together other times, too."

"So they walk their dogs together." I let too much skepticism into my voice, because she flushes a little.

"Sure, I see what you mean. But, you know, she's a teenager, he's got to be forty-five, there they are chatting away. I don't know, I just thought they were unusually friendly together."

"That was your first impression," asks Tony, "that there might be something inappropriate about their relationship?"

She so much prefers Tony's soft, indulging voice, I'm getting her shoulder now.

"I don't want to put it that way. But that was my first thought when I saw she was missing. I thought I should tell you, you know. Oh and he's got a foreign accent. British, I think."

Oh, foreign? That's a slam dunk then. We can probably hang five other unsolveds on him. Somehow, Tony has drifted into the space between her and me.

"Have you got time to pull the tickets on both of them for us?" he says to her.

"Oh sure. I'll do it right now."

"That will be great. Thanks a lot."

She smiles and walks off happily in her snug pants, but Tony has been careful to switch his eyes to his computer screen. "Could be something," he says without looking up at me. Several witty responses occur to me, but I manage to say nothing, a rare case of engaging filter before mouth.

Walking down the corridor to the bathroom, I detour into the Weisz murder war room to see if there's any new material on the boards. Even now, these crime scene photos shock me. I've seen some tough stuff, but these are different. The close-ups of the garden implement clearly show shreds of the victim's guts and his bright pink Brooks Brothers golf shirt on the spikes. The "Made in China" stamp on the metal is in sharp focus. A pair of white Adirondack chairs keeps peeping into the shots, bizarrely suggesting an outdoor furniture catalog. Again I think this is not the work of your disgruntled landscaper. This is personal. And the fact that the family has nothing to say about that is suspicious to me. That's why I wanted to be the one to interview the daughter. The department is so busy tippy toeing around the Weisz family they can't see it. It's the money. This is Webster; if you've got money you're obviously a good guy.

"Haven't you got your own case now?" Beanbag Paterniakis has entered behind me. He has to lean back a bit to counterbalance his expanding gut and it causes him to waddle.

"Hi, Sam. Just looking to see if there are any developments. Any leads outside of the landscaper?"

He ignores the question. "I heard they pulled the Kentucky dude off patrol to help you," he says. "Must be important."

He smirks at me. It's not a pretty sight. There are many questionable mustaches in the department, but Beanbag's is particularly egregious. It has areas that appear to be discolored by food that remains after he washes his face.

"I'm going to have to throw you out of here now," he says, waddling me toward the door. "Strict limits on information access on this case."

Bite down, Bradley, and get moving. This is all about something that happened two years ago, right after my promotion to detective. There was an evening barbecue at one of the detective's houses, half the department was there. By ten o'clock, events arising from intoxication were breaking out. I was wearing jeans and a shirt that I suddenly felt was too tight. Self-conscious, I took my margarita out of the floodlit area and stood under a tree in the semi-dark yard where I could be an observer. In a few minutes a hand alighted on my waist and I looked around to see Beanbag and his mustache at my shoulder in the dark.

"Great party," he said, standing close, looking toward the shenanigans in the light.

His hand rested on my hip for a few beats. Then it drifted upwards off my jeans and eased under the edge of my shirt so that his fingers were on my skin. I could have gotten out of it without damage but I was a real rookie then.

I turned to him and I said, "Oh, please." Not oh please, give me more, but oh please how did you even begin to think this would ever happen?

He turned his head away and moved off smartly. It all lasted about five heartbeats, and I still see his anger every time he makes eye contact with me.

Back in the squad room, Theresa is hovering around Tony with a proud smile.

He looks up at me. "Amber Zajac's fine for the unleashed dog has not been paid. She's delinquent."

"How about the mysterious Brit?" I ask.

"Leonard Miller," says Theresa. "Forty-seven. Lives around the corner from Amber Zajac. Here's his address. Paid his fine promptly. He had only one other file item, a ticket for illegal dumping three years ago."

"One case of illegal dumping and an unleashed dog," I say to Tony. "Not exactly the gateway drugs to child abduction."

"But if he talked to her often he might know something."

"And if she slammed out of her house in a temper, his place might have been the closest stop. Maybe she's friendly with his kids or something."

I call Sgt. Hendry. The canvass group recorded no one home at Leonard Miller's address when they called.

7 p.m.

To get to Leonard Miller's house from Amber's you would walk north up Wilton Lane. A block before the school, turn left onto Bristol, which is a dead end and forms a little enclave where the houses look more expensive and the yards are larger, with more trees. Miller's house is set back, screened from the road by trees and shrubbery. The heat and humidity have backed off a little and the evening light is soft enough to make memories with. Some teenage boys are walking up the middle of the street doing clever things with a soccer ball and being conspicuously loud. One shouts 'fuck you' at his friends but really to offend the houses and the sprinklers on the green lawns and two middle-aged joggers laboring up the hill.

Tony presses Miller's doorbell. A dog barks and moments later her gray face appears in the glass pane next to the door. It takes a while for a human to follow. Leonard Miller opens the door and a waft of cool central air hits us.

"Mr. Miller?" I show him my shield. "Webster Police. Can we have a word with you?"

"What's happened?" BBC accent.

"Amber Zajac. She lives down the street. Do you know her?"

"Yes. What about her?"

"She may be missing. Have you seen her recently?"

"No, not for a week or so."

"Can we come in?"

"Of course."

At the police academy we had an instructor who said we should aim to retain the first impression we get of a witness or suspect. He said that's our only true, unadulterated picture of what the person is really like. As soon as we start to accumulate information on any subject there's interpretation going on which distorts the memory. Every time we open a memory, we change it.

So, first inventory of Miller. He's a big man but not tough. Heavy in the body but gaunt in the face. His hair is gray but he still has all of it. Mid forties, maybe. His movements are shambling, not vigorous. He looks tired, exhausted, even. And he's been drinking—still is. He leads us into the living room and there's a bottle of whisky and a partially filled glass on the coffee table next to a paperback novel. Not a sound in the house. No voices, no TV, radio. I have the sense that we're interrupting something, although absolutely nothing seems to be going on.

We sit on a sofa across from Miller. The dog approaches me for a nuzzle but Miller says something soft to her and she stops, eyes on him. He gestures with his head and the dog walks across and lies next to him. It's a remarkable interaction.

"Amber's been out of touch with her parents. They're concerned," I say. "How do you know her? Is she friendly with your kids?"

"I don't have any children."

"How about your wife—does she ever chat to Amber?"

"My wife no longer lives here. She returned to England last year."

That hangs in the air. I keep my eyes on Miller to encourage him to continue, but he looks away. After a moment, he reaches down to scratch the dog's head.

"So you live alone here?"

He nods.

"How do you know Amber?"

"She walks Bella for me sometimes." He indicates the dog.

"Do you sometimes walk with her?"

He shakes his head. "No. We met her up there with her dog. That's how I ended up asking her if she wanted to help me out sometimes with Bella. She brings her own dog usually and collects Bella and takes them both up to the park."

"How often?"

"It varies, maybe once a week on average, more when I'm working on a bigger assignment."

"When did you last see her?" I am doing all the talking; Tony is unobtrusive on the sidelines.

"Perhaps two weeks ago."

"So she has a key to your house?"

"Yes. Well, she knows where I hide the spare key outside the house. She doesn't take it away with her."

He swirls his glass and swallows the last of the whisky. The ice tinkles. Good quality glass. Personally, I would not drink in front of detectives who were interviewing me, guilty or innocent.

"You haven't seen her, even passing in the street, the last few days?"

"No."

"Did she give you any indication that she might be unhappy?"

31

He pauses. I say nothing.

"Nothing that would cause her to run away, if that's what you mean."

"Sir, you shouldn't try to pre-judge whether your information is relevant." Tony doesn't say it aggressively like a cop; he says it like a doctor recommending improved lifestyle choices to a patient. "Did you feel that Amber was unhappy in any way?"

"Really, I know nothing about her home life."

"But she never talked about running away, definitely?" Tony asks.

"No. Definitely."

"Boyfriends?"

"Never discussed."

"Well, what did you talk about, Mr. Miller?"

"The way Amber and I got talking was through my accent. We met at the park with the dogs. She asked me where I came from. She's read a few English authors. She's also into a lot of English bands."

The blinds on the windows are down but they face west, so he has a legitimate reason for keeping out the setting sun. We sit there. The dog watches him. If he moves his hand along the back of the couch, the dog's eyes go with it. Whatever happens in this house, the dog knows it.

"May I ask what you do for a living, Mr. Miller?" Tony asks.

"I'm an insurance adjuster."

"For?"

"Self-employed. I have some of the big insurers I work for regularly."

"How did a citizen like you end up with that illegal dumping ticket?" I try to say it lightly, but regret it right away, because Miller's eyes change.

"In England," he says, "there are often big recycling bins in public parking areas outside pubs and filling stations. When we first moved here, I didn't know how things worked. There are those big bins outside the Shell station on Quaker Lane. I assumed they were for public use. We had lots of cardboard boxes left over from the move, so I went to dump them there. The staff saw me, but they didn't say anything to me. Next thing there was a police car in my driveway. They had taken my license plate. I explained it was an honest mistake and I would retrieve the stuff, but your guy ticketed me anyway."

"That was inhospitable of him," says Tony.

Miller stands up. "If you checked my record before you came here, then you didn't come to see if I could help. You came to see if I am involved in some way. I'm not. So why don't I let you go now?"

"Look, Mr. Miller," I say, "You've got to admit it's a little strange that she was friendly with you?"

"Only in America," he says.

"What's that mean?"

"You have a national psychosis about inappropriate relationships. You name laws after victims which gives them a maudlin sentimentality and suddenly remote possibilities become everyone's fixation."

"You don't appreciate our fine country? What makes you stay?"

"I appreciate that it isn't England. Is there anything more?"

Suddenly the dog is up and heading for the door, and we hear footsteps and voices on the porch and the dog barks excitedly. The doorbell rings.

"That sounds like my neighbors," says Miller. "We often walk together at this time. I need to take my dog out." He goes to the door. Tony gestures his head at me silently: let's go.

A couple is on the front porch with two dogs.

"They wouldn't let us go by without collecting Bella!" says the woman. She's wearing ill-advised running shorts. I'm thinking it's more likely that she and her husband couldn't walk by without knowing why our car is there. Although it's an unmarked cruiser, there's a blue light in the back window and most people know the gray Crown Vics we use.

"These are detectives," says Miller. "Amber from down the road is missing."

"I know!" says the wife. "Apparently someone came to our door this morning. I wasn't there, but the sitter said."

"What happened?" the husband asks us. Their faces are eager for information. His dog's leash is wound around his legs.

"Thank you, Mr. Miller, we're on our way," Tony says, keeping me moving.

In the car, he says, "You want to take a drive around, get a feel for the place?"

"Sure."

There's a message on my cell phone from Hendry. The canvass team has gone off duty. Nothing from the sex offenders, nothing from the hospitals.

Up the hill on Wilton Lane, we pass an elementary school and some town recreation facilities, two soccer fields, some lumpy tennis courts. This is where the dog walking apparently takes place. We park in the school lot. Two elderly women walk past our car in animated debate.

"Is that Russian they're speaking?" Tony asks.

"Yep. There's an apartment building at the top of this street occupied almost entirely by Russian Jews who were brought here under a charitable program in the eighties. That deli on Farmington Avenue next to the Laundromat, all Russian stuff. Let's take a walk."

On the tennis court, a mother patiently hits balls to her kid who wings them over the fence with delight. The boys we saw earlier are playing soccer with a bunch of other teenagers. There's a nest of empty plastic water bottles which have been thrown at, but not in, the trash can.

"His wife's left him," I say. "He has no kids. His best friend is his dog. He drinks alone. And he became hostile when he heard we'd pulled his record. If there was a crime here, I might suspect him of it."

"Part of that is the cultural differences, I think. Maybe he's just a loner since his wife dumped him."

"I guess. There are basically two possibilities for his involvement. If Amber's a runner, then maybe he's helped her, he knows about it, given her money, something like that. Or he's a full-on sex criminal and he's got her in the basement. Did you get a real feel for either of those?"

"I don't rule out that he knows something," says Tony. "But I don't get a dangerous vibe from him."

"Me neither."

Quite the little community spot, this park. Parents with kids at the swings, a group of older kids playing Frisbee, an old man making painfully slow circuits of the running track around the lower field, and at least a dozen walkers. The grass is recently mowed.

"If you think about it," says Tony, "Wilton Lane is like the dividing line between prosperous Webster and the part that slides into Hartford. Everything west and north of here is bigger and better houses. Go a few hundred yards the other direction and you're into the tanning salons and tattoo parlors and then into New Park Avenue, which is drug-score central."

"Detective di Giorgio? That part of Webster you just dissed? That's where I live."

"I didn't diss it. I only said it's at a comparative disadvantage."

"*Mixed* is the polite word you're looking for, detective. It's almost all multi-family rentals where I am. Where we are now is where the estate agents bring families who want a Webster address but can't pony up half a million. But their property taxes are still killing them and they don't want these immigrant kids shouting fuck outside their houses."

My phone rings. Cynthia's name on the screen.

"Just calling you before I take off," she says. "Nothing on your cell phone yet. The computer—aside from several nasty pieces of malware—there's nothing. Someone has gone through and deleted the browsing history and defragged the disk."

"Is that unusual?"

"Not really. Listen, I've got a date, so I'll speak to you in the morning."

I relay this information to Tony. "Does this tell us anything about Amber?"

"More likely the father," he says. "He was very reluctant to give up the computer. It's probably got his tax dodging records on it."

"Let's call it a day. I need to do five miles tonight."

9 p.m.

The so-called balcony of my apartment is just big enough so that I can string my hammock. It's a good place for a beer after my run, and it's where I think best. The subject of my thinking right now is that I am a shitty person. Amber Zajac could walk into her home this evening and tell her parents she's over being pissed at them and we should all breathe a huge sigh of relief. But in a deep, horrible part of me I want this girl to be missing. I want a real case. And it's a simple truth of being a detective that we only get career opportunities when someone else's life goes bad.

I ran away myself once. Junior year. Three of us had been

caught shoplifting. Correction—three of us had gone shoplifting. I was the only one actually caught, carrying a $19.99 pair of slutty panties. Yes, there was this guy. He was cute, not especially, in the range I limited my expectations to. But he had a way of resting his eyes on me that would hit me like a hockey check. This resting of the eyes business conveyed to me that here was a creature of my own age who, instead of jabbering through teenage life like a witless chicken, actually had possession of himself.

Anderson. Yes, he had a last name for a first name, which kinda sealed the deal. It was completely logical to me then that a guy with two last names would have possession of himself. I had this recurring daydream that Anderson would find me in an enormous bathroom, and I would happen to be wearing just the slutty underpants like the pictures in *Cosmopolitan*, and he would think that I was like the girls in the magazines, who were all unattainably gorgeous. I would never have considered actually buying such panties, but stealing them was somehow justifiable. All I needed was an enabler, who came in the form of Marissa, a black belt manipulator at age sixteen. We set off to the mall on a Saturday morning together with her sidekick Kimberly, jauntily discussing what items to lift. They enthusiastically approved my choice. We split up in the crowded store and then reconvened at the escalator for the innocent stroll out the front door. When we were stopped, it turned out I was the only one carrying.

They didn't press charges. My mother subjected the security staff to such a torrent of hysterical nonsense that they just wanted to get us out of there. In the car, she went on a rave about what it said about the family. By contrast, my father said nothing, which I took as a comfort. It was Monday at school that was excruciating. Naturally, Marissa allowed details of my choice of merchandise to escape her lips, and this information was rapidly disseminated across the student population. My life became unbearable in a matter of hours. The faces coming toward me down the hallways were like demons. Every glance was distorted by my knowing that they knew. Whispers and murmurs swirled around me. Anderson looked away when he saw me.

At lunchtime, there was a scuffle in the bathroom that I didn't start but did finish. The school called home and my father came to get me. He flirted with the principal's secretary. On the way home he took me for ice cream at Family's. I stared at a triple-decker while he told me about scrapes he got into at my age, absent-mindedly pouring salt and pepper out onto the table and mixing them together with his finger. His large workman's fingers were never quite clean but extremely dexterous. He used his pinkie finger to hollow out the little mound and I realized he was mixing cement and builders' sand—the hollow in the middle was where you pour the water before you start to shovel the mixture together. I had seen him do this when he was working on our house. He pulled a wad of paper napkins from the overstuffed dispenser and wiped it all away. After this there was no further way of postponing talking about me, so he said, "Look Donna, it must be hard for you, I know you're not the prettiest."

My father was—is—a good-looking man. Life has always offered him attractive females. All other females, the plain ones, were to him no more distinguishable from one another than zebras. I suddenly realized why my father had made so little fuss about the shoplifting. He had sympathy for the lengths a plain girl had to go to. He was going on about how I mustn't feel angry at the world, but I wasn't listening by then. When you're a kid, you have trouble keeping ideas at their right size; the image of myself as an ugly protuberance on my family expanded with every second we sat in that Family's, an establishment I have ever since avoided.

When we got home my mother said she had arranged a special

consultation with a therapist at seven that evening, to intervene in my decline into a life of violence and kleptomania. I can still remember how I felt: I simply could not continue to be at that location on the planet without exploding into fragments. I collected together all my cash and walked out of the house in the baggy sweatshirt, pants and sandals I was wearing. I got a ride to the station and lurked about until I boarded the bus to Boston.

That drive east from Connecticut to Boston was one of the events that shaped who I am today. Deep inside I knew I was going nowhere, but for the two hours that the road was sliding away under the vehicle I was in charge of my destiny. It was dark and cold by the time we got to Boston. I walked in my broken sandals, hugging my sweatshirt around me, anxious that I looked conspicuously displaced. Nothing happened. No boys approached me. No pimps tried to recruit me. No concerned citizen pointed me out to a passing cop. I was just another body in motion through a city with bigger things on its mind. I stood at the dockside and stared into the cold, greasy water. I bought a falafel and ate it sitting on the sidewalk in a light rain as people swarmed past me. I walked until my feet hurt and then circled back to the bus station. I slept on the bench there and took the first bus back in the morning. There were recriminations, but I had given my parents enough of a fright to keep them muffled. At school, I cared a little less. I needed that night to learn just how indifferent life is to our wails and moans.

So now I'm lying here wondering if Amber is on her bus to a small discovery as well, and if life will treat her as kindly as it did me. For just as I made it through unscathed, other young women are quickly devoured. I try her cell. Voicemail. The parents might forget to call me if she came home, but I hesitate to call them and check.

Suddenly the mosquitoes are all over me. I roll out of the

hammock and go inside and rummage in the refrigerator for some vegetables that haven't gone soft. At home I eat mainly vegetables—that way, if I eat fast food on the run at work it balances out. Chop broccoli, carrot, zucchini into a bowl; microwave two minutes; splash with olive oil and balsamic; serve. Minimum time, minimum wash up. You get used to anything. I don't think I've ever turned on the oven.

I'm still awake at two o'clock, lying on my bed scratching a mosquito bite. I don't have A/C and my noisy $29.99 fan just moves the same stale, hot air around. Maybe it's not a mosquito bite; maybe I'm just itching from anxiety.

By day she is a feral sprite, roaming the house and the yard in bare feet, uncombed hair streaming. She can play endlessly on her own, up and down the ladder to the tree house, bumps and scratches unnoticed, talking to herself about the world she creates as she proceeds. The blond hair, which her mother will never cut, is wheaten-hued with deep vitality.

But as the afternoon progresses, the child changes. She stays closer to her mother. Alone in her room after the light is out, she is afraid of the inky corners, the space under her bed. Afraid even of the cold regions under her comforter, she curls up tight.

She's afraid to be awake and afraid to go to sleep; she doesn't want to be trapped alone with herself in the dungeon of sleep, unable to wake. It has become so that she can barely tell nightmare from reality. By the age of five, she is accustomed to spending long stretches of the night awake, watching the pattern of shadows on her walls, alert for any sensation that her imagination can conjure into terror.

Despite Amber's fear of the dark, she is not allowed a night light. Her father forbids any lights on through the night; it is a waste of electricity. Amber's father is a relentless saver of money in ways that make life harsher without producing noticeable improvement in the family finances. With a red Sharpie, he draws a line on the thermostats indicating the maximum permitted heating level: 64 degrees; Amber spends her childhood winters wandering the house with a comforter draped around her.

But at least she is allowed to sleep with her bedroom door open. In the early part of the night when her parents are still up, light from elsewhere in the house reaches her and keeps the fear at bay. Later, even with all the lights off, she knows the gradations of darkness that mark the doorway and the passage beyond—her escape route.

There comes a night when Amber awakes to find that her room is so dark it can only mean the door is closed. And there's an unfamiliar sound—a slight scratching somewhere in the room. Her heart bangs in her ribby little chest. She is trapped, too fearful to put her feet to the ground and make for the doorway. Then something slimy touches her foot. She tries to vanish into the tight ball of herself, but the thing touches her again. Her terror of the thing is suddenly stronger than her fear of placing her feet on the ground and she makes a run for the door and the sanctuary of her parents' room. But the door does not yield. She is locked in the room. The beam of a flashlight snaps into her eyes, blinding her. Then her older brother Kris swings the beam under his own face to create a mask of shadows, and he growls like a monster. Finally her fingers find the wall switch and she snaps the overhead light on. There is Kris, dangling the toy-store slime in her face.

He points at her skinny legs. "Look, you've pissed yourself!"

The following Sunday, when Kris is given the chore of sweeping the fall leaves, Amber slips down the side of the house, where a pile of natural stone is left over from the spring when her grandfather Mikolaj built an outdoor barbecue for them. Amber chooses the heaviest stone she can carry. She hefts the stone across to the base of the large birch tree. This tree, with its peeling paper bark and huge white limbs holding up a massive canopy, has been a ballast in Amber's world since she was laid out under its shade on a baby blanket. It is a thing of infinite wonder, a constant, like a third parent. When she climbs up onto its limbs she feels like the tree is cradling her in its arms.

In the branches above her is the tree house, also built by her grandfather. She needs one hand for the ladder up to the tree house. With the other hand she makes a sling of her dress and totes the stone up in that. She sits patiently in the tree house as Kris works his way toward her.

The stone strikes Kris on the collarbone and she experiences an exultant rush of retribution from his scream of shock and pain. Her next memory is of her father standing below her, and the memory picture she has is of a human with anger physically bubbling out of him. She remembers thinking about staying in the tree house forever. She doesn't remember how or when she came down. She does remember her Aunt Rita saying repeatedly, "She could have killed him!" as Kris is led away to the car for a trip to the hospital. She recalls the exact tone of that "she" for years. It placed her outside the boundaries of the family, like an exile.

DAY TWO

Wednesday. 7 a.m.

The printer is out of paper. And the paper supply is locked up. Of course. We're in a police station. I've spent an hour making up a poster of Amber and now I have to wait until the admin comes in to finish it. I couldn't sleep so I came in at six, hoping that the report on Amber's cell phone would have come in overnight. Nothing. But the poster has turned out well. The photo is perfect—it's just a candid family shot of a teenage girl with all her half-formedness and vulnerability, but she has a light in her, the bright eye of a pixie curious about the world. She looks out from the photo and she grabs you.

I call Tony and we agree to meet for breakfast. I leave a message on Cynthia's desk to press her on the cell phone, then head out for the diner on South Main. I'm a fan of breakfast, but we're only halfway through the eggs when dispatch calls.

"Detective, there's someone on the line who says she has information on the missing girl."

"Put her on."

Tony drives us to the address on Maple, which is a block or so west of Amber's home. It's a house that jars on the eye. It's been tastelessly extended and has a McMansionesque portico added at

43

the front door, out of keeping with the simpler New England co-
lonials on the street. There's a basketball hoop on the driveway
and a dark blue Audi convertible on one side of the open double
garage.

A woman in her late 30s opens the door. Holds herself like
she's used to getting attention from men, and her eyes go straight
to Tony. A ten-year-old boy, handsome but sulky-faced, stands
right behind her. Before we can speak, two golden retrievers de-
scend on us, barking and jumping.

"Harry! Sally!" the woman shouts as the dogs devote themselves to transferring hair and spittle onto our clothes. I think of
Leonard Miller's touch-screen control over his dog. "Throw them
out, Tim."

The dogs are ejected and the door closed.

"I'm Valerie Ingerson," she says. And then to the boy, "Tim,
you need to go and play outside, okay?"

"I don't want to," he whines.

"Go!"

Slowly, he goes.

"It's a long hot summer vacation," she says, leading us to the
living room. A moment later a basketball cracks loudly against the
metal backboard; some screws on that hoop could do with tight-
ening.

"Tell us what you know about Amber Zajac, ma'am," I say.

"Everyone was talking about it at dog group this morning. Apparently you're investigating the guy who lives behind us here,
Miller—"

"Hold on," I say. "What group?"

"Oh, there's just a bunch of us who meet every morning over
on the fields at Wilton Lane to walk our dogs before work."

I can see she likes the look of Tony; there's a small flexing of
her shoulders which projects the breasts forward.

"There can be fifteen dogs there sometimes. Anyway, Leonard Miller didn't come this morning, and then Elizabeth told us you guys were at his house yesterday?"

"We're interviewing a lot of people," I say.

The dogs commence a frenzied barking outside. "Here's my husband," she says. "He's been at the gym."

Behind our cruiser, a Dodge truck encrusted with chrome embellishments has pulled into the driveway. You could tow Westfarms Mall behind it. At the police academy, where there were just a few of us girls, we used to say the bigger truck the shorter the fuck. There's something slightly comical about Mr. Ingerson climbing down out of this monster truck because he can't be more than five foot seven. We watch him striding to the front door—a turbo-charged small man whose over-zealous shoulder work at the gym has left him looking cartoonishly disproportionate. The dogs, I notice, fear to jump on him, probably because he has established boundaries in relation to his hint-of-Mafia lounge shirt and pressed slacks.

He's an inch shorter than his wife. He sticks his hand out to Tony. "Hi, Matt Ingerson."

"Detective di Giorgio. This is Detective Donna Bradley, who is in charge of investigating Amber's case."

Ingerson reluctantly moves his eyes to me; not a guy who likes to acknowledge female authority. He has very hairy arms and the assessing gaze of a reptile that eats its prey whole and so has to get accurate measurements.

"I told them what we heard," his wife says to him.

"Is he involved?" Ingerson asks me.

"We're talking to anyone in the neighborhood who might have had contact with Amber. What is it that you want to talk to us about?"

"Him. Miller." He points out the north windows. "We share a

boundary, so we have some experience with him. He's the kind of guy who when he turns out to be a criminal, you realize you knew it all along."

Maybe I'll get more sense from the wife. "Mrs. Ingerson, you told the despatcher that Mr. Miller had had some kind of contact with your son that bothered you?"

"Yes."

"Did you make a report?"

"Didn't need to," her husband answers. "I told him that if he ever spoke to my son again I'd work him over so hard he'd have to go back to England for some of that free socialist medical care."

"What did he say to your son?"

Mrs. wants to answer but Mr. is having none of it.

"He took Tim into his house, middle of the afternoon, sits him down and starts a conversation with him. This is a nine-year-old kid, alone with him in the house—"

"Hold on. Are you saying he tried to entice your son into his house somehow?"

"Timmy was in his yard and—"

"Why was Timmy in his yard?"

"The people who lived there before, they were fantastic, they used to let Timmy cut through their yard to get home from school. Otherwise he has to walk around the long way. There was no fence between us then. Miller moves in, a few weeks later, he's at the door complaining to us that our dogs are pooping on his lawn. In the summer, the fence goes up. It's like six foot tall. Do you notice that the back of the fence faces our way? That's what he's like. So when school starts again, Timmy can't cut through. Except, Timmy's not a wimp, he decides to try and go over the fence. Next thing, Miller's got Timmy inside, offering him milk and cookies, talking shit in his ear."

"And ask yourself," Valerie Ingerson chips in, "what is Miller

46

doing home alone in the middle of the afternoon? You add it all up—"

"He gave your son milk and cookies?"

"Not literally," the husband says. "I think he offered him a soda. What I'm saying is the subtle persuasion, the pedophile tactics."

"Matt, you can't use that word," Mrs. blurts. "We're not sure—"

"I didn't say he's that. I said it's that kind of thing they do."

"So then you went and told him to lay off?"

"No, that was after the second time. Miller just shouted at him that time."

"Your son climbed his fence again?"

"He's a strong-minded kid! It's a good thing!"

I can virtually see Ingerson urging his kid to piss off the neighbor.

"How about the Zajacs? Do you know them?"

"We know them." Mrs. Ingerson is careful. "Not close. They're struggling a bit financially, I think. Rosemary—the mother—she's been very ill. Honey, you did something with him once, a few years ago?"

"We did one house together," says Mr. Ingerson, "but I knew three weeks in that it wasn't going to work out. He's just not a businessman. He takes too long, wants to do everything perfectly, doesn't stay on top of the numbers. He's just not meant to do anything more than Sheetrock and paint."

"Isn't there a living in that?" I ask.

"There is, but after his father died he took over the property development business, screwed it all up. He bought some rental properties in 2007, top of the market. You could get any loan you wanted then and he got the numbers wrong. Then the recession. Things go very bad very quickly if you're not sharp. His father was good, apparently, but the gene didn't pass on."

"Do you think he had a beef with anyone?"

"No. That's his problem. He needs to have more beefs with more people. He lets people push him around."

My phone is vibrating in my pocket.

"Okay, well, thanks for calling in with your information," I say. "We'll let you get back to your day."

"What are you going to do about Miller?" asks Ingerson.

"On the basis of your information, nothing," says Tony. "But I am going to advise you to discourage your son from trespassing."

Whoa, Tony. You have poked the reptile with a stick. And look at the wife, she's glowing like a lantern at the sight of someone getting in the face of her husband the bully.

"Jesus Christ," he says. "Fine. Let the asshole carry on. We tried."

And with that, Mr. Ingerson snatches up his gigantic ring of keys and strides out of the house.

On the way to the car Tony says, "I left half a really good breakfast for that."

"Text from Cynthia," I say. "She's got the cell phone report."

When Tony's pissed off he drives faster. Wouldn't have thought so.

"She was a bit of a sparkler, though, wasn't she?" I say, "And you really got a response out of her." He ignores me. "Come on! I saw the way she looked at you. Women go for you," I blunder on, "it's good. Useful, I mean. They open up to you. Didn't you think she was hot?"

"You know, my very first thought when I got you as a partner was relief at the fact that we wouldn't be giving a score to every female we encounter."

"I'm just trying out the buddy talk thing with you."

"It doesn't become you."

"Copy that."

48

Cynthia hands me the fax of Amber's cell phone records.

"Call and text numbers," she says. "No activity since Sunday night, not even incoming."

"How likely is it that a teenage girl has her phone switched off for more than a day?" I'm thinking aloud.

"Zero," says Cynthia. "The phone is lost or broken, or the girl is." The callousness of this remark riles me; cops use gallows humor to get them through grim situations, but I don't think Cynthia's desk job entitles her.

"I'll still request that the carrier advise us if and when the phone is used," she continues, oblivious, "and put a tower log watch on it so that if the phone is used again, we can get an approximate location."

"Thanks."

"Also, my intern did a thorough web search. Your girl might be the only teenager in America without a Facebook page."

"Jeez, we're not having much luck," Tony says.

"Well, you've got her recent call list there," says Cynthia, "that's like the autobiography of any sixteen year old, you should be done with the case by lunch time."

"Have you thought of becoming a detective, Cynthia?" I say to her icily.

"I'd make a brilliant detective," she says. "But I can't stand violence."

Tony and I work backwards from the most recent call. The last logged call was Sunday at 10.43 p.m. I call it, no reply. A few incoming texts during Sunday, but very little usage.

"Again, doesn't fit with typical teenager," I say to Tony.

"Maybe she was running out of battery, didn't have a charger."

"But they said she was home Sunday."

"We need to check that with them, but let's see if we can get anything from these calls first."

We share the list and check each number we call. I get voicemail three times—too early for most teenagers. Then I get a girl called Rebecca who immediately bursts into tears when I tell her Amber's missing and moments later I have an irate mother on the phone lecturing me on police procedure. And that's Webster in a nutshell—live their entire lives blissfully remote from crime, but as soon as they get a hint of one, they want to write a letter to the New York Times about the method of its investigation.

I try another number. After three rings the message clicks in, reciting the number and asking me to leave a message. He gives no name, but I recognize that accent. It's Leonard Miller. I check back to the call list: Amber called him last Thursday, 3:26 in the afternoon.

I show Tony. "Miller said he hadn't seen Amber for at least two weeks. She called his house last Thursday."

He points at the list. "Call duration, six seconds. She probably got the answering machine, didn't leave a message."

"Yeah, but why's she calling him? He calls her when he wants her to walk the dog. She doesn't have a reason to call him." I run my finger up the list. "Incoming, incoming—look, here again. Outgoing. She called him. July twentieth. They're back and forth. What's that about?"

"I don't know," says Tony, "but if she didn't leave a message, he might not even know she called. Right now I think our best shot is finding a friend she's in contact with regularly."

Mrs. B, the stringy but durable pensioner who serves as the detectives' admin, is bearing down on us with an armful of posters.

"I'm going to leave you with the phone calls for a few minutes," I say to Tony. "I want to get a few of these posters up in the square and at the library—there's a lot of kids hanging around there."

"Sure thing."

Tunxis Square is the shopping and eating area that was recently developed right next door to the police station. There's a large Barnes & Noble, where the manager agrees to display one of Amber's posters right at the entrance. I figure the upscale clothing stores with their carefully landscaped window displays are not going to want a poster of one of life's potential failures spoiling the effect, so I don't even ask.

The Webster Central Library is on the other side of Tunxis Square. I show the poster to the librarians at the front desk but no one recognizes Amber. I ask to see a list of the books that Amber checked out.

"Can't do that," says the librarian. "Since that privacy case, we delete past borrowing records."

I strongly doubt that. More like the record is made unavailable to the public, but I'll bet the library techie could tell me every book checked out of this library since Windows was invented.

"The library has a teen room," she says, pointing to the rear of the library. "You should put a poster up in there."

A large warning notice is posted on the door of the teen room that pretty much covers the whole spectrum of normal teenage behavior: cursing, bullying, noise, distraction, alcohol, drugs—all will result in immediate expulsion. Despite this, there are indeed a couple of teens in the teen room, girls doing homework with laptop computers. There's a shelf of DVDs—this is where all those bad high school movies come to die. I show the poster to the librarian who runs the room.

"Sure, I recognize her. Amber. She's missing? Wow."

"Maybe."

"She's a bright kid. She used to come here a lot a few years back, haven't seen her much recently. That's not unusual. When the boobs come, the books fly out of their minds. It's mainly middle schoolers here."

"She ever have any issues?"

"No. We know all about troublemakers. She wasn't one. I can sort them at a glance."

I watch her make space for our poster on the notice board, and I can see a couple of the kids taking an interest. Something to text about. The thing is, a kid who frequented the library, even if it was only until she was 14, doesn't line up as a kid to get into something stupid.

Heading back to the station I route past the Grindhouse and get us coffee. There are three thin women in their dazzling Lycra workout gear sitting together—the most expensive gym in town is right next door. I show them my shield and then the photo of Amber. I tell them she might be missing, ask if they know her. Their reaction is to instantly forget about Amber and start babbling about the safety of their own children. They're up and heading for the door, pulling out their cell phones to call the sitters, as though the information I have given them might itself be contagious.

"How's it going?" I ask Tony as I walk back into the squad room.

"Something out of synch," he says. "I tried that last number she dialed Sunday night again. This time someone picked up. It's a pizza place in Old Saybrook."

"On the coast? At eleven o'clock on Sunday night? The parents said she was home on Sunday night."

"Exactly," he says.

"We need to talk to them again."

"Such as?" I say to him.

"She doesn't think first." His eyes come to mine. I don't like looking into this guy's eyes. There's just too much calamity in there.

Tony takes his arm and steers him firmly. "I'm going to walk you to the house now, Mr. Zajac."

As Zajac stumbles away with his stooped shoulders thrusting his head forward, I find his wife looking at me intently, as though she doubts I'm capable of taking her pain away. Then she turns and follows her husband into the house.

Her mother takes her to the priest once a week, on Thursday afternoons through the late autumn, until the first snow.

She and the priest have talks. He smells of mints, but not only of mints. He insists that she look at him and pay attention while he talks, so she comes to know in close detail the properties of his face. Her impression is that the priest's face is made not of flesh, but of some sort of putty. His skin is often damp, even in the cold afternoons. He is so large and so full of flesh and sounds and expressions and smells that she's not convinced he's even the same species as her, this man of God. His ear lobes are massive and fleshy and the ear holes are deep and black, as though rough mines have been excavated in the side of his head. His breathing is ponderous as he talks about obedience and cleanliness of the soul. About evil, how to know it, how to fight it.

She remembers little of the content of these talks. When her mother brought her to him, the first touch of his eyes on her was a condemning look, as though he saw written on her face the story of her crime and heard her brother's scream of pain. The priest could have said anything after that, it would have made no difference.

55

At the end of each talk, they read from the Bible. He comes around and sits next to her, close to her, pointing out to her with enormous fingers the words he is saying. The texture of the black cloth of his robe is rough against her skin. Then they kneel in the first pew for a short prayer, asking for guidance.

At home after these meetings, her parents will ask her what the priest said. She knows she is supposed to have learned something from the priest, but she doesn't know what it is. She can repeat fragments of what he says, but it has no reality to her. What is real and memorable is the silence of the church, the smell of the wood, the difference in the light near the high ceiling, the world of echoes.

For several years Stan and Rosemary Zajac watched their young daughter warily, as one watches an unpredictable animal. It was never spoken of as such, but they were afraid of her, of what emotional contaminant lay within her and when it might erupt again. In the architecture of the family, she was set at a slight distance, as if to give them time to react if she became dangerous.

It is her grandfather who leads her away from her fear of the dark. As with everything, he has a practical approach to it. One night he takes her into the living room and asks her to look out of the window.

Tell me what you can see.

Nothing, it's dark outside.

Then he takes her into the dark yard and they stand outside the same window.

What do you see?

She can see everything inside the brightly lit living room.

Can someone in the living room see you out here?

No.

If you're ever afraid, the dark is your friend, it's where you can hide and watch others.

All very well, but there are noises in the night that she's afraid of, too. So, one night when everyone else is asleep, he takes her and sits her in the dark living room and they listen.

What's that cracking noise?

At night, when the house cools down, some parts of it contract and move a little bit.

He shows her that if she sneaks down the hallway in the dark middle of the night to the bathroom and turns the faucet suddenly, the sleeping water jerks awake and bolts noisily down the pipes making the house shudder.

So by the time she is ten, Amber is drifting from room to room in the dark, her path lit only by the discarded light from street lamps and the glow of the clocks on electronic appliances. Her fear has been reversed; she loves darkness now. She loves how sometimes the dog pads up to her and silently touches his cold nose to her leg, a fellow traveler of the dark. Sometimes she opens the sliding door to feel her bare feet on the cool patio stone. She can spend so much of the night awake that she enters a state of exhausted trance. She has turned a fear into a comfort.

Stan Zajac's accidental gift to his daughter was his refusal to pay for cable TV. Amber found books. At first they were just a means of postponing the moment of switching off the light at night. From there, she simply fell down the rabbit hole into the rhythm of words and turning pages. She came to know the wonder of leaving her own body as she drew another world up from the ink on the page, a world more vivid for having been made from the implements of her own imagination.

It's just short of a mile from Amber's house to the Webster library. When she's nine and ten, her mother brings her. By the time she's twelve, there she is striding along Farmington Ave, one or two afternoons a week, with her book bag, straight-backed, the wheat-colored hair in a bouncing ponytail.

She loves the library and stays as late as possible, not just because of the volume of worlds into which she can escape, but because it delays returning home. In her house she is limited and confined. Out in the world, she can be anything.

On these library days, her step is lively, her chin up. Puberty has come early. She's got something to show the world. What adolescent boy could not notice her, the skateboarders and bicyclers, slouchers and athletes, heading home from school, hanging out in the long summer evenings?

As Tony drives us away from the Zajac's house, I deal with my voicemail messages.

"Got something from one of the numbers on her call list," I tell Tony just as someone answers my return call. "This is detective Donna Bradley. You called me back?"

"Yeah, um, you left a message about Amber earlier today? She just texted me."

"What's your name?"

"Jenna Brodky."

"What did she say?"

"'It's cool at the beach. You should be here.' I tried calling back, but I got her voicemail."

"Where are you, Jenna?"

"At home."

"Give me your address. I'm coming there now. Then text her back and ask her to call you."

She lives on the west side of town on the long ridge that separates Webster from the Farmington River Valley.

I call Cynthia. "A friend of Amber's just got a text from her."

"Yep," she says. "I was just going to call you. It came up on the alert about ten minutes ago."

"Do they have a location for the phone?"

"On it. Take about an hour."

I tell Tony. "If she's happily texting from the beach, then she's alive, she's apparently not under threat, we just got to find her, right?"

"If," he says.

Up here, the homes back onto a large chunk of forest that covers the watershed for the reservoirs.

"Theresa told me she darted a bear up here last year," Tony says as we cruise along Jenna's road, checking the house numbers.

"Really? Didn't hear about that. I'm impressed."

"It was trying to get at the dog through the French doors."

If you want the beautiful view over the Farmington Valley you build on the west side and you have to deal with the blazing long afternoon sun. Jenna's house is on the east, early mornings, early sunset. Jenna and a watchful mother escort us onto a large wooden deck with a view over the forest. We sit around a table with a pitcher of iced water.

I look at Jenna Brodsky and I think this is why they have private schools and elite colleges. She is that other species, knockdown good-looking, eyes clear and calm and smart, polite, and the whole burnished package sits perfectly against a backdrop of easy wealth. Her mother, groomed like a racehorse, watching her handle us, as though this is a teaching opportunity in deportment.

Jenna hands me her phone, with the message on the screen:

Cool at the beach. You should be here ;-)

It's timed at 11:52. I copy it down exactly into my notepad.

"Did you text her back?"

"Yeah, she hasn't replied."

"Were you supposed to be at the beach with her?"

"Not really," she shrugs. "Kids were texting about a party down there."

"Where?"

"Saybrook, I think."

"But you said no?"

The mother interjects, "As a rule, we don't allow Jenna to go on these mass sleepovers. You don't know whose house it is, sometimes there is no parental control at all."

"I understand. So Jenna, were you and Amber good friends? Best friends?"

She tosses eleven pounds of glossy hair to dissuade me of this notion.

"I mean, I like her. She's smart and really sweet when she wasn't with the idiots."

"The idiots?"

"In her freshman year she had a problem. She was a scholarship kid. Wrong clothing labels, cheap phone. There are kids at Wycroft whose parents are foreign ambassadors and billionaires and stuff like that. Anyway, there was something embarrassing on her Facebook page."

"What was it?"

"Honestly, I can't remember. But kids were talking about it for like a day, laughing at her."

Yep. Been there. Kids recoil from what they see as tainted. Their sensitivity to who is "like" and who is "other" is finely tuned.

"So she kind of withdrew, you know," says Jenna "and then ended up with the idiots."

Jenna's mother leans into her daughter. "You need to tell them, Jen."

Jenna takes a big breath. "Amber hangs out with the kids, you know, who drink. And do drugs. The potted plants—pot-smokers. There was a rumor that she was a supplier."

"That's what you heard? That Amber was supplying drugs at the school?"

"Yeah, like, I never saw it, I can't say for certain, but that's what I heard some kids saying—if you wanted to score, you should talk to Amber."

I look to the mother. "Did you expect this, Mrs. Brodky? The kind of money you're paying I would expect the school to have no drugs."

"Less drugs, perhaps," she says with a mirthless smile.

"And the people who would have been at this beach party?" Tony says to Jenna. "They were the kind of guys who might have been her customers?

Shrugs. "I really don't know?"

"How many texts do you get from her a week, say?"

"We don't usually text, maybe occasionally. That was a bit out of the blue."

"I think what may have happened," says the mother, "is that some boys tried to encourage Amber to get Jenna to the party."

Jenna, the sought-after gem. Amber the intermediary.

"Do you know anything about Amber's relationship with her parents? Happy at home?"

"I've never met her parents or been to her house. I don't know."

Tony's phone rings and he steps away to answer it. The mother takes this opportunity to discreetly consult her watch.

"Then how did you and she become friends?" I ask Jenna.

"So at school you can be friends with different people in different ways? There's like your tribe that you hang out with all the time, and then there are other people you just talk to about certain things. Like someone you might be on a sports team with. Amber and I were in English together and her stories were amazing. And she would talk about stuff that she had read that no one

61

else had read. And she could be really funny. She had this way of saying 'quoth the Raven' about things. You know, from Edgar Allen Poe? But she used it in a funny way. Like, ironically?" She glances at her mom for confirmation gets a small nod in return.

"If Amber was spending a few days with a friend—say, a boy—do you have any thoughts on who it might be?"

"No, sorry."

Tony rejoins us and gives me an eyebrow that says we have news. The mother, who wouldn't miss a glance from across a football field, stands and pushes her hair behind her ears.

"Jenna," I say. "I want you to think. Come back to me with a list of kids from your school that you think might be friends with Amber."

She's nodding but not listening, glancing at the mother.

"Are you listening to me, Jenna? This girl's life might be in your hands. She might do some things you don't like, but she hasn't had your advantages."

Bang. Now she's blushing. Not at the possibility of being uncharitable, but at being thought uncharitable. "Of course! I will! I'll do it now."

"Thank you. You're our best lead right now. Call me, okay?" And I top that with a long look at the mother.

I meet up with Tony outside.

"What's happened?"

"Cynthia," he says. "Verizon did the tower track. That text to Jenna was sent from Webster. Right in town."

I flip open my notebook.

"You should be here," I read out to Tony. "I can't see how that's a typo or an auto-correct thing."

"She wants Jenna to believe she's at the beach when she isn't," says Tony.

"So there's something more between these two girls than Jenna is saying?"

As we enter the station, I spot Captain Donald trying to escape down the corridor without anyone from the detectives' room intercepting him.

"Captain!"

"Found her?" he says, walking on.

"No. Sir, I need more resources. There's complications."

He stops in the middle of the corridor.

"The parents lied about when she went missing. She's actually been gone longer than we thought."

"I'll get Mrs. B to allocate you a war room. The bodies you got from patrol yesterday, you can keep them. I can't give you detectives, that's the way it is."

He's gotten to be head of department because he makes decisions quickly.

"We need to get publicity, sir. I know the chief said—"

"Do it. But talk to Mac first. Let him guide you on dealing with the media. Email me a summary at the end of today."

"Thank you, sir."

"How's it going with di Giorgio?" he interrupts. Suddenly those hooded eyes are interested in what I have to say.

"Oh, I really like him."

"Yeah? Where's the wedding list?"

I blush. Then I blush some more because I am so frikken furious with myself for blushing.

"Very competent and easy to work with, is what I should have said."

"Relax, Bradley. Find that girl." And he's walking again.

Roger "Mac" MacKenzie is a 50-something captain who floats around in the air near the Chief. I don't know exactly what he does, but he must be good at something because he has the respect of the troops despite being bounced upstairs to a non-operational role. Shortish but powerfully built guy with a real freckled, Scottish look. His style is to treat all cases, no matter how serious, in the same jaunty, irreverent manner.

"This is what we're going to do," he says after I've outlined the case to him.

"We'll call a press conference for one hour from now. Short notice, very few reporters will actually be able to attend, and they'll make do with the release we send out. That buys you some time before you have to field a bunch of difficult questions."

Stubby fingers make bullet points in the air. "This is the definition of a press conference. It's an event where you tell reporters the information we have decided in advance to give them. End of definition. Nothing else is conveyed to them, no matter what questions they ask."

"I've been to press conferences before, sir."

"It's different when you're the one standing up there. It's different when they're asking you personally why you haven't found this kid yet. It's very tempting to start explaining yourself, and three sentences later you've handed them a stick to beat you with."

"Okay."

"I'll write a draft of the release, you read it, tell me if I've got anything wrong. While I'm doing that you practice this phrase, 'It's too early in the investigation to speculate.' That is your song. Basically you're going to keep singing it until this girl is found."

He offers me candy from a bowl on his desk.

"The fact that we've already got one bad case on our table makes you vulnerable. Something new helps them keep the other story alive. Webster is overflowing with crazy people, that kind of nonsense. These New York reporters that are watching the Weisz case? Pythons.

"Realize this," he says, now shepherding me to the door. "There will come a point in any case when you are so enraged by what has been done to your victim and her family, when you're tired and confused and you want to lash out or burst into tears or both. That's the moment when one of the pythons will slither up to your elbow with a cup of coffee and a look of camaraderie and a gentle word about what you must be going through. And she'll quietly drape her coils around your body and five minutes later she'll have constricted you to death."

"Why are you saying 'she'?"

"The female is deadlier than the male."

"Thanks very much, Mac."

"Present company excepted."

"Again, thanks."

Mac's mustache is a model for others to follow. Trimmed very short and clean. I must commend it to Beanbag.

The war room is just a room separated from the detective's squad room, but it will give us a place to organize the increasing streams of information coming from different sources. I set one of the patrol guys, a youngster named Flynn, to setting up the display board, filing and computer.

Tony is doing his paperwork. There's not much actual paper any more, except for the notebooks we carry. The case records are templates you fill on the computer, but we still call it paperwork. A lot of officers let everything accumulate until it absolutely has to be done, but in two days I've leant that Tony is meticulous on this subject.

"Mister Neat and Tidy Casework, aren't we?"

"I'm mister been there, done that, got the reprimand, been crapped on by the judge on the witness stand. I had a case fall apart because the defense hired law students to go through every single piece of investigatory paperwork. They found an error in the address on a search warrant. The guy walked."

"Judges who buy that kind of thing should be prosecuted themselves."

"Either way, it makes you very keen on neat and tidy case-work."

So I sit down and do mine, too, to occupy the time until the press conference.

Every evening in the house on Wilton Lane, Leonard Miller takes a bottle of single malt whisky off the shelf next to the olive oil. One shot followed by another. He drinks the first one quickly, neat—it's his transport from the world where he maintains appearances. The second is nursed, water added. And that's all. His meds don't play well with excessive alcohol. Two whiskies a day, nobody's idea of oblivion, sweet or otherwise, but it's a staging post, something he can use to get through the end of the day.

Bella knows this time of day, too, because they eat crackers and cheese together. The dog presents herself like a sphinx on the carpet next to him. Her back legs tucked in, front legs extended, nibbling the crackers like a debutante. Television he can't stand. It seems to Miller like one massive, screaming asylum. He reads, mostly history, worlds far removed from this one. He and the dog sit together most evenings with the whisky and the snacks, keeping each other company. Miller reads his book until the natural light goes and then sometimes sits there unmoving into total darkness. It is not uncommon for night to come and go without him turning on a single electric light. He is not always sure what happens to him in the bad nights. The boundaries between reality and dream are moveable. He no longer resists it. These are his nights. He has woken up in every room in the house.

Whatever happens during the night, he is at his desk at 8:30 every weekday morning, whether in his study on Wilton Lane or at one of the insurance companies that use his services. He works a full eight-hour day, more when necessary. When his body or his mind assail him during work, he simply continues.

I like to run the streets; you see the stuff you never notice from a car window. As Tony pointed out, I live on the wrong side of Webster—the south end, literally the wrong side of the tracks. In the row of stores south of my place, the shoe shop has been replaced by an operation that will buy your gold jewelry, fronted by a tough-guy Russian who runs unintentionally comical ads on local TV. Next door, the Vietnamese restaurant is gone, there's just an abandoned space still emanating the smell of exotic herbs. I tripped and fell two weeks ago—the road surface needed work at the end of winter but it was never done, and now the heavy storms of summer have scoured out deeper erosions. Some are marked by traffic cones, some not. Groups of pre-teenage boys wander unsupervised. There's a gang in this area that calls itself the NBA—after New Britain Avenue—and the twelve-year-old wannabes hoping to catch the recruiter's eye start out with petty vandalism they can tag and brag about. All of this three miles from Tunxis Square, where the restaurants are heaving with people willing to pay $28 for an entrée.

I push the pace the last half-mile, and then stand under a cold shower for ten minutes. I really need to sleep tonight—last night I only got about four hours. I eat the soup and quinoa bread I picked up on the way home and then take a glass of cold milk with me to bed—a routine that sometimes works.

Not tonight. You know when you try not to think about something? It becomes the thing splattered on the windshield of your consciousness. I'm undergoing a kind of horror at myself for the way that I felt last night when I was so gung-ho about having this case. A poverty of evidence is frustrating; contradictory evidence is frightening.

Mac was right about the press conference this afternoon. The few reporters who attended all asked questions that implied a lax investigation, and it made me furious. I felt alone and vulnerable in front of them and doubted myself. In the middle of it, I glanced to the side and saw Tony watching me with the same suppressed anxiety that parents have when watching their 8-year-old on stage in the school play. Or that's what I thought I saw. I don't know. Because there's evidence from my past that I infer things that people are thinking about me—negative things—which may not be true.

I don't get along easily with people. It's been that way always, probably because I'm an only child. Never had the tumble of siblings, the feeling of a team that has to stick with me. Anyway, the point is my relationships in the department have never been very close. I don't form lifelong friendships with officers I am randomly teamed with. But I'm feeling I can really trust Tony. And that feeling carries with it a counter-feeling that I mustn't fall for feeling secure. We all get to the age where we start to learn and accept what's fucked up about ourselves and how to work around it. Here I am now, thirty-three. I love my job. Maybe too much. My captain said that to me once during a review. But even though I've risen up the ranks, fitting in has remained something I've had to consciously work at. The other officers never told me their life stories while we were killing hours on a stake out. It never affects the job, it doesn't affect me—except here I am thinking about it.

With Tony di Giorgio things are turning out different. I feel like I have communication with the guy. Take that interview with Leonard Miller yesterday, for example. Tony must have led hundreds of interviews in his time, but he felt no need to butt into mine. I just know if I had been partnered with almost anyone else in the division, they would have been interjecting all over me. Also, a lot of male cops try to physically intimidate interviewees, but Tony just sat there with a neutral demeanor. It was his complete concentration on Miller's face that discomfited Miller. It was good teamwork. I am lucky to have gotten Tony. I know that now. But I still know what everyone else in the squad thinks. He's my babysitter.

It's obvious I'm not going to fall asleep, so I get out of bed and pull on some clothes. Twenty minutes later I'm walking into Planet B, a bar a quarter mile south of Amber's house. It's a welcoming place, unlike most of the over-designed Webster restaurants. The tricky elf at the back of my mind has persuaded me to believe it's conceivable that someone in here would know something about Amber. Or I could use some anonymous time on a beer and a conversation with anyone about anything except Amber. Either scenario would work. It's even conceivable to the elf that we could meet a half-decent guy. Because we'd give it up for a night's sleep in an air-conditioned room.

DAY THREE

Thursday. 5:00 a.m.

Like three hours' sleep. Once a week on trash collection day there's an Asian guy who comes at dawn rattling a steel shopping cart down the street, foraging for returnable bottles and cans in people's trash bins on the sidewalk. I leave my soda cans out in a separate paper bag on the sidewalk, but he still forages noisily through all the other trash bins.

So, at 5 a.m., I am out of bed doing a hundred sit-ups in reps of twenty. Then arm work with the 10 pound dumbbells. Speed, not bulk. I'm in the war room before six so I can be alone and quiet with the information that came in yesterday and overnight. Flynn's done a good job of summarizing everything on the display board—each line of inquiry and its outcome. But it still adds up to shit.

And at 6:50, here I am in Mrs. Riaz's severely tidy kitchen again. Showed up much too early at her door, but she was up and dressed. The same vase, with fresh flowers, stands on the table. The coffee is good.

Mrs. Riaz comes back into the kitchen.

"I've woken her, she'll just be a few minutes," she says. "I have to leave for work in twenty minutes."

Catriona's mother is an impressive individual—great posture, muscle tone, an aura of competence, no bullshit.

"Mrs. Riaz, do you have anything to tell me about Amber that might be useful?"

"I don't see her much anymore. Catriona used to hang out with her a lot before, but not so much anymore."

"Since she went to private school?"

"A bit before that, actually."

"Any reason? Off the record."

"Look, I'm a single mother. Catriona has to come home to an empty house when I'm at work. So I'm a bit stricter than other parents. There were some kids they were hanging around with in eighth grade that I didn't like. Older kids. I talked to Catriona about it and she agreed to make some distance from them. I know she sometimes dresses like a pole dancer but she's basically got good instincts."

The doorbell rings. That was fast. "That'll be my partner," I say. "I'll let him in."

I called Tony maybe twenty minutes ago to tell him I was coming here. I thought I might get to do this alone, given the time of day, but he's standing on the step shaved and dressed like he had been standing at the phone waiting for my call.

I introduce him to Mrs. Riaz. "Catriona will be with us in a minute," she says.

"What made you cautious about those kids Catriona and Amber were hanging out with?" I ask.

"Really, I am not accusing anyone of anything."

"I understand."

"Our girls were thirteen then. These new friends were older and they were Lander kids, not from Travis High. I bust my butt to pay for this house so that we're in the Travis district. Lander gets the kids from down by New Britain Avenue, I don't want to sound like I'm discriminating, but there's a higher risk of problems with those kids."

Now Catriona comes in with a robe wrapped around her, hair mussed. She gives me a furtive look. She knows already that I've got her.

"Let's all sit down," I say. Mrs. Riaz puts a mug of juice in front of her daughter and then sits as well. "Catriona, Amber's been missing more than two days now. She could be in real danger."

She's playing with the friendship bands on her wrist. "I spoke to a friend of Amber's yesterday who told me she might be involved with the sort of people who do drugs?"

No intention of meeting my eyes.

"Does that sound like the Amber you know?"

Mrs. Riaz looks at her watch.

"You're going to be late for work, mom."

"Just answer the question, Catriona," Mrs. Riaz says.

"Like I said before, I don't see Amber much these days. But we went to Hendricksen's for ice cream in spring break, and she was just different, you know, from what she used to be. Like she was over confident. Kinda zingy, you know?"

Raise my eyebrows at that. "Zingy?"

Mrs. Riaz can't stay seated any longer. She takes her mug to the sink and rinses it with flashing hands.

"Very excited about everything," says Catriona. "I asked her what's up with her and she said that things were much better at the new school now. But, I could tell something wasn't right. I've seen it in other kids, the ones who are going to get in trouble. Something about them changes. That's what she was like and I got scared for her." She turns to her mother. "Like Renata."

"Who's that?" I say.

"An older girl they knew," says Mrs. Riaz. "She met a guy who played in a band, ran off with him in her sophomore year at school, came home a year later with needle marks and a little bump."

Catriona's eyes are starting to brim. Her mother hands her a tissue. The kid takes a glance at her mom but there's no amnesty yet. "A few days later she came around in the afternoon. She said she wanted me to meet some guys up at the park. So we walked up there. Two guys arrived in a car, like a new BMW. Rich kids. They said let's go to the reservoir, but the guy with the car, he didn't want to take the dog."

"What dog?"

"On the way up to the park we went by this house, Amber walks the dog there, so we took it with us."

"Okay, so then?"

"Anyway, in the end we did take the dog in the car. We parked far away from the other cars and Amber pulled this little bag out of her purse and she had pot in it—"

Mrs. Riaz lets out an explosion of breath.

"I didn't smoke any!" Catriona wails.

"You were there! In public!"

"Mrs. Riaz, please—"

"Mom, I'm not interested in drugs and I don't like the people who mess with them. Honestly."

I hold up my palm to try and calm the scene. "Catriona, that's okay, I know it's hard to tell on your friend, but you've got to keep in your mind that this is the way to help her."

Hands balled on her hips, Mrs. Riaz is shaking her head as if she's not buying any of it.

"So she and the boys smoked some weed and then you came back home and everything was okay?"

"Yes."

"And when did you next hear from Amber?"

"Well, she texted a few times, but I didn't reply."

"Why not?"

"I was pissed at her for that day."

"Because of the weed?"

"No. I mean, if I got pissed at everyone I know who smokes weed I wouldn't have any friends. It was because, you know, I felt she was using met...like she only took me along for the boys..."

"They wanted to meet a hot friend, right?"

"They kept telling me I should come and hang out at their house, there's a pool, bring your bikini, blah, blah, they were so gross." Now she's furiously wiping away the tears. "I feel bad saying this because of what's happened."

Mrs. Riaz plops the entire box of tissues onto the table in front of her daughter, muttering something in Spanish that I don't understand but the gist is in the delivery: you're crying now, wait till the cop lady is gone.

I take out my pad and pen. "Catriona, I want you to relax for a minute. Don't talk. Just think. Take this pen. And write down for me the names of those boys. And the older guys you used to hang out with at Lander. Back when you and she were still friends?" I push the pad and pen over to her.

She hesitates. I can see the lean, hard muscles working in her mother's arm as she firmly taps her finger on the pad. Lots of light weight reps in those arms.

"I'm just trying to remember!" The words burst out of Catriona and she snatches up the pen. I shift my seat slightly so I can see what she's writing.

Guys with BMW:
Brandon ?
Eric ?
Guys from school:
Donnie Alvarez
Angel
Z-Z

Catriona turns the pad so it faces me. "Donnie was the guy we knew best. He introduced us to the other two."

"Who was the oldest? Who was the leader?"

"Z-Z. He had a car. I don't think he was in school much."

"You can't remember his real name?"

"That's all anyone ever called him. He had a tattoo like that on his arm."

"Like two Zs?"

"Yes. Maybe they were supposed to be thunderbolts, I don't know, but he was Z-Z."

"They ever take you to any of their houses?"

"We went to Donnie's a few times." Glancing at her mother. "Just in the afternoons, not at night."

"Do you know where any of these guys are now?"

"Donnie's in school. I see him but I don't talk to him. I don't know about the other two." Her robe is gaping slightly as she leans forward and her mother steps behind her and swiftly repositions it.

"I'm sorry I didn't tell you this when you came that day, but it's hard, you know."

"You're right," I say. "Nothing you've told us today would have put us any closer to finding her. It's okay."

But misery has descended on Catriona, the polite and obedient hottie who I'm betting will end up a pillar of the community like her mom. The tears stream down her face. So now's the time.

"So, Catriona, that day, when did you first see the pot? At the reservoir or before?"

"At the reservoir."

"Amber had it in a purse or something?"

"Um, yeah, the old denim bag I think. The one she's been using for years to bring her books from the library."

"Did she have that bag with her when she arrived at your house?"

"Sure. I don't specifically remember. But she must have."

"But when you stopped to get the dog? Did she leave the bag with you while she went into the house?"

"I don't think so."

"Can't you remember?"

"No. Not exactly."

"Did she come from her own house to yours that day?"

"I think so."

"Do you think Amber would keep pot at her own house?"

"I didn't think about it. I guess she wouldn't. There are some parents who don't take things so seriously, but for her it would be risky."

"When I looked at Amber's room it was very neat and tidy. You couldn't hide anything in there."

"Yeah, she's like that. Because the rest of the house is so messy, usually, I guess."

"When you took the dog back that day, did Amber take the denim bag into the house?"

She thinks a moment. "They dropped me off first. I asked them to because I wanted to get away from those boys. I said I needed to be home."

"And, Catriona, did you guys actually walk the dog that day? You know, give him exercise?"

"No, he just came along for the ride."

"So, do you think that Amber really went to the house to get the dog, or is it possible she used it as an excuse to go into the house and collect the pot?"

"I don't know," she says, but I can see the possibilities bouncing in her eyes. "Do you mean she kept her stash there, without the owner knowing?"

I shrug.

"It would be clever, like her. She would enjoy doing that because it's clever. She's like that."

I stand, pick the pad from the table and give a glance toward Tony to see if he has anything. He doesn't.

"Thank you, Catriona, Mrs. Riaz, you've been very helpful."

Walking out to the street, Tony says, "Good work. How did you know she had more?"

"Teenage girls always know more than you think. That's one of the laws of nature." I hand him Catriona's neat little list of names. "These top two, the rich kids, I'm sure they must be from that school. Maybe you could get onto that advisor and see if there's an Eric or a Billy in her class. Or in the whole school. She probably hangs with boys older than her?"

"Sure. What are you going to do?"

"I'll get the daily report to the captain out of the way and then check if there's been any action on her phone, and so on."

The truth, but not the whole truth.

"Where's Detective di Giorgio?" says Captain Donald.

"Following a lead to some boys Amber hangs with."

I have wrangled my captain and an Assistant State's Attorney named Angelique something or other into a room together and now I have to sell them a story.

"The missing girl is Amber Zajac. We've got a school friend named Jenna who was the last person we know who communicated with Amber. This girl says Amber hangs out with the kids at school who do drugs. Catriona, Amber's friend from way back, says that in the spring she saw Amber give weed to two boys. On the way to meet those boys, she saw Amber go into Miller's house and get the marijuana. Miller works during the day. Amber has

77

access to his house to walk his dog. Amber keeps the marijuana in his house. Her parents are strict, not to mention a bit crazy. This is a safe place where she can hide her stash. So my question is, can we get a warrant for Miller's house on that basis?"

"I'm confused," says my captain. "Are you looking at Miller as a pedophile-type abductor, or as a drug dealer?"

"Do they have to be separate? If he's supplying her drugs, or even condoning her use of them on his property, then he is corrupting her. Possibly as a means of taking advantage of her in other ways."

That hits home with him. Because he can see the headlines.

"Has Miller got a record?" asks Angelique. Although she's young, early thirties maybe, she has a cool assurance.

"Not in this country. He's British. We put in a request with the police there."

"And you've interviewed him and he denied knowing where she is?"

"Yes. But we have another couple who lives behind him who says he invited their ten-year-old son into his house. Alone."

She frowns. "Is he gay or straight? I'm not an expert, but don't pedophiles stick to one or the other?"

"He used to be married but he's got no kids, and now he lives alone with a dog. So, indeterminate."

"You need to get on the phone to our friends in London," Captain Donald says, "this guy could have a sheet there."

"Look," says Angelique, "I think if you go to a judge and say he might be a drug dealer or he might be a pedophile, that's difficult to act on. These are two completely separate types of crime. You have the girl collecting weed from his house, right?"

"Yes," I say.

"She's a minor?"

"Yes."

"That's enough then. Go with a drug search warrant. If there's nothing, then you're back where you were, no worse. If there's drugs in his house, then you've got him in an interrogation room, you can ask him whatever you want."

Captain Donald is nodding like a cheap toy dog. He's impressed with everything about our Angelique, and so am I, but I have to get out of here before she asks me how solid my witness is.

"Hang on, Donna," he says. "Listen, I'm going to have Pengelli execute the warrant."

What the fuck? I look that at him. I don't say it, but I leave him in no doubt.

"It's consistent with the basis for the warrant. It's a drug case. He's the drug specialist. It'll add weight to the warrant."

"You want me to hand my guy over to other detectives who don't even know he exists?"

"Look, if he's guilty on drug issues, that's what we would do anyway. If he isn't, but there's something relevant to your case, then you get him."

I have to eat it.

"I'll call him in," says the captain. "Why don't you start drafting his warrant application? He'll appreciate that."

Things develop rapidly. I've never worked with Pengelli but his rep is solid, he gets results. He has a Roman nose and the kind of arms you only get by doing curls while you catch up with everything on your DVR. He doubles as leader of our SWAT team, but he doesn't overstep, as far as I know. And he apparently has his go-to judges, because he has a search warrant for Miller's house before Tony even gets back from Amber's school.

Pengelli rousts out his favorite wingman and a marijuana

sniffer-dog handler. They take three marked vehicles and several uniforms, Pengelli being a shock and awe kinda guy.

I can't sit and wait so I go for a walk around Tunxis Square. When I get back, Tony is sitting at his desk in the war room.

"Get anything from the school?" I ask him. But he's not interested in that.

"Can you give us a minute?" Tony says to Flynn, who's processing paperwork at his computer. The kid gets up and goes, closing the door behind him.

"What's up?" I say.

"How did you get a warrant for Miller's house?" The volume of his voice is still soft, but the tone is not.

"I told the captain and the state's attorney Catriona's story and they agreed there was likely evidence of marijuana in Miller's house."

"To get a judge to sign the warrant, you must have offered a witness willing to testify with direct knowledge of it."

"Direct is open to interpretation."

"Not to me. I didn't hear Catriona say that Amber got the pot from Miller's house."

"Pretty much."

"No, you suggested it to her, and then she agreed that might be the case."

"She just didn't work it out for herself."

"That's the point. It had to be worked out. It's a deduction. Not a pure evidentiary fact."

"It's exactly the same as what a prosecutor would do with a witness in court!"

"Bullshit. And you know it. Were you absent the day they gave the probable cause lecture?"

Now my eyes are stinging and the only way I can stop that from progressing is to let myself get angry.

"This is what I know." I make myself look straight at him. "Amber's been missing three days. My faith in the idea that she's just dissing her parents is fading fast. And if this turns out badly I don't want to think that I didn't help her because I was worried about the rules for a warrant."

"That's why they have the rules. So that officers who are convinced they know the answer can't start framing things up to their liking. You need to learn that."

"Oh, and you know what I need to learn because you've been put with me as a babysitter! Do you think I don't know that?"

"If that was the brass's intention," he says, "nobody said anything to me."

"Oh, please, you can't see the setup?"

"Sure I can. What I don't get is your resentment. So you've got a babysitter. Boo hoo. It happens all the time. And you just proved you need one. Do you think this will ever hold up? If they charge him? His lawyer will trash that warrant in a second. Then it's much harder to pin him. Did you think of that?"

"I didn't. Because pinning him is not my priority. Finding Amber is. Finding her safe. If we save her from whatever shit she's in, we've done ninety percent of our job. The important ninety percent."

And at that moment, the police radio kicks in. Pengelli's movie-actor style voice comes over.

"I'm bringing Mr. Miller in. He's holding at least twelve ounces in his basement."

The timing is preposterous.

The sniffer dog went in the house–after Miller had secured his own dog in the garage–and immediately dragged the handler down the basement stairs. Now Miller is sitting in the interview

81

room waiting for his lawyer. And I am in the war room with the following items, neatly evidence-bagged, on the table in front of me:

* one scuffed and faded denim bag with shoulder strap, with "Amber Zajac" written in marker pen under one of the pocket flaps.

* twelve dollars and twenty-seven cents.

* an inexpensive ankle bracelet, catch broken.

* two sheets of paper, folded and dog-eared, which contain a print out from an Internet site of "The Raven" by Edgar Allan Poe.

* a business card from Ink Dreams, a tattoo parlor on Parkside Road with, on the back, a sketch of a raven, adapted from the gothic image at the head of the poem.

* three hair-ties.

* several sticks of gum.

* a small pack of liver treats for dogs, unopened

* one plastic Ziploc bag, containing marijuana, weighed and tagged by Pengelli at 14.5 ounces.

"I hear Pengelli got a solid arrest?" Captain Donald says from the doorway. I point at the marijuana bag. "Fourteen point five, intent to deal. I think we've got him where we need him."

"Anything there to tell us where she might be?"

"No."

"Next step?"

"He's in the process of lawyering up. Then Pengelli's going to interrogate and charge him formally, then I get him."

"Where's your partner?"

"He just stepped out."

"You need him in there with you."

"Of course."

Actually, I don't have clue where Tony is. He walked out after Pengelli gave us the information over the radio, and I haven't seen him since. But I'm relieved to learn that he has not been in the captain's office telling him that I massaged the warrant.

Miller's lawyer arrives and turns out to be Bob Gisk, who I know to have an okay reputation. I'm watching through the window as Pengelli steps Miller through the booking process with admirable swiftness. Felony drug possession. Tony shows up next to me. I open my mouth to ask him where he's been, but then I can't do it.

"We're getting Miller when Pengelli has him charged."

Tony just nods, watching the scene through the glass.

Miller is adamant he knows nothing, has never seen the bag or the contents before. Repeats the explanation about Amber having access to the house to walk the dog. Within half an hour he's been charged and processed, but it's too late for him to get a bail hearing tonight. The lawyer starts talking about Miller going home on his own recognizance, that's when Tony and I walk into the interview room.

"I'm sorry, Mr. Miller, but we have other questions for you." I turn to Gisk. "You may not have made the connection, but the Amber Zajac who purportedly owns the bag found in his house is the same Amber Zajac who has been missing for four days now."

A good lawyer can roll a hit like that without any twitching. He turns to Miller and elevates his eyebrows a hundredth of an inch. Miller nods.

"I see," says Gisk. "Can I have some time with my client, then, please?"

"My dog is still locked in the garage," says Miller. "Can I go home and tend to her and come back in half an hour?"

"Of course not," I say.

"She can't just be left there," he says.

83

"Surely you have someone who normally handles this for you?"

"Yes," he says. "Amber."

"I'll get Animal Control to handle it," I say.

He looks alarmed. "She can't go to the pound. Weimaraners get separation anxiety. Can I have some time to contact neighbors or someone from the dog group then?"

"Out of the question," I say. "You are not leaving the station and you are not communicating with anyone except police officers and your lawyer. Animal Control will collect the dog and assess its condition, and we'll go from there."

Tony goes to dispatch and asks them to get Animal Control around to Miller's house. Then we are two-on-two across the interview desk with the recorder running, the official interview preliminaries dispensed with and Captain Donald on the other side of the glass.

"I'm going to begin like this," I'm leaning forward toward Miller, forcing eye contact. "Amber has been missing several days now. She is at risk, severe risk, until we find her. If you know anything that can help us, and you don't tell us now, that's on you. Understand?"

"I'm not hiding anything from you," he says.

"You told Lieutenant Pengelli this is Amber's denim bag?"

Gisk jumps in. "That's not what my client said. The bag has Amber's name on it. He has not seen it before."

"Although it's in his own basement?"

"It's a big, unfinished, poorly-lit basement," says Miller, "with a lot of stuff in it. I use it only for storage. If there's heavy rain I go down to check the sump pump. If a fuse trips, I go to the board. Otherwise, I never go there."

"So she hid this bag in your basement without your knowledge?"

84

"I can only assume so."

"How would she do that? When would she get an opportunity?"

He shrugs. "Any time that she walks Bella for me when I'm not there."

"She has a key to your house?"

"I told you that when you came to my house."

"Please answer for the record."

"Amber knows where the spare key is hidden outside the house."

"So you're asking us to believe that when you're not there, Amber wanders freely around your house, down into the basement, where she can keep stuff with the confidence of knowing you won't look there?"

"I once asked her to help me move a table down the basement stairs. There were some cobwebs. She commented it looked like no one ever goes there. I told her I never do. I guess she saw an opportunity."

"You didn't tell us that before."

"It didn't come up."

"Did you know that Amber was involved in drug dealing?"

"Of course not! And I still don't. I'm sure the kid just got mixed up in some stupid thing."

"Did she bring other friends to your house?"

"Never. That I know of."

"Did she tell you about her friends?"

"No."

"Nothing?"

"Obviously she may have mentioned small things. Nothing significant."

"There seems to be more and more things you didn't tell us when we interviewed you."

"Look!" Miller stands but Gisk quickly pulls him down. "You know whose fault that is?" he says. "Yours. You didn't come to me for information with an open mind. You came to my door that day with the idea that I was a suspect. You came for information that would confirm your preconceived idea."

"Why would we do that?"

"Who knows. Maybe somebody should do a doctorate on it. I need to go to the bathroom."

The interview is suspended so that everyone can use the facilities. When I get return, Miller is back in the interview room and Theresa is waiting for me in the corridor.

"I'm going to take his dog home with me," she informs me.

"Whoa, I'm not happy with that."

"Why not?"

"Because you're a police officer. We should be creating a hostile context for him, not giving him succor."

"Succor?" she repeats.

"Is there no other option?"

"The pound is closed now. She's a wonderful dog," she says, "and not guilty of any crime."

In Theresa's world, dogs have a bill of rights.

"Okay, take the dog for one night. Put it in the pound tomorrow. Or wherever. But we don't provide babysitting services for suspects."

Off she goes, and Tony and I head back to the interview room. Another hour. As far as we can tell he never lies, and he never contradicts himself meaningfully. Over and over the mundane stuff, trying to break his self-control. I hand over to Tony, who goes through the same questions again, while Miller's three hundred dollar an hour lawyer examines his manicure. At quarter of nine, Gisk decides he's earned enough for today. He looks at his watch.

"Can you give my client a break now?"

My only satisfaction is that Miller will not be heading to Logan airport tonight—it's too late for him to get any kind of bail hearing. He'll overnight in the station holding cell and get an audience with a judge tomorrow morning. He obviously hasn't eaten and it's the town's responsibility to feed him, so I order in pizza for all of us. And Miller's dog is well provided for, that's a comfort, presumably curled up next to Theresa, which would make her the envy of every Webster PD patrolman.

"Hey, Tony." He's in the war room packing up when I come in. "I got you some pizza."

"No, thanks," he says.

I pull up a chair at his desk. "We can't have this thing hanging over us."

"I'm not angry any more," he says, "just forget it." He's going for his jacket. "Are we going to advise the parents of developments tomorrow morning?"

"Ah, yeah, I guess that should be first," I say.

"Okay, then, meet outside there at eight?"

"Sure."

"Okay, take it easy."

And he's out the door, leaving me sitting alone beside his desk.

By the time I get home my pizza is cold and my half-gallon of milk in the refrigerator is sour. Tonight I could see the merits of a live-in boyfriend. It would be good to just talk through the day with someone. Someone who could get the knots out of my shoulders. I'm going to break a rule and drink alcohol on a weeknight. My dad never had a big problem with alcohol, but he also never let the sun go down without a cold one. And I've always felt that his generally lax attitude to getting things done was related to this. But sometimes for me the only road from a really bad day to a better perspective passes through three margaritas. This is not a quantity that a single woman can drink in public without attracting vermin, so I keep the fixings at home. Also, at home I choose the music and tonight I need my best buddy Liz Phair thumping in my ears. It's a matter of occasional distress to my neighbors that my idea of recuperative music is the kind that cracks the caulk on your drywall but they never complain and it usually lasts only for a short time.

I like to make the margaritas just so, with the crystallized sugar hard on the rim and some mint from the patch growing wild through the fence behind where I park. It takes me longer to make them than to drink them. The smack of the lime on my tongue makes me remember: *succor*. Out of nowhere and into my mouth. A good word for an English teacher, perfect in the context. Terrible word for a cop trying not to sound like an English teacher.

Miller. I have to face it that we got nowhere with him tonight. I'm terrified that I just don't have the experience—or perhaps it's the imagination—to see how everything fits together between him and Amber. I have to restrain myself from driving back to the station and saying to him "just cut the shit and tell us where she is! Put yourself and a lot of other people out of misery."

But the guilty ones are either so wrapped up in their own pain that the lives of others don't even register, or they're psychopaths, in which case there is no pain, no guilt, and no soul. Is Miller one of those? I looked into his eyes many times tonight, trying to divine the answer to that. And he looked back into mine, as if he, too, were looking for something.

Now I'm out of mint, but not out of tequila.

Mikolaj Zajaczkowski was an American patriot before he ever set foot on its soil. The idea of America was magical to him from the time he started to read the newspaper in his village in eastern Poland, twenty miles from Chelm. When he walked to school in the aching December cold he dreamed of California. On the wall of his bedroom was a color picture torn from a magazine—a blond model standing next to a gleaming double-door refrigerator. It was the refrigerator that captivated Mikolaj; it represented to him everything about freedom and enterprise.

By the age of twelve, he was already working after school with his father on small building projects. Mikolaj was born with an innate understanding of viable structures. Loads and gradients and the properties of building materials came to him like sacred visions came to a shaman; he could look at the plans for a building once and go from there. Tools sprang to life in his hands and he was laying perfect lines of brickwork before he was old enough to shave.

Mikolaj loved the idea of America because it was a place like him. A place where things happened fast, where work multiplied itself in value. A place where you could apply energy to a pile of materials and end up with a structure that paid you back forever. Mikolaj was born onto this earth a fully formed capitalist—but at a location right in the drowning vortex of mid-20th century communism. He knew it was up to him to correct this misplacement.

He arrived in America in 1956 with his wife Wioletta and a son, Stanislaw, aged five. Although the immigrant practice of shortening long, consonant-loaded Eastern European names had declined by the fifties, Zajaczkowski submitted the paperwork to become Zajac. In his mind, this was like putting the edge of his trowel to his name and giving it a smart crack—Zajac was a stubby, practical, half-brick of a name suitably trimmed for his foundation in the new world.

His English was poor, but his sketches and scale plans were articulate. He was exploited at first, but he knew it, and he also knew he would consume his exploiters from the inside out. He

89

proceeded upward on line upon line of perfect brickwork, seamless drywall, flush tiling. America fulfilled him just as he had known it would. In ten years, the mason had changed his destiny and propelled his family to a new life.

And yet he found himself unable to bring every aspect of his life to the state he desired. He had expected that his son would transform into a typical American boy, one who steps out of his front door every day with the expectation of success, and by doing so, make it so. He had placed the boy in the right spot at the right time. Mikolaj felt that if such an opportunity had been created for him, he would have set off on the adventure of American life like a racehorse. But the boy Stanislaw seemed perpetually alarmed by the busy frenzy of his new country. Even as a teenager, he carried himself with the stiff immobility of a peasant burdened with the yoke of communism.

Mikolaj blamed his wife. Wioletta had brought the cold and the stubbornness with her on the plane like a plague. She declared a dislike for the American way, and withdrew into her home as if it was a walled Polish village surrounded by vagabonds. She wore her Catholicism like an armor to the world and whispered in her son's ear. Mikolaj saw her doing it, saw the words creasing his son's brow and putting apprehension in his step. To Mikolaj, his wife increasingly resembled a piece of Polish sausage, a repository for all the indigestible bits of Polish tradition and history and uneducated superstition rendered together.

In his frustration, the mason's strong hands were hard on Stan in childhood. He tried to cuff and prod and even whip the boy into a forward gait. To no avail. The boy was dull, he was sullen, he was pale and clumsy. In the nights when Mikolaj suggested the making of another child to his wife, she gave him a round answer: I want no more American children. We go back to Poland, we can make Polish children.

So Mikolaj threw his energy into the bricks and mortar, growing mildly prosperous in the years of American plenty. And it was no surprise to him when his grandson Kris became another heavy-limbed dull boy, even though he had never touched Polish soil or felt the cold or seen the drab color of a line of women waiting through a winter's morning for bread. It was only when Mikolaj saw the wild life in the eye of his wheat-haired granddaughter that he felt his journey had finally born fruit. Despite the pain of his arthritis, he climbed the tree in his son's yard and built her a wooden house in the leaves so that he could sit on the porch and watch her.

Mikolaj's long journey was rewarded. By thirteen, Amber was exceptional in school, her grades near perfect. She was one of those selected ones, the ones that teachers smile over while uttering the names of Ivy League colleges. Amber wrote a dark fantasy story that won a statewide contest, and she was offered a scholarship to an elite private school. That was the American way, that was why the mason shepherded his family out of the cold dark reaches of eastern Poland: so his grand-daughter's blond hair could shine in the American sun as the world admired her.

DAY FOUR

Friday 7 a.m.

Hangover. That bitter regret at the loss of self-control. I slept a few hours, but it doesn't feel like it. I know what it was about—alienating Tony yesterday left me with that desolate feeling from childhood.

Force myself out onto the road for a run. Perspiration pops out of me immediately, stinking of the alcohol that still lingers in my body. Back at my apartment, I realize I forgot to go to the Laundromat. The only clean khakis I have are tight on me. No breakfast in this place, no time to get any.

I'm twenty minutes late and Tony's already parked outside the Zajac house. He gets out of his car as I arrive. Greets me with a smile, which I return.

"Going to be ninety six and humid today," I say. That's what you do to paper over—talk about the weather.

"Let's try and split them up," he says. "Get them to talk separately, maybe something will come out of it."

No response to the doorbell. The house is positioned toward the front of the lot, so there's an extensive yard in back. We walk down the side of the house and come to a back porch enclosed with large glass windows. Inside, Stan Zajac is sitting in a chair, staring out of the glass across his back yard. He's wearing boxer shorts and nothing else. He has a concave chest and a lot of prominent bones. He's flossing his teeth with a brutal thoroughness that is hypnotizing. After a moment, Tony taps on the glass with his car key. The Labrador, previously unnoticed at Zajac's feet, explodes into barking and flies out through the open sliding door to meet us. From down the slope in the yard comes a cry of despair from Mrs. Zajac as a thousand birds fly up in disarray.

"Oh, Stan!" she cries out. "I told you to keep him quiet!"

Stan Zajac isn't listening to her. He's staring at me, trying to suck the news out of my eyes, my facial expression. There's blood on the side of his mouth from where the floss has ripped into his gums.

Down on that lawn, there must be a half a dozen birdfeeders hanging on poles and from tree branches. Mrs. Zajac has been sitting down there with the birds. This is how they tick through the time that their daughter is missing. She hurries up the stone steps to join us.

"We haven't located Amber," I say, rehearsed, "but we do have new developments."

I show them a photo of the denim bag and Mrs. Zajac nods in recognition. I step them carefully and selectively through what we know from the search and from interviewing Miller, making sure they hear that it's just one move in the investigation.

"Do you understand that at this stage we have no proof or even indication that Miller is directly involved in Amber's disappearance?"

They nod.

"The gentleman we are investigating lives near you. I know you might feel the impulse to get involved, but you must resist it. Don't think of going to his house to confront him—"

"He's not in custody?" she says.

"He is at the moment, but he'll probably make bail this morning," says Tony.

"Don't even go for a drive past his house," I say. "Please, that's very important, do you understand?"

I'm trying to catch Stan Zajac's eye, but he's staring into the yard.

"You get squirrels taking from your birdfeeders?" I say to Rosemary Zajac.

"All the time," she says.

"I've got a solution for that. Come on, I'll show you."

We walk down the slope of the lawn. There's a beautifully built stone barbecue, but run-off from a down-pipe has eroded the ground and washed away some of the grass. Dried bird shit is splattered on the back of the chair where she's been sitting.

"First," I say to her, "because you've put these stakes into the ground at ninety degrees, they're too stable. If you put them in at an angle, there's some springiness in the metal that makes the birdfeeder bounce around when there's suddenly an extra weight on it. Doesn't matter to the birds because they're light, but makes it harder for the squirrel to stay on it."

I uproot one of the stakes and plant it in again at an angle.

"Next—this is my mother's patented trick—put some Vaseline on the stake. It's quite fun to watch the squirrels sliding and slipping and the stake bouncing."

I don't know if she's listening to me or not. She's staring at the stake, or past it.

"Mrs. Zajac, did you know about Amber using marijuana?"

Mrs. Zajac pulls up the stake and re-inserts it into the ground the way it was before. "She's a teenager. She doesn't talk to us about everything."

"I find it hard to believe that you don't have some notion of what she did and who she was with."

"Can't you find some way to do this that isn't about tearing my daughter's life apart? Do you think she would want that? You're talking about her as though she did something wrong! As though she's a criminal you're trying to catch."

"Well, the last time we were here your husband did say to me that Amber could be impulsive. Some teenagers do become excessive risk-takers. Did you see any of that?"

"I've told you everything I can think of."

She turns away from me and starts walking up toward the house. The birds are already back at the feeders. A substantial tree house sits solidly in the branches of a tree, a beauty of a big birch. Someone who knew what he was doing built this tree house. But it's been left untended and the elements are steadily annihilating it.

Tony and I head out to the street where we left our cars.

"I didn't know this side of you," Tony has an extra soft voice he uses when he wants to kid me, "the bird-watching expert."

"I just made stuff up. It was a way of getting her on her own. Did you notice when we first told them about Miller? They didn't seem to really latch onto it. It's like they don't see him as being involved."

"Could be, but I've also seen victims' family members who take virtually no interest in the case. They're just defending themselves. They either don't want to know or they're frustrated about being kept at arm's length by us, so they shut it out. It's good for us. It's worse the other way, when they're on your phone twice a day or organizing their own search parties. Did you get anything from her?"

"Nothing specific. She's very defensive about Amber. I mean, that's the way she should be, but it's more than that."

"Such as?"

"I don't know. I'm not a psychiatrist. Or a mother."

Neither of us says a word about yesterday's argument.

10 a.m.

At the Hartford Superior Court on Lafayette Street we're meeting the uniforms from Pengelli's drug team who have transported Miller to his bail hearing. The bus from the correctional center has arrived just before us so the side entrance is congested, and they decide to take him through the front door. There's no need to cuff him; he's as docile as a lamb.

Directly in front of the main entrance to the courthouse a burger wagon is doing raging business.

"Hey, detective!" Manny calls to me from his window in the wagon. "I got that sauce you like."

I wave back at him but keep walking. It's true I am a former patron of Manny's wagon, but today I need to get quickly away from the smell of it; last night's tequila is still vividly with me. When I was a rookie beat cop I ended up here plenty of times escorting the deadbeat re-offenders. There's a class of people for whom the courts are part of life, often from childhood. Some are congenitally criminal, some resort to crime from desperation, some have endured childhood horrors that leave them maladapted to society and some simply don't have the wit or resources to organize their lives without falling into chaos. They become regular visitors to the courts, regular customers of the bail bondsmen who flash their cards at the court entrance. The lifetime re-offender never has the cash to pay his fines or his bail, but is often equipped with a smartphone and hundred-dollar sneakers.

How Manny and his tubby little wife got the sweet permit to park their wagon right outside the courthouse, I asked him many times, and all I ever got was a smile. I'm sure he's paying freight to someone, but he can afford it. He's got a lock on all the marshals and clerks and bondsmen and lawyers.

We are assigned to 2-B, a small courtroom used to rapidly

dispose of a long docket of bails, continuances and referrals. And Angelique has done her work well—we're right up near the top of the list. Which turns out to be not early enough. Tony elbows me and uses his eyebrows to indicate a woman sitting on the small bench reserved for the media, notebook in hand.

Yes, we want the media's help in broadcasting Amber's disappearance and bringing in possible tips. No, we do not want the media to take an interest in Miller's arrest. We want to be able to proceed without having them second-guessing our every move.

"She doesn't look like a budding Woodward and Bernstein," I say.

"Maybe there's something else she's interested in on the docket."

The good thing about this courtroom is that it's a fast-moving river of obscure docket numbers and legal process jargon which happens rapidly between the clerks, prosecutors and a revolving roster of lawyers, and the whole thing is difficult to follow from the public benches. After a tax cheat, a drunken driver who's skipped his correctional training, and a sex offender who failed to register his change of address, we get to Miller.

The thing that catches the reporter lady's eye is the bail that Angelique asks for—one hundred thousand dollars. Miller's lawyer immediately starts contesting that, telling the judge that Miller didn't even know the drugs were in his house, he doesn't use drugs, good job, no priors, blah, blah, blah. Angelique counters with foreign passport and no ties to the community. The reporter is listening but not writing.

In addition to his lawyer, there's a guy who's arrived to assist Miller, a friend or maybe a relative. Miller proves to have the necessary funds for bail. He's asked to surrender his passport and his lawyer makes no issue of it. Miller's going to be back home in a couple of hours.

"My phone's buzzing," says Tony.

"Mine, too, but I want to hang on and see if the reporter takes an interest."

"I'll see you outside," he says.

Sure enough, as the next case is called and the uniforms set off with Miller to the cashier's window, the reporter scuttles after Angelique. I sidle over. Angelique is good. She stands tall and looks the reporter directly in the eye without a flinch, perfecting that whole would-I-lie-to-you thing.

"Off the record? He's not a dealer, he's just a grown-up who should know better and we want to remind him of that."

"But a hundred thousand dollars?"

"He's got it." She shrugs.

Reporter lady looks at me. "Are you the detective on the case?"

"No, Ma'am, I don't do drugs."

Across the top of her head I see Tony standing in the door of the courtroom. There's a look on his face that causes me to leave Angelique and the reporter standing where they are.

He guides me clear of the crush around the courtroom door and then turns to me. "Hartford PD's got a body at the dump down in Hartford. White female."

It's like walking into a glass door I didn't see. I stop hearing the buzz of the courthouse around me. I can't find anything to say.

"Come on," he says quietly, "I asked them to hold everything until we get there."

We're silent in the car as we take 84 east across the top of Hartford then 91 south for two miles along the Connecticut River. Soon after we exit the Brainard Road off-ramp we are snarled up in traffic. There's a mile-long backup of dump trucks snaking towards the trash incinerator plant where we're headed. I reach out and stick the flasher on the roof and Tony uses short bursts on the siren to keep us moving.

got some superficial stuff, need an autopsy to be sure. But she does have bruising on the neck."

I step over to the body and kneel down next to it. I force myself into the procedure—observe and note systematically. The double bagging has been cut completely open by the techs and it seems there was nothing else with her inside. She is in denim shorts with a pink belt, and a faded T-shirt. The techs have already bagged her hands to preserve any DNA evidence under her fingernails. Decomposition and tissue loss is advanced, but not advanced enough. Even though the flies and maggots have already started degrading the orifices and moist skin surfaces, I can still see the slender, adolescent shape of her, the stream of blond hair.

I've made it through car wreck scenes and a fatal house fire. I've seen a human body broken and lifeless. But the sight of this body gets me in that deep place of my soul I seldom visit.

The face is swollen and the maggots around her eyes have turned the flesh black, but there's still a ghost of human expression, the same curious pixie outlook on the world that made people stop for a moment at her poster. Two luminous green flies dance around in my view, the clammy humidity and the smell are all over me like a drunk's embrace. The loader is making that strident beep-beep-beep every time it backs up. I think my mouth is still talking, but I can't hear what I'm saying. I'm light. There's a faint shrill sound somewhere and Tony's voice saying "Donna" like it's coming over a small transistor radio.

The next thing I'm aware of, I'm in the reclined passenger seat of the cruiser. The A/C is blasting over me. Tony is holding a bottle of water at my face. And a furious burning shame is erupting in me as I realize what's happened.

Throwing up is one thing. Most cops do it at some time. But fainting? That's just fucking girlish. Tony must have carried me to the car like a child.

"Jesus."

"Take it easy. It's the humidity. Drink." Tony offers me the bottle.

"Just fucking shoot me now."

"Come on. Did you skip breakfast? Blood sugar or something."

"Did I puke?"

"No. You just went down in complete silence. Very composed."

I trigger the seat into the upright position and a wave of light-headedness hits me again, but I stay conscious. I drink some of the water, lukewarm and soapy. I can see the uniformed patrolmen from Hartford have positioned their bodies to face away from me, which could be out of courtesy but also seems to delineate the difference between them and me, between the professionals and the fainter. I'm furious at not being able to render undone what just happened.

"Maybe you should just sit here for a while," Tony says.

I could do that. I could sit here for a couple of days with the A/C on me while I carefully process what I feel. But I can't sit here for another two minutes and continue to be a law enforcement officer. I know that. If I don't get out there right now I will become a legend across the state. Cruel nicknames will be coined for me. Not the prettiest, and not the toughest. So I wipe the feverish cold sweat off my face and neck, take a final swig of water, and push myself out of that car into the heat. Test my legs. I pour some more of the water into my hand and splash it in my face, wipe it around. Then we walk back to the scene. I dare not look at her. I just force myself to talk.

"You okay?" asks Shaved Head. Grin. Fuck off.

"That's her," I say. "Amber Zajac. Missing eight days from her home in Webster."

I pull out a photo. None of them even glances at it. "So she's ours. We'll take it from here." Shaved Head is still smiling. Like

I'm a kid to be managed.

"You know you crossed the town line getting here, right? This is Hartford."

"That's not the definition of jurisdiction. This is not the original crime scene. You get that, right? The doer didn't bring her here to kill her. She was killed somewhere else. The dump is yours, the body is mine."

All the while I have the taste of metal in my mouth and too much saliva. Tony says nothing to support me, just stands half a pace behind my shoulder, a position he seems to like when we're face to face with others.

"Haven't you guys got your hands full on that side?" says a patrolman who must have worn shoe inserts to make the height requirement. One of the techs chuckles, although I notice Shaved Head is above that.

"You got a person of interest yet?" asks Shaved Head.

"No," says Tony smoothly before I can start mouthing off about Miller.

Shaved Head smiles and shrugs. "So you don't really have a clue where the crime was committed? My boss is territorial. We'll process here. The body goes to the M.E. either way. You come up with anything concrete, let's share."

The thought of passing care of Amber off to these gum chewers is appalling to me at this moment, but it's pointless to argue.

"You'll notify us of anything material you find here?"

"Of course. And we'll leave the family visit to you. You already know them?"

"Yes."

"Let's go talk to the driver who found her," Tony says.

"Just a minute." I want to see her again, fix the scene in my mind. There will be crime scene photos but I pull out my pocket camera and take some photos of my own so I've got reference with me when I need it. Or a reminder. Nine times out of ten, she would have gone straight into the fire, no trace, no DNA, and the only thing left would be the eternal doubt that she might still be out there somewhere. A wave of shivering passes over me, despite the heat.

The driver who found Amber is sitting in an air-conditioned office, playing with his cell phone and no doubt figuring the overtime he's going to rack up.

"How the hell did you even spot her in all that?" I ask him.

"Blond hair. Nothing else like it. Bit of luck, but you do develop an eye for stuff. See a lot of dogs and cats. But of course if the bag hadn't ripped she would have sailed straight through."

"Is there a way of telling the source of this trash?"

He shrugs. "More than sixty towns send their trash here. It saves them landfill issues."

"Including Webster?" I say.

He nods. "I can tell you everything on this platform came in since Friday. Boss can give you the towns that delivered in that time frame, I guess, but bigger towns send something every day—different parts of the town on different days."

Back on the tipping floor, a large Ford truck, gray, unmarked, is backing up to where she lies—the body transport from the M.E.'s office.

"They're not going to give us anything from this site, you know that?" Tony says.

I nod. "No point in hanging around here, then."

As we're driving out of the plant gates, I hear one of the front-end loaders start up. The good folks of Connecticut aren't going to interrupt throwing shit away just because we found one of their kids in the trash.

"Let's get something cold," Tony says, turning into a gas station.

Ten minutes later he swings us through the gates of the Charter Oak Landing Park.

"Where are you going?"

"Let's take a break before we go back," he says. He parks the car so we're looking directly over the big river. "You should let the captain know." Then he gets out of the car with his Pepsi and walks off to look over the river, notably out of earshot.

I want to avoid a full disclosure with my captain right now, so I call Mrs. B and ask her to inform him about Amber. Between the A/C and the cold soda, I feel a bit better. My adrenaline is telling me to get going, but Tony is staring out over the river like he's got all day. I get out of the car and walk over next to him.

"It's a shame what they've done here," he says. "I used to come fishing with my dad. He worked at Pratt & Whitney, just across the river there. We launched a little outboard about a mile down. This river gave birth to Hartford. When Mark Twain lived here, ocean-going vessels came right up to this landing."

No longer. Now the eight-lane 91 overpass casts a pall on everything along the riverfront, its concrete feet stomped down indiscriminately on the land. Someone made a brief effort to keep the narrow strip of river shore alive. There's a paved walking path and some decking and a drinking fountain. But beneath that highway shadow, anything attractive withers. This is now an area for cheap motels and the stuff no one wants to see: off-track betting and auto body shops. Tony's read the thoughts right out of my mind, because he says, "Rest in peace, Mr. Twain, this would have brought tears to your eyes."

"The river's pretty though," I say.

"I'll take you out one day, if you like."

"Pretty to look at. I don't want to go on it."

We both know why we're dawdling here at the edge of a river—because the next order of business is the worst. We have to go and tell Mr. and Mrs. Zajac that their only daughter has been found stinking in a thousand tons of trash after being raked over by a front-end loader.

I look at him until he turns to face me. "You knew it would end this way, didn't you?"

He turns back to the river.

"Just tell me."

"I didn't know any more than you," he says. "I've just seldom seen these things turn out well."

"I just always held out hope, you know."

"That's a good thing."

"That's a rookie thing."

"So you're a rookie. You can't skip that. You don't want to skip that. Being a detective isn't a thing you get born good at. You learn it. If you skip the learning process then all you're good for is being promoted to a job where you get in the way of the real detectives who didn't skip it. You want that?"

"What I want is to not lose this case. And me screwing up like a rookie makes it easier for them to take it away."

"What happened to you today was not a screw-up. It was human."

"We have to go and tell them," I say.

"But first we have to shower and change."

He's right. And even that might not get rid of the smell.

There's a sprinkler going in the front yard of the colonial on Wilton, waving slowly back and forth, some of the water falling uselessly on the driveway. A remote region of my brain thinks how I would have set the sprinkler so it didn't do that.

In my pocket I have a folded leaflet produced by the Office of the Chief Medical Examiner. On the inside of my wrist I have a red, inflamed rash from something I brushed up against at the dump, some paint stripper or something that was there in the trash along with Amber. There's still a white noise behind everything in my ears from when I fainted. I've consumed two large Diet Pepsis but I'm still feeling like at any moment my consciousness could just step away from me.

Mrs. Zajac opens the door and right away starts with a kind of small gasping noise before I even open my mouth. She's reading every detail right off my face. She knows why we're here so soon again after this morning. Then he's flapping behind her in the doorway, that clumsy, bony, wild-eyed bird, and I hear my voice reciting the litany, regret we have bad news.

They bring us in the house and the platitudes continue to flow from me in an effortless monotony, very sorry for your loss. I pull out the Chief Medical Officer's leaflet and hand it to Mr. Zajac. "Information for families" it says on the front under the state crest, and at the bottom in italics: *Please accept our sincere condolences on the loss of your loved one. We recognize that this loss brings deep sorrow and is one of the most stressful times in life.*

The two of them fall into a baffled silence over the leaflet. There's a paragraph, welcome to many but not to all, that says it's not essential for them to make a personal identification. The state stands ready with alternative methods to confirm that the body in the bag is that of the girl with the pixie face who used to build dens out of comforters here on their living room floor. I want to urge them to take up that offer, but I can't find the right words.

Mrs. Zajac looks up at me and I'm flooded with the idea that I should rush this woman to the hospital right now. Her skeleton seems about to cut through her papery skin and only her eyes are alive. She's looking down at the floor as if it's about to give way at any moment and murmurs, "Is she in one piece?"

I see the maggots in Amber's eyes again. You could give me

107

twenty-four hours and I couldn't produce a response to this question. Tony's even tone comes from over my shoulder.

"Yes, she is, Mrs. Zajac."

"I want to see her."

"There'll be an autopsy tomorrow," Tony continues. "After that the state Medical Officer will let us know about further arrangements."

There's a soft, seductive tug on me to just drift out of this room, out of this case, and let Tony handle it all. This is what drug addicts feel when they seek the refuge of oblivion. It's too much, this woman's pain. If we were still chimpanzees she would bite our faces off for bringing her this news. And that would be fine by me right now.

We go through the motions. The contact numbers for Victim Services. The encouragement to keep telling us anything they remember and most gruesome of all, me muttering something about getting the perpetrator, don't you worry.

I am walking across the parking lot from the station to the town hall. A tinny wail of music issues from a speaker inside a plastic rock located among the decorative plantings. "Take it Easy" by the Eagles. Despite that, Webster is efficiently run. It takes me ten minutes to get a schedule of the trash pick-ups for the whole town. Twenty minutes later, Tony's driving us through the west side of town, scanning the crossroads.

I point toward a side street. "There's one."

We turn left into a road lined with green trash bins, which I have seen plenty of times but never paid much attention to. Further up the road, a trash collection truck is working.

We're right behind the truck now as it rolls up to a green bin. A mechanical arm reaches out, grabs the bin, swings it in a 180 degree arc over the back of the truck. Gravity does the rest; the lid of the bin falls open and a cascade of black bags falls into the truck. The mechanical arm replaces the bin and the driver moves on.

Tony shakes his head. "If you were designing a way for home-owners to dispose of bodies, this would be it. There's no human involved in the collection, so smell or heft are not going to attract attention. When the bin empties into the back of the truck, the driver can't even see it. And half a minute after that the compactor has mixed it with everything else, no traceability."

"We need to know what day of the week they collect at Miller's house," I say. "We really need an accurate time of death from the lab. And we need a warrant for Miller's trash can."

He looks across at me. "You know what you need?" I can think of a couple of things. "Some down time. A good night's sleep. Take your foot off the gas for a while." I start to object, but he shakes his head. "I'm buying you a burger and beer, and then you're going home."

He was right, although two beers seemed to hit me like six. Now it's 9 p.m. and I'm at the Laundromat. There's a neon tube flickering, strobing sickly off the grubby white walls. It doesn't stop the dumpy woman from reading her People magazine, and it doesn't stop the Asian student from pecking speedily at her laptop, and it doesn't stop the attendant from sipping noisily on the ice in his plastic cup, but it's driving me nuts.

Normally I drop my laundry for a service wash, but that's only available during the day and I desperately need clean clothes. Clean sheets. Clean everything. So I got to sit here tonight. I feel like I've been in a car wreck. The clock that's been driving me for 72 hours has stopped. Amber the pixie face is on a steel gurney in the cooling room. She's dead today and she'll be dead tomorrow.

What's the rush? Mrs. Zajac's skin and bones are the way they are, I can't change that. Hell, the captain will probably take the case away from me now that it's a murder investigation. I haven't heard from him since I left the message with Mrs. B.

My dryer is vibrating noisily as it speeds up, trying to shoulder its companions aside and make a run for the highway. The attendant looks up, shouts across at me, "Hey, Lady! Your stuff's unbalanced, you need to distribute it more evenly."

When I was a student of the liberal arts, we called that a metaphor.

She didn't run, but walked rapidly away from her house. Walking helped to calm her. Her left cheek was still tender from where her father had slapped her, but that was the least of the sensations roiling her. She took the first left to get off Wilton then stopped and tapped a text message into her phone. She doubted they would come after her, even if they noticed she was gone—they'd think it would be good for her to cool off.

She walked over to the English guy's house. His car was in the driveway. That meant she couldn't just use the spare key to get in and grab her bag from the basement, which was a problem—the boy would want his weed.

Sometimes she felt a twinge of guilt about Mr. Miller. He paid her well for the dog walking and he was always so polite—"courtly" was a good English word for him—and kind to her. He took an interest in her but made no judgments. But she needed somewhere to stash her supply that wasn't at home or at school, and the English guy's place was perfect, because he trusted her so completely.

She walked on to the park. Two wannabe skater boys were practicing beginner moves on the curbs of the car lot. Down the slope, a number of runners and walkers were circling the old running track. Two dogs she recognized were walking with their owner. There was maybe an hour of daylight left. A shipment of cooler, lighter air had come in from somewhere and provided a respite from the humidity.

She continued across the field to the swings and seated herself on one of them. It squeaked as she started to go back and forth. She must have been on these swings hundreds of times over the years; there was comfort in the familiar, rhythmic arc of their movement. She kicked hard with her feet through the bottom of the arc, building speed.

She should have thought to bring some stuff—money, some clothes—but she had been in a rush to get out of the house. It was as though the house was about to explode from all the crap in her life, and her father's gaunt face and his incessant bitter voice and the smell that had been in the house ever since her mom got sick. The squeaking protest of metal on metal from the swing became shriller as she threw her upper body back and forth to build momentum. Ground, sky, ground, sky flipped before her eyes as her arc got higher and higher. She had that feeling in her head—of when things became too difficult to think about she just went straight to the extreme and did the worst thing she could do. That way, she avoided all the thinking. And there was a kind of satisfaction in throwing a decision into the face of worry. It was like, don't fuck with me, because I am prepared to go further than you can imagine.

She heard a child's voice calling. There was some slack in the chains at the top of the arc as she exceeded the horizontal. Ground, sky, ground, sky, hypnotic rhythm. *Stop, you're going to hurt yourself*, an alarmed adult voice called.

Amber let the swing slow, kicking up pieces of the wood mulch as she used her feet as brakes. It was a mother with a boy—about five, plump—standing beside the swing. On the running track, two of the walkers had stopped to watch as well.

"You'll break the swing," the child reprimanded her. "It's dangerous."

Amber got off the swing and knelt down next to the boy.

"I'll tell you a secret," she said, catching the child's hands in her own. "Do you know what's dangerous?"

The mother put her hand on her son's shoulder to ease him away, but Amber held onto his hands, her eyes on his, down at this level where it was just their two sets of eyes.

"Being frightened. That's what's dangerous. Never be frightened."

"Come on, Daryl," now the mother put both hands on the boy's shoulder and turned him firmly away.

Amber pulled out her phone and sent another text, and then walked over to the grassy bank where she could see the parking lot. She lay on her back on the grass and waited for him to arrive.

Three years ago she found her grandfather lying on the stonework of the porch with spit coming out of his mouth. She touched his face and he made an inarticulate sound she still remembers exactly. Four days later they turned off the life support. She didn't feel that much at first, that's how she remembers it, but in a few months it was like things around her just slipped into a shapeless heap. There was no one left who knew how the story of the family should go.

DAY FIVE

Saturday 8 a.m.

At Whole Foods, where they make a good hot breakfast. I pick up a newspaper as well, and find a seat as far from other customers as possible.

Bottom right of front page. "Body found at Hartford dump."

No identification, no age, no gender even. I'm wondering if this was an act of mercy by our Hartford PD colleagues or just good luck, when my phone rings. My captain has also been reading his morning paper.

"It must have been a rough day for you yesterday," he says.

Yeah, did you hear? I fainted in front of my colleagues. Otherwise routine.

"I'm okay, sir."

"I'm sure you are, but I want you to take the weekend off anyway. Give yourself a break."

"I have the autopsy this morning."

"After that, then. And do not respond to any media inquiries."

"Are you taking me off the case, sir?"

"Don't jump to conclusions. We'll review the case as we would with any homicide. Monday morning. Understood?"

"Yes, sir." Suddenly I'm not hungry.

The state Medical Examiner's building is on the campus of the University of Connecticut's John Dempsey Hospital in Farmington, not more than a few miles from us, but I've never had cause to go there before. I'm getting out of my car when my phone rings.

"Detective Bradley?"

"Hello, Mrs. Zajac. How can I help you?"

"We'd like to see her."

"Have you really thought about this, Mrs. Zajac? It can just add to your pain."

"We want to see her. It's our right."

Well, that's not strictly true, but no point in going down that road. "I'll talk to the medical officer and call you right back."

When I walk in the door, everyone's already there. Shaved Head from Hartford PD has that annoying smile again as he introduces a sidekick I don't remember from the dump. I'm reminded how big he is—Shaved Head—like a block of muscle. Wish I could remember his name, it puts me at a disadvantage. Then I shake hands with two state detectives. This is setting up to be a pissing contest. I'm feeling like I've got freshman stamped on my forehead, so I keep quiet.

I take a seat next to Tony on a hard, budget-conscious sofa and turn my head to his ear, sotto voce. "They want to come see the body."

"The parents?" He shakes his head. "Nothing good can come of that."

"I know, but she's pretty adamant."

I see Shaved Head watching us. He grins when he catches my eye. Dick.

"What do you think?" Tony asks.

"He's the kind of person who if we say no, will end up shouting in the station."

"You'll have to let them do it."

A small, neatly-made man enters the reception area. "Police officers for the autopsy of Amber Zajac?" When six of us stand up he looks disapproving. "What's going on?"

"There's a little ambiguity over jurisdiction," says one of the state cops with a smirk.

"I'm Dr. Hemingway. Will you follow me?"

I step up. "Just before we start, Doctor, could I have a word with you." I try to steer him away from the others, which he doesn't like.

"The parents are pushing to see the body."

"We have a viewing room downstairs."

"What condition is she in?"

He shrugs. "We can clean up her face okay. Tell them to come at ten."

The elevator takes us down into the basement. Then we go down a long a corridor. I can hear the buzz of a bone saw. Through a set of swing doors, we step into the busy autopsy room.

"Everyone get suited up," says Dr. Hemingway. "Then join me at the table on the far left."

A young tech assistant hands out white one-piece coveralls. I've used these a dozen times at crime scenes and never had a problem, but today, of course, I catch my foot in the elastic crimp at the ankle, lose my balance and go down. Shaved Head's massive hand is immediately in front of me. I take it and he hoists me off the floor with the ease of a power winch.

A doctor standing nearby at the wash-up sink looks at me with a wolfish grin and says, "First autopsy?"

I nod and turn away from him, but he sings out, "Virgin in the house!"

There are some cheers and stares from the tables where people are working.

"All right," Dr. Hemingway voice is not loud, but it is authoritative. He leads us over to a counter on the side of the room.

"Before we begin on the body itself," he says, "let's look at the clothing that was on the body when it was found. Denim shorts and a T-shirt. No footwear, no underwear, no bra. It's possible that this was how she was dressed at the time of death, but it could also indicate that she was hurried dressed by someone else, postmortem. That's your department. Now let's get started."

As we approach the body table, I catch Tony glancing at me. Actually, I'm going to be okay. What's lying on the cold stainless steel table before us is no longer Amber, it's just a repository of evidence. Everything here is functional, impersonal, sterilized. The table surface slopes to a drain to carry body fluids away. The instruments are heavy and metallic, their sounds magnified. In addition to the six of us, there's the tech and a tall, handsome young Asian guy, who I take to be a med student.

"Let's begin with the postmortem interval," says Dr. Hemingway. "The technicians at the scene collected the insect material from the body that will provide one measure. That's already gone to the lab. But because the body was moved between death and discovery, PMI is difficult. This morning, I collected the vitreous humor for another measure." He looks at me. "Do you know how that works, Detective Bradley?"

"No, sir."

"That's the fluid from the eye. By comparing the potassium content of that with the potassium in the body, we can get a measure of how long since death, because potassium settles in the eye much slower than elsewhere in the body."

I still don't fully get it, but I nod to get him to move on.

"So we'll have to get back to you with a time of death estimate. Now let's do the external examination. First of all, note that the left side of the body is darker than the right. There's quite a distinct line. That's collection of blood on the lower side, so she lay on her left side—pretty much undisturbed—for some time immediately after death."

Dr. Hemingway has hands as small and quick as a squirrel and they move along the surface of Amber's naked corpse with complete ease. My pen is dry and I have to scribble vigorously on my notepad to get the ink flowing. I'm the only one taking notes.

"We can see there's no indication of trauma on the front of the body." He motions the tech to help him and they carefully lift one side of the body so we can see her back. "And none on the rear side.

"This grazing damage on the hip is postmortem." He looks at me. "We can tell that because although the skin is broken there is no blood. She went through the trash process, that sort of damage is to be expected. So on the torso we find no superficial indication of cause of death. The legs have nothing of forensic interest.

"Next. Your victim was not a virgin. She had had sex recently but there is no particular indication of violence to the vaginal area." Dr. Hemingway's hands move in the air above the pubic area. "We've collected a standard rape kit," he says. "No indication of infection. Moving to the head. The damage you see to the face is postmortem. On the left side of the skull, above the temple, here's a contusion from blunt force before death. From this pattern of injury, I don't think she was deliberately struck with a weapon. I think she hit her head, or she was aggressively manhandled and her head was struck against a wall or floor, for example. Now, the neck."

Hemingway's small, dexterous hands slip behind the neck of the corpse and he lifts it just a half inch so that the head tilts back and the neck is lengthened. Like an instructor guiding a ballet dancer into the perfect pose.

"We can see indications of significant compression of the neck. It's not uniform, not a ligature—bare hands. Premortem, confirmed by the bruising. Notice this mark on the right, how it extends upward, like a smear mark? The victim struggled, and the assailant's grip slipped. Conceivably that's when he struck her head against the hard surface, either to subdue her, or in the course of regaining a grip. I say 'he' because strangulation almost always requires a significant disparity in strength between victim and attacker.

"Contrary to popular understanding, strangulation does not cut off blood flow to the brain. It's the other way around. Arteries are tougher than veins, so when there's compression of the neck, the veins carrying the blood away from the brain are constricted first. But because depleted blood isn't getting out, new blood flow can't get in to replace it, and the result is the same—oxygen starvation. Cerebral ischemia follows."

He leans over the face and with a practiced movement flips an eyelid inside out.

"To confirm strangulation, we check for petechial hemorrhage, and we find it here inside the eyelid.

"Mr. Desai!" Hemingway has spotted the med student surreptitiously glancing at the screen of his cell phone. "Explain to the detectives, would you, how strangulation produces petechial hemorrhage."

"The capillaries are the smallest vessels in the body. When there's a pressure buildup, they're the first to rupture."

"Put the phone away, please." Hemingway turns back to us. "We can be eighty percent sure of everything I've told you so far. Of a more speculative nature, I've got some thoughts arising from the exact position of these other bruise marks. Anyone?"

Shaved Head speaks immediately. "Sleeper hold."

"Exactly," Hemingway nods. "It's not definitive, but you can work on that." He steps over to Shaved Head and places his small hands on that thick neck. "If I am facing you and I try to strangle you, my thumbs are naturally to the front of your neck, where those deep bruises are on the deceased. But the other bruises at the carotid points on the side of neck suggest that this attacker changed his grip. Loss of consciousness can occur within thirty seconds of closing off the blood circuit. But death requires longer—at least two minutes, for which the sleeper hold is ideal." He releases his hold and says to Shaved Head, "Perhaps you would demonstrate, Detective?"

Shaved Head steps behind his partner and straps an arm around his neck, elbow directly to the front, locking the sides of the neck between the forearm and biceps. The other arm is used like a lever to tighten the grip.

"Did they teach you that at Police College, Detective Bradley?" Hemingway asks.

"No."

He nods. "It was cut from the Connecticut training manual in the nineties. Too many cases of unwarranted force by officers. Some states still teach it. So one scenario here is that the assault started face to face. But to finish the job, the assailant flipped the body round and held it from behind. In that case, and I stress it's by no means for sure, your perpetrator could be law enforcement, military, martial arts, in that area."

"The assault was not planned," Tony says, more to himself than to the room.

"Exactly where I was going," says Hemingway. "This assailant knows how to kill efficiently, but he starts out like an amateur. So maybe when he starts, he's just spontaneously angry, he grabs her by the neck as an act of fury or temper. He might just as well have slapped her or punched her. But only after that does he take the deliberate action of killing her."

The astringent clarity of Hemingway's analysis is having a strange effect on me—he's put me right in the scene, my mind is climbing all over the possibilities.

"Maybe he wanted to stop her talking," I say.

"She knew something?" says one of the state detectives. "He couldn't let her tell anyone what happened."

"No, I mean, at first," I say. "You said he could have slapped her or punched her—that's what most men do to women they want to subdue. But this guy, whatever it was that sent him into a rage, it was something she was saying to him. He acted to shut off her voice. Could have been, I mean."

Hemingway gives me a quick look of approval. "Well, I'm going to leave that to you detectives to sort out. We'll report on the rape kit and the material from under the fingernails. The trash bags in which she was dumped will also be processed, although they don't look promising. I'll try to have everything back for you before the end of next week."

"Let's wait outside for the parents so we don't have to chat to these guys," I say to Tony. But as we're walking out of the building, Shaved Head comes over to us. Smiling.

"We got no fingerprints off the trash bags, and nothing from the surrounding search."

"Thanks for letting us know."

"Any progress on your side?"

I shake my head.

"How'd it go with the parents? Must have been tough."

I look him straight in the eye. Is he fishing for information he can use to take the case away from us, or is he just breezing? Did he listen in on my chat with Dr. Hemingway about the viewing?

"Sure."

"Obviously we've had some media interest," he says. "So far no one's linked it to your case, and I said nothing."

"Thanks."

"But they will soon."

Is there any occasion solemn enough to stop this guy from grinning like daddy's favorite son?

Sitting in the car waiting for the Zajacs to arrive, I'm thinking about that look Hemingway gave me at the end that made me feel like I had gotten my Ph.D. in deduction. It was a small glimpse of what it might have been like to have a dad who took an interest in me. Someone like Shaved Head's dad, maybe.

Mr. and Mrs. Zajac both look slightly drugged, which they quite possibly are. We shepherd them into the elevator and take it down without a word. Dr. Hemingway is waiting for us as the elevator door opens and he takes over smoothly, inserting himself between the parents and with a gentle touch of his hands to their backs, moving them along the corridor.

"In the viewing room," he says to them, "there will be curtain across a window. When I open the curtain you will be able to see through the glass, and Amber will be on a gurney on the other side of the glass."

Neither of them says anything.

When we are facing the curtain, I notice that Crazy Bird positions himself slightly behind his wife, as if to let her shield him from the impact of what they're going to see. Dr. Hemingway lets them settle, and then presses a button. We can all hear the slight whir of the electric motor that opens the curtains, a sound which I am sure many who stand here live with forever after. There are sharp laundry creases in the starched pale blue sheet that covers Amber, right up snug under her chin so they can't see the strangulation marks. Mrs. Zajac shuffles her feet briefly as though a small earth tremor had momentarily unbalanced her, but they have no other reaction. Maybe ten seconds go by. Then she turns away and he follows her out into the corridor, heading for the elevator, not a word.

Up in the reception, she stops and turns to us. He keeps going for the outside.

"Thank you," she says to none of us in particular.

As we come out through the revolving door, Stan Zajac is standing with his back to us, looking down the steps and over the parking lot. And abruptly he throws back his head and explodes into a burst of unintelligible speech, fluent Polish curses possibly. His wife quickly steps up and catches him under the elbow, propelling him down the steps like a club bouncer. At the bottom of the stairs he stops for another short volley of shouting at the sky.

Then they're in their car. And I'm now okay with my captain ordering me to take the weekend off.

DAY SIX

Sunday 9 a.m.

Wake up feeling dead. The case is like a congealed mess on me. Sundays, I usually visit my mom or take her out, but I'd really like to avoid that today, so I call Tony and suggest we prepare for the review tomorrow.

"I thought the captain ordered you to take the day off?"

"You got other plans?"

"I'll be with my mother this morning. This afternoon, Theresa asked me to go with her to walk with her dogs at Powder Forest."

"Really? Have you asked your doctor if you're healthy enough for sex?"

"I'm not that old, Bradley."

But quite a lot older than her.

"Anyway," he says, "it's not like that. She's lonely."

"With that body?" Shut up, Bradley.

"Because of that body, maybe. You've got a prejudice against her."

So, we're both spending Sunday morning with our mothers. I love my mother but I hate spending time with her. Maybe not hate, but I have a problem with it, the first being I have to go and see her at the house I grew up in.

When I was five, my father moved us out of the suburbs to a dilapidated house surrounded by trees in a semi-rural area near

Tolland. He had a grand plan to buy cheap, renovate and sell at a big profit. He talked a lot about capital gains, which he deemed a superior form of income. The renovation commenced with great enthusiasm. A builder friend came over and they ripped open the east side of the house, where the siding was decaying. But my father's momentum soon flagged and when the first snow came, the east side was still exposed behind the flapping plastic. Only a threat from my mother to move out got that solved. The plan for the new kitchen was impressive, but three years later it was still a half-finished mess.

I grew to hate the house in the woods. The bus ride to school took me every day on a bleak tour of houses in decline like ours, houses with decaying RVs in back, illegal power lines strung to outbuildings. The place down the road from us had a large pond; fetid and stinking in summer, icy and desolate in winter. The two boys who lived in the house there were taken away from the parents, I never heard why. There was a summer when every second kid seemed to have Lyme disease and mothers were panicking. I was taken to the doctor one afternoon when all I had was allergies. That day, I stuffed a Cosmo magazine from the waiting room into my bag and took it home.

So I don't like to hang around the house when I see my mom, which is fine with her because what she likes is to go to the mall with me. My father hasn't lived with her for a couple of years. No divorce. He went to do a contract job in New Jersey, which became a contract job in Florida, and by mutual agreement they now have a remarkably successful separation, without rancor on either side as far as I can tell. He drops by and gives her some money from time to time and Mom has kept her job. She's financially strapped like everyone else these days, but the roof hasn't fallen in. On the one hand I'm quite impressed by the unconventional way they've handled things. She's not bitter, but I can't really call her happy either. My father is fine as far as I know. He's a simple man. These are the things he enjoys, in descending order: an attractive new woman flirting with him, measuring up a room for a renovation job and discussing ideas about how to do it, handing off that job to someone else when it gets tricky, and going for a couple of beers with the guys. I'm pretty sure he's still getting all those things, and I seriously doubt he goes to bed alone. He phones me sometimes—more often since I made detective. At first he didn't know how to relate to me as an adult, but I have never once confronted him with his shortcomings as a parent, and that has enabled us to maintain a certain level of communication. Yeah, I do have a kind of ache for there to be a family home for me to go to with some nostalgia and memories, but what you gonna do?

Mom and I wander around the mall. She likes to look at stuff she can't afford—clothes and shiny kitchenware, mostly. She doesn't even seem to mind that she can't afford it. She's happy just that it exists out there. One of her uncompleted tasks of parenthood, in her opinion, is to endow me with a sense of style, so we hover at the Ann Taylor window while she points out the merits of clothing we both know I will never buy, even if I could afford it.

Then we go to Olive Garden for lunch and I pretend to be sharing her bottle of wine. We have a limited range of conversation, as by mutual agreement we never talk about my work. She catches me up on people I've long forgotten about. When the alcohol hits her inhibition center, she starts making allusions to my "love life." This always happens and it always annoys me.

"Actually, I had sex with a guy I met in a bar Thursday night."

She stares at me. I smile evilly.

"What was that like?"

"He was okay. Or I was drunk enough. He didn't smell and his

125

room was air-conditioned. I made that a mandatory. It's so hard for me to sleep these days. Most of all I just needed the good night's sleep."

Her mouth is pinched, a look that takes me back to age four. "I don't know what to say. Why do you do this to me?"

"Why do you always ask about my love life? If I want to tell you, I will."

"I never asked about your love life!"

"Yeah you did. In that round-about way."

So there, I ruined her whole day like a petulant child, and it's only three o'clock. I drive her home and decline to stay for coffee, saying I have to go in to the office. I am becoming anxious about tomorrow morning's case review with the captain, so I can easily generate two good justifications for going to the station. I need to be current with everything that's flowed in over the weekend, and I should make sure the war room is ship shape for hand-over if they take the case away from me.

And here's Tony, sitting in the war room.

"What happened to your stroll in the woods with Theresa?"

"Fun. She's fitter than me."

Something in his manner.

"What's up?" I ask.

"I was just about to call you. The Brits just faxed through the report on Miller."

"Any dead girls in his past?"

"Yes."

Right news. Wrong expression on Tony's face.

"Who?"

"His daughter. Killed in a horse riding accident three years ago. She was twelve."

I keep looking at him. "That's it?"

"That's it. He's clean."

Realization is coming upon me in fragments, like little missiles. He's watching me.

"It explains a lot about him," I say.

"Sure."

I don't want to meet his eyes. "So I came in to catch up, but I think I'll just head home."

He nods. "I've written up everything, we're good for review tomorrow."

Instead of going straight to my car, I walk across Memorial Road, onto the grass of the small parkland they've developed along the Trout Brook. People from the new apartments in Tunxis Square are walking their apartment-sized dogs. A skinny man is doing slow tai chi moves. I sit on a rock that has been carefully placed here by a landscaping designer to look natural.

One reality has been ousted by another in its entirety. Everything that made Miller suspicious before, now makes him innocent, even sympathetic. None of the other facts we know has changed, yet they all mean something different in the light of this new lone fact. Miller's strange isolation from the world is no longer indicative of someone who might have preyed on a teenager, but of a father groping his way along the journey of incurable grief.

I feel afraid and alone. I tricked myself like a child into a conviction I wanted to have. Self-doubt is a fire in me. I know clearly now why the Chief has been reluctant to give me a case lead, why I don't deserve it.

My phone rings. Tony. I let it go to voicemail. I get off the rock I'm sitting on and walk further down the incline towards the Trout Brook in case he comes looking for me. The vibration of an incoming text: Tony advising me to tell the captain today rather than leave it until tomorrow. He's right.

Miller is not just no longer a suspect. He's a victim. Of me. Of my incompetence.

My phone rings again. Jesus, Tony, leave me alone. It actually physically hurts to be this wrong.

It was cold and wet and miserable, in the way only England can be. No direct sunlight for what seemed like weeks and the sense that, this time, summer may actually never make it all the way around the calendar. The woodwork of the indoor show ring felt soft and porous to the touch and the forest behind the parking lot was dark and dripping.

The new horse, Archie, a nearly black gelding, was big—16 hands—but it had been agreed, with Gracie growing so fast, that they would buy her something that could take her through the next three years. Like buying school uniforms a size too big. They had been at the show over five hours when it came time to tack up Archie for his final round. All the events had been crowded with entrants and the hours had ticked by as each young rider did a circuit of the jumping course. The first course was too easy, producing too many clear rounds going through to the next elimination. But Gracie was excited. For the first time she had a competitive horse and Miller knew she was itching to turn the tables on some Pony Club rivals who had always defeated her in the past. This event could be an easy win for Archie. He was fast and sure around the jump course, and all Gracie had to do was steer him and stay on.

Afterward, Miller would realize that he had been afraid of this horse from the start. Archie was athletic and without vices, but he had a way of doing things in his own time that suggested to Miller that the horse was managing his relationship with humans, and not the other way around.

At the third jump—a 2-foot-6-inch double with flowerpots on

each side which Archie could easily have cleared from a standing start—the horse changed his mind. Perhaps the group of riders in his sightline distracted him on the approach, or Gracie's seat on him was not sufficiently familiar, or his joints were hurting from standing out in the damp for five hours. He stopped stone cold one stride from the jump. Gracie, who had been properly taught to project herself into the jump with every muscle, was pointed almost horizontally forward on his back. For a moment, she flew.

Usually, to be thrown clear was better; being dragged by a heel caught in the stirrups was considered more dangerous. Accidents were not uncommon in the Pony Club, but kids are flexible and mostly they walked away. Sometimes a wrist or a collarbone was sprained or broken. What happened to Gracie was a freak accident, it was said; she probably hit the ground with the point of her chin, snapping her head back. Miller's inescapable burden of fragmentary sounds and images from that day included the small yelp that his wife, Helen, gave as Gracie clattered through the woodwork of the jump; the way Archie trotted away to the exit chute, stirrups flapping, and Miller did not think about him again for the next hour; the irrevocable stillness of Gracie's body as he ran towards her; how the damp wood shavings on the jumping track got inside his shoes.

That had been followed by a period at the hospital, in the antechamber of death, a time of elaborate torture, the doctors dithering with their technical options and their ethics and their skills in family relations. It was in this interlude that Miller had lost any remaining connection to the world he had previously known. After unrecalled days and nights, he and Helen did some murmuring and nodding and then the functioning of certain machinery was adjusted, and their daughter officially ceased existing.

DAY SEVEN

Monday morning.

And back where I started less than a week ago: in the chief's office. Ominous location. A routine review would be just me and Tony and Captain Donald. Mac is also present. I'm here to get fired.

"You had a tough week, Donna," says the chief.

"Yes, sir."

"Trial by fire. You doing okay?"

"Absolutely fine, sir."

"You can't take your cases personally."

Shut the fuck up now. In front of my partner.

"No, sir."

I'm sure I look different than I did last week, but so does the chief—and the captain. The pressure of the Weisz case is wearing them down.

"Captain tells me that you now think the English guy is not a suspect?"

"There was a lot about him that looked suspicious before, sir. He lives alone, drinks to excess, appears to be isolated in the community. That's a strong correlation to the profile of a sexual predator. But when you learn that he had a twelve-year-old daughter who was killed three years ago, then a lot of that profile

130

looks different. Now he looks more like a guy trying to survive."

The chief nods. "Question is, why didn't you know about this daughter before?"

"Because my first interrogation of him was poor, sir. We asked him if he had children. He said no. Technically, that answer was true, of course. I'm afraid I didn't take it beyond that."

"It was too attractive to have him fit the profile you already had for him."

"That's about it, sir."

"But he did have a felony quantity of marijuana in his home?"

"Yes, sir."

"What's that about?"

"Our current guess is that he probably didn't even know about it. The victim had a key to his house. She regularly walked his dog for him. She was probably using the house as a safe storage place."

"You resolved the jurisdictional issue with Hartford?"

"No, sir. We need to establish where the murder took place. The autopsy didn't yield anything on that."

"You've really tangled up your fishing line here, haven't you?"

"Yes, sir."

The chief pushes his hands through his hair. "Well, Donna, Captain Donald recommends that we let you keep the case. I don't know if that's because he doesn't want to hand such a screw-up onto some other unlucky team. Anyway, we're going to give you a bit more time."

"Thank you, sir, I appreciate that."

"But—and this is a big but—we have to manage the media very carefully on this. This is another unsolved murder, and we have enough problems in that area already."

Indeed.

"Mac will handle all media, refer all inquiries to him."

"Yes, sir."

He turns to Mac. "The minimum. Girl found at dump is missing Webster teenager. Nothing more."

"I've talked to Hartford about it," says Mac, "and we've agreed to coordinate. Use the jurisdiction issue to delay further updates."

Music to my ears.

"Doesn't mean they won't be watching. So you need to be seen to be active, Donna. Get people doing things."

"Yes, sir."

Pengelli's in the armory cleaning an automatic rifle.

"That your take-home?" I ask him. Rates a grin.

"What do you carry, Bradley?"

"The usual. SIG two forty-five."

"That all?"

"I don't mix with your type."

"Can you strip, clean and reassemble it in the dark?"

"Neither can I skin a deer in a foot of snow."

"It's a good way to get an appreciation of the weapon. Hey, sorry to hear about your girl. That's a tough one."

"Yeah, thanks."

"You keep the case?"

"Surprisingly. That's why I'm here. I need another angle of investigation. Although you've pinned Miller on the possession, I believe he knew nothing at all about the marijuana. The girl was using his house. If she's a dealer at that sort of quantity, she could easily have gotten into trouble."

He's already nodding in agreement. "What have you got on that?"

"Not a lot. You ever heard of a dealer kid goes by Z-Z?"

"Rings a bell. But he's not big time."

"Too small for you, huh?"

"Look out the window, Bradley, you'll see the I-84. We're right on the highway, halfway between New York and Boston and all the major routes to northern New England. More drugs go along that road than organic food. That's what I'm focused on. But I've got a guy on the payroll who knows most of the local players. Name's Addy. Ugly shit. Jamaican, but he's hooked up with the Ricans, they seem happy for him to have some of the casual market. I'll give you his cell number but he seldom picks up. Best to go looking for him if you're in a hurry. Sometimes he hangs out at the movie place on New Park, catch that after-crowd. Depends what's showing. Otherwise, try after ten at that row of shops along Kane Street, the munchies crowd heading to Burger King. It's a good location for a dealer because there are ramps both east and west onto the highway right there. He'll be sitting in a blue Camry, nose facing the exit."

"Thanks."

"Where's your partner?"

"He's around."

"Give you some advice? Don't come talking to other officers without your partner. Keep everything shared. Don't isolate yourself. If you've made a bad call, it isn't like the whole squad room is staring at you. Sometimes you screw up and turn over the ball, it's football, not a holy judgment on you as a person."

I'm shocked to realize that the status of our case is so widely known. And kind of amazed to be getting well considered advice from Rambo Pengelli.

"You're right. Thanks."

I'm almost out the door, when he says, "Hey, Bradley. They're running a SWAT training course down at state in the fall. You should sign up for it."

"Yeah, right."

133

"I'm serious."

I look at him. He is. I wave him off. "You just want me because I've got no dependents."

"No, I've seen your range scores."

"I'll think about it."

"You think too much, Bradley. It's a chick thing. Lighten up."

Back to the Pengelli we know and love.

On the web, checking the listings of movies currently showing at the multiplex on New Park Avenue. There are basically two kinds of movies these days: stupid girlie ones and stupid tough guy ones. Maybe it was always that way. Two of the stupid tough guys ones end around 10:30. That's our demographic.

"So let's be there around ten," I say to Tony.

"You think this dealer studies the listings like you?"

"No, but his customers might make arrangements to fit."

"Worth a try," he says. "So you want to get dinner before? My treat."

"No way, we split it. Where do you want to go?"

"Is there decent Mexican food anywhere in this town? That's one thing I miss from down south."

"The authentic local cuisine of this area is Italian. You should appreciate that. How about Asian, there's a place not far from the movie house?"

So at 9 p.m. we're sitting in the Eastwize Diner, with the grubby neon lighting and plastic-topped barstools and too-small tables and time to kill.

I put down my fork and take a big breath. "I've got something to say." Ideally, that should be followed with a swig of tequila, but we have only water. "Official apology. I'm sorry. I really screwed up with Miller. I should have listened to you."

No protesting, no forget about it, don't mention it. He's going to let me talk it through.

"I just got into a state of mind, like some kind of conviction. Stupid. And I'm going to go and apologize to Miller."

He shakes his head immediately. "Not a good idea. If you set off down the track of apologizing to every innocent civilian who gets trampled in one of your investigations, you'll be wasting a hell of a lot of time."

"I'm going to screw up *that* much?"

"It's not about you. Investigations are messy. Collateral damage is unavoidable. If you worry about it, you'll get distracted. That's why there are rules about investigative procedures. You can't be making moral judgments along the way. Your job is to follow the scent along the path of established practice."

"Have you considered writing a text book for the academy?"

"Are you saying I'm ready for retirement?"

My phone rings.

On the other end, "It's Bryan. From Hartford PD."

For a moment, I have absolutely no idea who Bryan from Hartford PD is, but then I realize it's Shaved Head.

"Oh, hi. Did you get something from the autopsy?"

"No, nothing yet."

Long pause.

"What's up?"

"I was just calling. See how you're doing."

"Pretty good. You?"

"I'm good." I can hear him grinning.

"Made any progress on the case?"

"Some."

"I've got a question for you."

"Shoot."

"Can I take you to dinner sometime?"

The restaurant is on fire. No, it's just the friction of me squirming in my seat.

"Bradley?" says Shaved Head on the phone. "You there?"

"Yeah. Well, we're kind of full-time on this investigation at the moment."

"Sure. I mean, you know it's unhealthy not to take a break. That's a proven fact."

"I'll look into it."

"I'll call you again tomorrow."

"That's too soon."

"And the next day."

"I have to do some police work now. Goodbye."

I put my phone back in my pocket. Tony has found something of immense importance in the laminated menu and has no interest in my phone conversation. Whatsoever. If you splashed water on my cheeks they would steam.

"That was the guy from Hartford PD. Shaved Head."

"Lieutenant Bryan Zellinger?"

"Yes. If that's his name."

"Bryan with a Y."

"With a Y?"

"Yup."

"Anyway. He asked me to go for a beer." Fudging that a bit.

"First-rate detective, by all accounts. Best clear record in his department."

"Whoa, have you been talking to him? Is this some kind of male cooperative —"

"Relax. No."

"So how do you know all this about him?"

"I take an interest."

"'I take an interest.'"

"You should try it."

I point my chopstick at him. "You say nothing about this. To anyone."

"You know me as a blabbermouth?"

"Taking no chances."

Tony grins at me. I am immersed in grinners.

"So what else do you know about him?"

"Do you ever read the stuff on SWAT operations in the state?"

"Not really."

"Zellinger is very active. Volunteers for a lot of ops."

"Oh, God, he's a cowboy."

Tony shrugs. "He's put in the time. Done the advanced cours-es. Been for out of state training. I wouldn't call him a cowboy."

"I dunno. I mean, obviously, we need SWAT people. But it's always a certain kind of guy."

"You're only seeing the surface."

"Maybe."

10 p.m.

Ten minutes ago Tony drove into the large parking lot on Kane Street in his personal truck and went into the Burger King. We didn't find Addy at the multiplex earlier, but now here's the blue Camry, parked away from the half dozen other cars, nose to the exit. I do a slow circuit of the lot in my old Honda and stop in the line of sight of the Camry so Addy can watch me when I make my approach.

I step out the car. I'm wearing jeans with a rip at the knee and a strappy top, which will keep Addy's mind from wandering to suspicious possibilities, if I say so myself.

I start walking across to the Camry and suddenly, unexpected-ly, I feel good for the first time in days. After all the fuck-ups on this case, this is a small act, which can, in itself, possibly go well. It's a nice evening, no stickiness, no bugs. Reminds me of when I used to go to the drive-in with my mom and dad when I was ten and they would let me and my friend Michelle go to the concession stand on our own to buy ice cream. We'd walk back in the dark between all the hidden lives in the cars around and with the massive images on the screen above and lots of things were possible. I'm not quite up to admitting that dinner with Shaved Head makes me feel this way.

Addy is behind the wheel of the Camry; his eyes watch me as I approach but his head doesn't move. Ugly shit, as Pengelli said. I lean down against the car window, with the edge of a $50 bill, requisitioned in triplicate, showing through my fingers. He's alone in the car, which makes things a lot easier.

"What's up, sister?"

"My friend told me you the man."

"Who's your friend?"

"Jenny."

"I don't know no Jenny."

"You Addy?"

I've got my badge in my other hand and I let him see it now.

"What the fuck." Not surprise, not anger. Just another day on the job for him.

"I'm not interested in your business, I'm just looking for some information."

His eyes skip past my face, trying to see back to my car.

"Yes, I have backup. Not in the car. But you don't have to worry here. I'm just looking for a guy. Kid called Z-Z."

"I don't know him."

The accent is Jamaican. When I'm amped, random facts fly at me: Greater Hartford has the second largest Jamaican population in the USA.

"But you know Pengelli right? My understanding is he lets you live in peace. I presume you want things to stay that way."

Our faces are less than twelve inches apart. I'm catching the jerk pork he had for dinner. His right hand is drifting around the junk on his passenger seat.

"Please keep your hands on the wheel, Addy. Check your mirror. Guy standing at the Burger King, he's with me. So don't get restless. This is not a problem for you."

"What you want with that Rican? He shoot someone?"

"Why? Has he got a history like that?"

"He got a weapon he likes to show people. I hear. Kid's in a hurry. He don't want to come up the ranks. Either going to shoot or get shot."

"What's he like with the girls? They go for him?"

Shrug. "He got his sluts no doubt. His people, they don't hold their women in very high esteem. Got no romance. Too many of them been fucked by their daddies."

I crinkle the fifty noisily to bring his attention back to the subject.

"Where do I find him?"

"Look, we don't mix, him and me, all right?"

"What, he take your customers? Situation could improve if he's off the streets."

"He like to show off that stupid ass black BMW Saturday nights. Along Parade Street where all the eating places are."

"Expensive wheels for a twenty-year-old."

"Only if he pay for it."

"Where else?"

Addy removes the bill from my fingers. "What you got for me besides this?"

"I can tell Pengelli you're a good citizen."

He snorts. "That a crazy man, but he play straight. Listen, Laundromat on Ferris Road in New Britain. I seen the car parked there a few times. I don't think the kid is inside folding his boxers. Maybe he got premises in that block."

"That sounds better."

"You get what you need, you owe me."

His eyes switch away from mine as the baseline of an over-amplified rap song reaches us like an earth tremor, and a hulking SUV swings into the lot.

"You step off now, officer."

Four large black men get out of the SUV. The lights go off on the vehicle but the music continues. I can see Tony detach himself from the wall of the Burger King and make his way to be closer to me. I put my shoulders back and my eyes down and walk straight for my car.

"Hey, baby." I keep my eyes on the ground. If I have to show these guys my shield, it will give Addy a career-ending, and possibly life-threatening, problem.

Tony's fingers touch my elbow; he's drifted up beside me, makes no eye contact with the men but gives them enough cause for hesitation.

"Man send his bitch to do his shopping."

"Maybe she get a better price."

"Maybe she work for it."

"No doubt dat."

"He doing all right by you, baby?"

And we're in my car.

The Wilton Lane dog group assembled without appointment weekday mornings, usually around 6:30 a.m. Signs at both entrances to the sports fields clearly stated that dogs must be on leashes but by unspoken agreement there was a period before work in the mornings when that rule was ignored, and local residents brought their mutts and released them to run together. The school didn't complain, the neighbors didn't complain, and Animal Control turned a blind eye during this period.

The group, in return, was self-policing. No one was in charge, rules were never mentioned, but there was a high level of compliance. Everyone cleaned up after their dogs. If an owner were lost in conversation when his dog pooped, other vigilant members would sing out helpfully, "Rudy's going!" Everyone carried spare clean-up bags.

There were occasional skirmishes between the dogs, especially when a new one was introduced, but these were resolved without injury to the dogs or to human relationships. It was generally held that vigorous socialization was a benefit to all the dogs, and no doubt to the humans as well—regular attendance ensured up-to-date neighborhood intelligence.

No one had ever been asked not to come. Yet those who didn't meet the standards of the group somehow got the message. Tough guys with aggressive dogs; owners who had been spotted not cleaning up; dogs and owners who could benefit from further training. These folks tended to drift away and either took their dogs elsewhere or walked them at different times. There was even a group contact list shared by email—organized by dog name first—used for barbecue invitations and news from former members relocated to California and North Carolina. Altogether, the dog group was a high functioning little civilization that the founding fathers would have been proud of.

Miller had come upon the group two years ago soon after he acquired Bella, and was quickly embraced *"although your membership is provisional until we see if your winter hat is funny enough."* They enjoyed his accent, they liked his dog, and they appreciated that he maintained the curb appeal of his house and thus enhanced the value of theirs.

Miller took up an outer-orbit location in the group; he fit in without being prominent. There were sufficient other contenders to lead the parade of wit and opinion. Some saw each other socially and visited each other's homes. Miller avoided that. The group enjoyed his outsider's perspective and he was careful not to overstep the boundaries for a resident alien.

Bella too was on the periphery of the dogs in the dog group, which was dominated by enthusiastic black labs. When they rough-housed, she skipped around them at a safe distance; when they ran in a pack, she was always a little behind, a cautious frown on her face.

News of Leonard Miller's arrest spread rapidly through the neighborhood. This is a place where people watch each other's houses, get concerned if a newspaper isn't collected off the driveway. Two police cars and a crime scene unit outside Miller's home on a Sunday evening had not escaped attention. Consequently there were plenty of alert eyes to watch him being walked out to the curb in handcuffs.

Tuesday morning, 6:30 a.m., Miller saw a change in the posture of the dog group members as he approached from the far end of the fields. The figures in the group perceptibly shifted closer together, backs were turned towards him. By the time he was 50 yards away, no one would look in his direction. He could hear their dogs being called in, and the backs turned to him seemed to form a protective carapace, like the shields of medieval foot soldiers held up to the rain of incoming arrows. He knew how this worked. Soon all the unsolved mysteries and imagined grievances in the neighborhood would come to lie at his door like old wolves looking for a cave in which to die.

Bella, oblivious, was scooting along the line of shrubbery against the school buildings, where sometimes a careless squirrel might be flushed out. Miller whistled her to him and clipped the leash onto her collar. She looked at him with her frown. Then Miller led his dog towards the lower gate, away from the dog group.

DAY EIGHT

Tuesday

Mac is in the doorway of the war room, carrying his laptop. Plunks it down next to me on the table, points at the screen.

Police may have lead on teenager's killer.

It's the headline of a story on a web site called CT-Online.

"Jesus. What's this?"

"I was hoping you could tell me," he says. "Didn't I tell you to stay clear of reporters?"

"Yes, and I did—"

He stabs his finger at the byline of the story on the screen. Bethany Kerry.

"I've never even heard of her. I've never heard of this web site. We haven't talked to anyone. Absolutely."

I'm scanning the first paragraph of the story. *A Webster man arrested on a separate charge may be connected to the disappearance of Amber Zajac, whose body was found at the Hartford dump on Friday.*

"So how did she get this?"

"All I can tell you is there was a woman in the media section of the courtroom at Miller's bail hearing. She asked Angelique about the case. I didn't speak to her. I followed the rules you gave me."

"I warned you. They're snakes. What about your partner?"

"He's completely by the book and very disciplined. It would

143

never be him. Surely this is a breach of media ethics or something?"

"You're behind the times, detective. Media ethics went down the same trash chute as the printed newspaper. On the Internet, the game is grabbing eyeballs at any price. If you read this article, it's carefully written. She hasn't given anyone anything to sue over, but she's still managed to create a sensational headline."

My cell is vibrating in my pocket, but I ignore it.

"What do you want me to do?"

"Close the case."

He snaps his laptop shut and heads for the door. My phone starts ringing again.

The town of New Britain has been a destination for immigrants to Connecticut since the English arrivals named it, but the sources change. So many east Europeans were coming here at one stage, my father's generation called it New Britski. Now, there are areas where the signage is only in Spanish. It has a lovely, well-respected gallery of American art, set in spacious grounds, radiant in the early morning sun. But drive five minutes from there and the green lawns are replaced by pitted parking lots and dollar stores. Second floor balconies have to be securely screened. Wide men are walking aggressive pit bulls on the sidewalk.

Ferris Street is the link between those two extremes, a broad fast-moving avenue littered with mini strip malls that were slapped up when times were good and now mostly stand empty. The Laundromat is in one of these, set back from the road a bit with a stretch of pot-holed asphalt in front, the white parking lines long faded.

Tony parks a little away from the building.

"It just occurred to me," I say as we walk toward the Laun-

144

dromat, "should we have checked in with the local cops before doing this?"

He shakes his head firmly. "Let's not complicate things."

His eyes are sweeping the location as he speaks, and suddenly I realize he likes this. The methodical, by-the-book guy who's been babysitting me for the past week is out of sight; this version of Tony is like a gun dog, nose to the breeze, nothing else on his mind.

The only other storefront next to the Laundromat looks long vacant, peeling signage harking back to the quaint era of the video store. The display windows have paper pasted on them from the inside. On the second floor, above the storefront, there are two windows draped edge to edge. Could be residential, could be office, could be a place to turn a big bag of merchandise into lots of little bags for the street.

We walk around the building. There are rusty steel steps up to a balcony that runs the length of the 2nd floor. The rear of the vacant store has a loading bay with a steel door.

Inside the Laundromat a Puerto Rican woman with a low center of gravity is loading the day's service washes. She looks at us, I can see the calculation sweep rapidly across her face: we ain't customers, we ain't neighborhood, we're cops. Her eyes flick across the parking lot.

"Good morning," says Tony, easy smile. "How you doing?"

"Yes?" She says, propping a large plastic laundry basket on her hip.

"Do you know a young man goes by the name of Z-Z?"

She buys some time squinting as though ponderously processing this foreign language.

"Black BMW," Tony adds helpfully.

"No, I don't know," she shakes her head.

"He's got a tattoo like this," Tony draws two large Zs on his forearm with his finger. She just shrugs. He beams at her as though she's been immensely helpful.

"What's upstairs?" He points upward.

"I don't know."

Liar, liar, pants on fire. It's in the way she turns aside, busies herself with the clothing in her plastic basket. Jeans and T-shirts grimy from a construction site, lucky customer, has a job in the American recession, can afford a service wash.

Now there's a sound from the vacant store next door. I can't work it out for a moment, but Tony swivels like a quarterback and is out the door and running. I scramble after him, taking the other way around the building. I've got the sound now: the grind of a steel door opening. I sprint along the empty shop front and reach the corner just as the black BMW swings into view from the rear of the building, coming straight at me, picking up some speed. The space between the side of the building and the property fence is wide enough for a car but no more. I step into his path, weapon up, and shout the command. He keeps coming, his face on the sight of my SIG and I can see him making a decision, the milliseconds are long and full of detail. I shift my aim three feet and blow two rounds into his windshield, then jump back behind the building. I hear the car scrape the side of the building and stop. Peep out: Tony is approaching from the other side, weapon-ready.

"Get out of the car!" he shouts. "Very slowly."

The driver's door opens.

"Slower," Tony shouts. "Hands first!"

The kid who comes into view is a scrawny guy, maybe 20, wearing only his baggy sweat pants. I'm quick to get up close to him. The adrenaline is jumping in me.

"On the ground, Z-Z!" I'm in his ear. He's wincing. "Where you going in such a hurry?"

"Going to the store, man, that's all!"

"Without your shirt?"

"It's hot, man."

"I'll take care of him," says Tony. "You check the car." He's worried I'm over-cooked, giving me time to cool off. So I do the car while Tony gets the cuffs on Z-Z.

"What you arresting me for?"

"Let's start with attempted murder of an officer."

"I didn't know she was an officer. She's just a chick with a gun to me!"

"She shouted *Police*."

"That don't mean she is! You come outta nowhere!"

There's a backpack in the rear seat of the car. I open it carefully with my fingertips. An assortment of marijuana and pills. I leave it and move on, but there is no weapon or anything else of interest in the car. One of my rounds is buried in the passenger headrest. I have to look harder for the other one, find it in the upholstery behind the rear door. Debate removing them, but decide not to. I can already see the procedural investigation into this.

"Narcotics in the car," I tell Tony. "In a backpack. That's probably how he stores it so as to be able to get out quick—just like this."

My heart rate has come down and now I can survey this kid more carefully. I can see the two Zs tattooed on his forearm, but they are nothing compared to the work he's had done on his skinny torso. There must be five pounds of ink on this guy. There's a crucifix around his neck and the mandatory oversize wristwatch on his left arm.

"Bring the backpack," Tony says as he starts steering the kid across the parking lot.

"Where we going?" says the kid.

"Our house," I tell him.

"What about my car? It's got no windshield, man! It's not secure."

Tony shoves him in the back of the squad car. "You're going to have half the New Britain P. D. looking over that car. It will be safe."

"Why you come looking for me?" Z-Z asks.

Tony treats this to a contemptuous silence. I follow suit.

"You got no probable cause for that search of my car," the kid goes on. "That's never gonna stand up."

Tony just gives him a two-beat look in the rear-view: where we're taking you those rules don't apply.

We get him to the precinct and cuff him to a table in Interview Three. For twenty minutes he's alone with his thoughts and a bottle of water. His backpack is in the corner. His wallet, key ring and other contents of his pockets are next to him on the table, except for his cell phone, which Tony took. Tony has been sitting in the war room going through that phone in detail, while I finish logging the paperwork required for a discharge of my weapon.

Then I enter the interview room and sit down opposite the kid with a pen and a pad. I just look at him for a while, give the kid a sense of gravity. You've stepped off the edge of your known world, little fella; there's no bottom to where you can fall now.

He could be as young as twenty. He has—I honestly don't know if there's a name for this—like a pencil line of unshaved whiskers coming down from his sideburns and following the line of the chin and up the other side. But very meticulously done. It must take time and care. The mouth is soft and his nose hasn't been broken yet.

"First, let's get your full particulars for the charge sheet, kid."

I pick up his wallet and get the license out and start copying down the name and address.

"Diego Escalante. Not as sexy as Z-Z, right? Where you come up with Z-Z?"

"Just a kid thing."

"The white girls like that?"

He doesn't flicker. "Listen, I never committed no crime in Webster."

"Maybe, maybe not. When you show us where you killed her, that will determine the jurisdiction."

"What the fuck!"

I'm up and in his face. "Hey! Diego! Language! You're not on some cheap drug bust now. You conduct yourself in a manner appropriate to these grave charges." This is just coming to me naturally, I don't know from where. I'm still high from the action. "I'll give you some advice. You want this to go well for you, don't use any curse words with Detective di Giorgio. He's a God-fearing righteous type from down south. He takes offense." I sit down again and copy out his address. "You a citizen of the United States, Diego?"

"Absolutely."

I shake my head consolingly.

"What?"

"Might have been easier for you if you had the option of extradition."

"Look, I don't know what the f— what you talking about!"

The door opens and Tony walks in. I stand up and quickly step away from the table, like even I am a bit nervous of him. Tony sits down, reads the information on the pad in silence. He holds up Z-Z's cell phone.

"So, Mr. Escalante. I don't find Amber's cell phone number in your phone. How did you keep in contact with her?"

"Amber?" he asks.

"Yes. Amber Zajac."

A beat of silence.

"The deceased," Tony adds deadpan.

149

"The what?" Z-Z's pupils dilate. "What the fuck you saying—"

Tony's palm slaps down on the steel table like a gunshot.

"No cursing," I remind him.

The kid's eyes are wild. "Amber's dead?"

Tony gets out of the chair and walks slowly around behind the kid. It's an old technique, but a good one—they don't like having the interrogators behind them, but they never turn around in their chairs.

Tony drops his hands onto the kid's shoulders. Massages him gently. "Can I see your hand, Mr. Escalante?"

The kid holds up his free hand. Slim, unmarked.

"You're not a fighter, are you, Mr. Escalante?"

The kid says nothing, the shoulder massage he's getting is approaching a sexual assault.

"You make it on your smarts, don't you?" Tony continues. "You're not an intimidator, not an enforcer. I don't like your chances in lock-up."

"Look, I don't know anything about anything with Amber!" he says like a teenager wailing in the principal's office. "Honestly, if Amber is dead, I know nothing about it. God's truth." And his hand goes to the crucifix that hangs around his scrawny neck, holds it between his fingers to vouch for the value of his word. Always fuckin' amazes me. Whether it's cheating politicians or defrauding businessmen, heartless killers or dime bag dealers, in their moment of bright exposure they all tap their tolerant God, little help here.

"I didn't hear from her for a while, I think it's because of the summer, you know, school is closed. Her business is slow."

"When you did hear from her, how was it done?" Tony asks.

The kid points his free hand at his phone on the table. I step across and hand it to him. He scrolls through the contact list with dexterous speed, hands the phone to me.

"That's Amber."

I look at the number.

"Diego," I say, "you're not in a position to mess with us. We know that's not Amber's cell number."

"I got her a phone. Different phone."

A whole new vista.

"And this here is the number of the phone you got her, that you used to communicate with her?"

"Yes."

"And that she used to communicate with her customers?"

"That's what I taught her."

Tony stands up, indicates for me to follow him out the door.

"Hey," says the kid, "can I use the bathroom?"

We walk out without answering. Captain Donald is lurking in the corridor outside the interview room.

"Detective Bradley," he beckons me aside. Here it comes. Tony walks over with me. "I understand that you discharged your weapon this morning?"

"Yes, sir."

"First time?"

"Yes, sir."

"And you did this outside the Webster limits?"

"Yes, sir."

"What happened?"

"The suspect was trying to escape, sir. He was headed toward me in a car in a tight alley. There was no space for him to go around me. I gave him the warning, advised him I was a police officer. He kept coming. I fired to stop him, not to hit him. The location of the rounds in the passenger side head rest and rear will confirm that."

Donald transfers his eyes to Tony.

"That's how it went down, sir. I saw it all." That's a lie. Thank you.

"And did we have a warrant for the suspect?"

"No, sir. We were there to question him only." That doesn't make him happy.

"But he was carrying a felony quantity of drugs."

"You advise the local department?"

"We had Dispatch call them when we were on the way back here. I filed the discharge notification right afterward."

"But you went in without telling them?"

I nod.

"I hope you haven't screwed this up."

He turns and walks away. I get coffee while Tony hustles Cynthia into urgent research and monitoring of Amber's second phone.

When we get back to Interview Three, the rookie patrolman who's watching ZZ through the glass says, "I took him to the bathroom. He says he wants a lawyer now."

Tony looks at him and nods briefly, then turns to me. "Okay if I carry on?"

I grin at him. "Keep doing what you're doing."

We walk back in. The kid opens his mouth to speak but Tony cuts him off.

"Don't say anything, Mr. Escalante. Just listen for a second. Your backpack over there? The only people who know about that right now are the three of us. That's a quantity of narcotics that will get a lot of people interested. Not just your New Britain cops—state, too. Those guys will chase your ass ragged for a year, guilty or not. But we don't give a shit about your backpack or its contents, you understand? Don't speak, just nod."

The kid nods doubtfully.

"That backpack does not exist at this moment. It's not even there in the corner. We're just here talking. But if you decide you want a lawyer now, then that formalizes this whole interview and, of course, that backpack comes right into the picture. Which means you never see it or its considerably valuable contents again. I don't want that to happen to you. Not because I love you, but because I need you. You say you didn't kill Amber and I believe you. But you may have information that can lead us to her killer, and that's all we want from you. That's the honest truth. Now, I believe you. Do you believe me?"

And such is Tony's presentation, such is the quality of his bearing, that the kid's face clears and he decides to trust Tony.

The kid fidgets for a moment, then nods. "Yeah, I believe you, man."

"So, Diego, do you want a lawyer at this time, or do we just continue chatting here?"

"I can go afterward?"

"Provided there's nothing else relevant to Amber's death that you've been hiding, yes."

"Okay."

"Good," Tony says. "So you had absolutely no knowledge of her death until today when we told you?"

"No."

"Did you have any problem with her?"

"No, I liked her! I had plans for her. She was going to be a good producer. Those kids she knows at that school, all rich families, rich friends, premium market. She's a loss to me."

"Let's talk about this phone you got her."

"Disposable. It's a business expense."

"I'm not your accountant. I want to know why you bought her a phone. She already had her own phone."

"No, I taught her. Separate phones. This phone is for calling me and your customers only, I told her. You keep your private life on your private phone. Then there can be no connection. She can ditch the disposable any time. No one can trace it to her. Pay as you go. You don't keep this phone in your house. You find a hiding place for it. Separate phone. That's best practice."

"Best practice?" I say. "What do you read, the Harvard Business Review?"

"I'm doing a business course at the community college."

"Yeah, right..." then I catch his expression. "What, for real?"

"Sure. It's like any business." He's cheered up immensely, his street strut is coming back.

"Jeez, Diego," I say, "we should put you forward for entrepreneur of the year, get a citation from the governor."

"So, Mr. Escalante," says Tony, "why don't you give us a breakdown of the product categories that Amber was dealing in?"

"She started on weed, obviously. Then oxy. Then we add cocaine."

"You front her?"

"Sure. Payment wasn't a problem with her. Those kids have the money. She told me there are live-in students at the school, from overseas—Chinese and Arabs and whatever? They have credit accounts with car services for when they want to go out. With Amber, it's clean fifty dollar bills."

"How long has this been going on?"

"About a year."

"You knew her from before, right?"

"Yeah, I had runners in middle school where she went. When I was just starting out."

"So then a year ago you suddenly thought oh, now that blond girl is ready to deal for me?"

"No way. Actually I forgotten all about her. She came to me."

"Come on, Diego."

"It's the way, man. She comes and says there's lots of kids at that school with money, she know I'm connected. I got proof of that. She had to find me through a friend. He'll tell you."

"What else? Heroin?"

"No, she didn't ask, I didn't push. She did ask for other shit I can't get."

"What's that?"

"That stuff body builders use. Steroids. And H ... H-G something?"

"HGH? Human growth hormone?"

"I think that's it."

"Did she ever tell you if she got another source for that?"

He shrugs.

"Any chance she was dealing with another supplier like you?"

"We never had a problem."

"When did you last see or hear from her?"

"Maybe two weeks ago she ask me for a stack of weed. Say she's got a big party at some house on the beach coming up. I delivered it to her."

"When and where?"

"I always meet her after her shift at the ice cream place on Parkside Avenue. It's late, I drive her home, she takes the supply."

"She tell you where she keeps it?"

"No, I asked her, she said she's got a safe place."

"Nothing from her since then?"

"Nothing."

"Okay, Diego, we need to know exactly who Amber's clients were. What can you give us on that?"

He shakes his head. "I don't ask, I don't listen, I never let them see me. That's the best way. The go-between is the cut-out, he goes down, there's no connection."

"How old are you, Diego?"

"Twenty-two."

"You been well schooled. Who did that for you?"

I can see him considering claiming to be a natural prodigy, but after a beat he says, "My uncle. He's gone now. What you doing, man?"

What Tony is doing is typing something into Z-Z's phone.

"I'm putting my number here in your contacts, Diego. See here, under Tony. Now you ever hear anything about what happened with Amber, you call me." He hands the phone to the kid, takes out his key and prepares to unlock the cuff on Z-Z's wrist. Then pauses. "We've had a useful chat here, I hope you take it seriously. I hope you will give us anything you hear, because you're still under a heavy load on this, you know that, right?"

"I thought you said you believed me?"

"I do believe you. But I can still get you if I need to. Diego, we got a new lady prosecutor here, she's good looking, smart, a dozen college degrees, the judges and juries love her. They just eat it up, whatever she's saying. It's like hypnosis. But this woman? Heart like a stone when it comes to bad guys. If she wants you, you will go down, guilty or innocent. You know what she'll say about you? Reckless endangerment. You put Amber in a situation where she got killed. You didn't pull the trigger, but you're involved."

"No way, man!"

"It's a valid charge. Check it out with your law professor at that community college."

The kid's eyes dart from Tony to me. His jaw is open as if words should be coming out of his mouth, but he doesn't know what to say.

"Look, man, sure, I'll do it. Because I liked her, you know. We had a future together. I was thinking even, you know, she could be a high-class escort sometime in the future, that's something I had in my head for her, too."

"Career development."

"Yeah. Because that's something I think of getting into in the future. Not the street girls. Upmarket. She had that class."

There you go. That essential blindness to the moral dimension. If he'd been born on the rich side of Webster, he'd be all set for Wall Street.

On the phone. Dr. Hemingway's measured tone.

"Do you see the contradiction, Detective Bradley?"

Actually, no, not a clue. The lab report on samples collected at Amber's autopsy is in front of me. You need a Ph.D. to read it.

"Not completely, can you walk me through it, Dr. Hemingway."

"The postmortem period as indicated by the parasite growth seems to be significantly shorter than that provided by the other indicators."

"Okay, and?"

"In such contradictions are opportunities for leaps of insight. One explanation is that the parasite cycle started sometime after death. Why would that be?"

"Because the body was in a sealed environment?'

"Excellent! Do you remember how the settling of the blood clearly marked the body, like a high tide mark?"

"Yes."

"What conclusion did we draw?"

"The body was left on its side, undisturbed, for some length of time immediately after death."

"Yes. Now if you look at the PM estimate from the analysis of the vitreous humor, that indicates a period of three days? That surprised me. The body, visually, was well preserved."

"So there were two days after she was killed where she was indoors, and parasites couldn't get to her?"

"That's right. But also, she wasn't just kept in a garage or a car trunk or anything like that. Flies are amazingly effective at getting

157

to where they aren't wanted. I think she would have had to be inside a building, somewhere pretty sealed off where the killer controlled access. And somewhere air-conditioned, or with a cool, stable temperature and low humidity. An environment that slowed decomp."

"A basement?"

"Possible, but even basements are accessible to flies."

"A commercial refrigerator, like a supermarket has?"

"Too cold. We would have seen signs pointing to that. You don't have to solve it now, detective, you'll know it when you see it."

"Okay, I get it."

"There's a usable quantity of human DNA from under her fingernails. So if you can identify a suspect and get DNA, that's useful."

"Thanks, Dr. Hemingway."

"Come and observe any time, Detective Bradley. Everything you need to solve a murder is in the autopsy room."

Seems I've made a friend. A weird friend, not the first, but one worth having.

In the war room, Flynn has mounted the photo board from Amber's bedroom on the wall, and added the photos I took of her room. He's screwed another large display board to the wall on which he's created the time line of the main events we know about. He's tracked each party with different colored sticky notes, which he must have bought himself because I don't see Mrs. B handing those out. Useful guy.

"Your new phone's a problem." Cynthia walks into the war room. "It's a cheap disposable. Small companies that don't have their own networks sell these. They lease space on the big networks. So tracking the usage is more difficult, plus there's another layer of bureaucracy that's less cooperative."

"Why?"

"Ask yourself, who buys disposable phones? Bad guys and cheating husbands. If that's your market, you don't get repeat business by ruining theirs."

"So, when, do you think?"

"Maybe twenty-four hours."

"If Dr. Hemingway is right," says Flynn, "that means the text to Jenna was sent after Amber was dead."

"By whoever killed her," says Tony. "That could mean the killer is someone who knows who Jenna is. Which means he's a kid."

"Or he chose a name at random."

"And why just one text as a decoy? Why not more?"

I'm still staring at Amber's display board. It reminds me of how neat her room was. How my search of her room turned up nothing.

"You know what?" I say to Tony.

"What?"

"We ... I ... had it completely back to front. I started out thinking that Miller targeted Amber. It was the other way around. She needed a stash house. His house was perfect. I should have got that when I saw her room. It was so unnaturally tidy."

"Hindsight is so useful when you want to beat yourself up," he says. "Let's go for a drink. Want to try Santa Cruz?"

"Thanks, but I can't tonight."

"Come on. Don't just say no. Let's go blow off the day."

"You worried about me because of the shooting? No PTSD. You're off the hook."

"Wow, just a friendly invite, no need to bite."

"Sorry, but I really do have something else."

His eyes come to me smartly. "Oh, really..."

159

"Shut the fuck up."

"So you cracked in less than twenty-four hours?"

"Shaved Head is a persistent man."

"You'll have to remember to call him Bryan."

"With a Y."

"Where you going?"

"Somewhere in Wethersfield. Frank's? I don't know anything about it. He chose it."

"Classic old place. There's a signed photo of Billy Joel on the wall."

"I hope it's not too pricey."

"He invites you to Frank's, then he's paying. He probably knows someone there. Gets a deal. You can order the steak."

"You think that's it? I thought maybe he was looking for neutral territory—you know, not Hartford and not Webster."

"He's not a suspect, Bradley, you don't have to analyze his motives."

Yeah, that's what you think.

Frank's is dark wood and clubby-feeling and gloriously cool. He's there when I walk in, just inside the door, occupying a lot of space with that wide body, chatting to the maître d'. He smiles the in-control smile.

"This is detective Donna Bradley."

"Welcome," says the guy. I don't get his name. This is all set up, as Tony suggested, to show me how connected Shaved Head is. Sorry, Bryan. He's got us a quiet booth at the end of the row.

Time and reality are still feeling loose around me, since the shooting. Those few seconds were so expanded and full of detail, everything else feels slow and trivial. Bryan is telling me a long story about his sister. My margarita is gone. It was full and then it wasn't.

The light over the bar catches a shiny point on his shaved skull as he talks. I read once that whenever we meet someone new, the body makes up its mind independently and instantaneously whether or not he's someone we would have sex with. We go through life seeing new people and being polite to them while deep within us the mating selector is going yes, no, no, yes, yes, no, no, no. We don't even register the ones that are no. The yesses we do, no matter how distracted we may be. It's like even when your house is burning down around you, if the fireman who carries you out is a yes, your body taps you on the shoulder and says "note to self."

My point is that when I first saw Shaved Head that day at the dump, my body sent me no message. Actually he irritated me. First off, the shaved head thing. It's okay if you're actually substantially balding, but the young guys who shave their heads because they think it makes them look tough, I just want to slap them. On the plus side, his skull is a nice brownish tan color, not that pale look of a guy who's been masturbating under a rock. Secondly, he behaved like a typical territory-protecting alpha male, so predictable, but I guess he could say the same thing about me. Dogs over a bone. But sitting here in this bar with that margarita inside me, I'm obliged to acknowledge an outbreak of lust on my skin like the brief blue flame licking across brandy cake. His wrists are like the things that connect train cars, but there's a boyish lightness to his movements. Most of all, he's actually having fun; he doesn't haul whatever case he's on around like a crippled relative after work. This date thing. It fulfills an aspiration in him—he's ordering for both of us. I've seen this in old movies.

"You'll like that," he says about whatever it is he's ordered for me. It's so quaintly gallant it actually makes me laugh.

He laughs, too. Easily.

"You want another margarita?"

"It's a week night."

"What? You got school tomorrow?"

"Okay, hit me."

He waves at the bartender. "So what happened to you today?"

"Well, I discharged my weapon."

"Really? Wow. Kill anyone?"

"No!"

"Were you trying to?"

"If I was trying to, he'd be dead."

That grin. "Of course he would."

"I mean, I know you SWAT guys are out there blazing off once a week, but some of us have to actually find the people for you to shoot at."

Still he grins. "Well, it's my good luck to catch you when you've got adrenaline burn. It's a glorious feeling, isn't it?"

Wow, he just looked right inside me.

"Come on, tell me exactly how it went down."

And of course I babble it all out, because I am still hyped about it. And he's so easy to talk to. A short old guy goes by, stops, and reverses comically.

"Hey, Bryan!"

"Hey, Sy! Donna, this is a friend of my father's, Sy Alderman. You want a drink, Sy?"

"Oh, sure."

He slides in next to Bryan and shamelessly runs his eye over my chest.

"Donna's a detective in Webster," Bryan says.

"You any closer to catching the guy who killed Nathan Weisz?" Sy asks.

"I'm not on that case, but no we aren't."

"Didn't you know him?" Bryan says to Sy. "You were in insurance."

"I was retired by the time he came along. Anyway, he's not one of us. He's a hired gun from North Carolina or somewhere, a corporate guy, not an insurance guy."

"Sy worked forty years for the same company," Bryan says to me, "Right, Sy?"

"Totally different world today," the little guy says. "Today, it's all about the quarterly results and the executive bonus. Short term. Insurance is long-term. Seven years of plenty, seven years of pain. The history of the insurance companies here in Hartford used to be a proud one. All the way back—do you know that New England General Insurance, as it was then, never laid off anyone in the Great Depression? For years, the leading CEOs in this town were known as the Bishops of Hartford. They lived in the community and they invested in the community. In the sixties and seventies, downtown Hartford was alive. You couldn't walk down the sidewalk at lunchtime it was so busy. Because the companies reinvested."

This is why I stay away from my parents' generation, because you will always end up hearing about the old days. But I like the guy. And he seems to like me, because when he gets up to go he puts his head next to mine and whispers in my ear.

Bryan laughs and says, "What's he saying about me?"

What Sy whispers in my ear is, "I hope I'm going to see more of you." And he leaves me with a wink.

DAY NINE

6.10 a.m.

My beeper goes. And immediately my phone. The department has a system for mass-dialing all staff phones with a recorded message in an emergency. As far as I know, it's never been used before. I hear Mac's voice telling me that the chief has called an all-hands meeting at the 7 a.m. shift change, no exceptions. I can't think of anything that would warrant it—even when Weisz was murdered we didn't do this. Maybe they're doing it because they've caught the guy? All hands celebration?

I've got nothing in the refrigerator so I swing by the diner on Parkside Avenue to collect a breakfast sandwich. I get to the station at five of, have to rush. Never seen the place packed like this. The meeting is in the main squad room, and I have to squeeze in at the very back. The chief and Mac and a few others are up at the stand.

The chief stands up and silence falls. He holds up a tabloid newspaper.

"This is this morning's New York Post," he says. "I'm going to read you the headline. GRISLY END FOR C-E-O. It's referring to Nathan Weisz. Accompanying this article are seven photographs. They are our crime scene photographs."

He shuts up while a wave of murmurs rolls out.

"Some parts of some of the photos have been covered over, but what's here is still very, very graphic. There's also a photo of the murder weapon."

There's still some noise. He waits for absolute silence.

"I don't have to tell you what this does to us as a police department. I'm sure you all get it. Why I've called you here is to say this. The officer or officers who leaked these photos will be found. He or she will obviously never work in law enforcement again and will never see his pension. But beyond that, anyone who helped or even knew about this, and doesn't come forward now, is going the same way. I am saying to each and every one of you right now, if you know anything, go straight to your superior officer. Right after the meeting—not an hour from now, not later today. Right now. All team leaders will be in their offices after this meeting. I'm telling you again, if we find out later that anyone who knew anything did not come forward today, that officer will be terminated. Secondly, refer all media inquiries, formal, casual, whatever, to Captain MacKenzie. The officer who did this betrayed everyone in this room. You should all be as angry as I am. Dismissed."

Naturally we all go straight to our desks and call up the New York Post web site. It's one thing to see crime scene photos on the board of a war room. But here in the context of sports scores and celebrity gossip, they are like a kick in the gut. The cheerful pink Adirondack chairs on the lawn behind the corpse provide a particularly gruesome contrast.

The Post has nothing to add on the actual murder investigation. The purpose here is pure gore-fest, despite coy references to how they've covered up the worst of the pictures. I guess the big urban operations like the New York PD work in the context of media scrutiny and controversy all the time and know how to keep functioning, but we don't get something like this more than once a generation. This is going to hit us hard.

The Catholic Church on Farmington Avenue, just east of the town center, is an imposing but unlovely slab of modern brickwork with a plaza of concrete in front of it, suitable for the mingling of a substantial congregation after Mass. I would have volunteered for Afghanistan to get out of this, but Tony is firm: we need to be at Amber's funeral to show support for the family and to do the routinely useless scan of attendees for possible perps. Everyone's gone in by the time we get there, except for a TV news crew, and the stooped figure of Mr. Zajac in an ill-fitting black suit, lurking under the solitary tree.

"They must have started. Why's Crazy Bird standing outside alone?"

Tony parks on the yellow line in front of the church and I put the WEBSTER PD sign on the dashboard. My only suitable dress is winter weight. The perspiration pops out on my forehead after five steps. Zajac moves from foot to foot as we approach, watching us. There's a cigarette in his fingers and a butt on the ground at his feet.

"You're not going in to the service, Mr. Zajac?" I ask.

He shakes his head.

"You want to walk in with us? Come on."

"I won't go in the church," he says.

"You don't have to be a Catholic, you know. You don't even have to be a believer."

"I'm Catholic," he says. "But when I go in the church it makes me feel nauseous. Every time. Sometimes faint. Once I vomited. It's better I stay out here."

This right here is why cops have to learn to dissociate themselves from the concerns of civilians. Because if I opened my heart to whatever is behind Crazy Bird's eyes I would never be done with it. As we walk away from him toward the church doors, I say to Tony, "Do you remember when they came to view the body? We came out afterward. He had his head back shouting? He was shouting at God. He's gone to war with God over this."

"Only one winner in that," says Tony.

Inside, attendance seems pathetically small in the massive space. Tony and I attach ourselves at the rear, neither of us participating in the singing or praying. When it's over we stay in our seats so that everyone has to pass by us on the way out. I make eye contact with Mrs. Zajac and nod to her, but she's in a trance.

Adults number about two dozen. Here's the idiot Ingerson, thumbing through his cell phone while walking in a funeral line, his wife looking the other way, projecting her breasts. Catriona, looking shattered, the eye-popping body stowed away inside a ballooning black dress; her mother, she's a survivor, straight back, this doesn't touch me. I think that's the librarian from the teen room. Then all the kids together, shuffling close to each other like sheep, except for a group of three longhaired boys at the back who might as well be carrying a sign saying potheads. There are boys here that make evolution look like a really hit or miss affair.

The transition from the cool gloom of the church interior to the baking white light on the plaza is shocking, and the grieving friends and family mill about as if stunned by the impact of it. Something is tapping at the door of my brain and I need to walk to sort it out.

I walk over to where Tony is talking to a bony-faced woman who he introduces as Amber's Aunt Rita.

"I'm sorry for your loss," I say. "It's like twice a tragedy when a child dies." Auto-platitude. There should be a guidebook for cops in these situations.

She doesn't look at me. It's Tony's eyes she wants on her. This guy—women of a certain age just love him. It's not always about

167

romantic or sexual attraction, he's just got some look or phero-mone that makes them feel safer or better or worthier.

"There was never going to be a place for Amber in this world," she says to him. "It sounds harsh, but that's what I believe. Do you know what I mean?"

He nods.

"I'm going to walk to the filling station on the corner," I say to Tony. "Pick me up there in ten?"

"Sure," he says.

I step away and there's Stan Zajac right in my line of vision again, standing alone at his own daughter's funeral, like a home-less person passing by who stopped to stare.

Stanislaw Zajac was his mother's son, she had seen to that. In America she poured her homesickness into the boy. She spoke to him in Polish to keep the language with him. She fed him the tra-ditional food and told him the old family stories. Her family had always been divided into those who went to God and those who went to hell. There was a badness in them all, but some con-quered it with faith. The others found their way to jail, or died violently, or destroyed the ones who tried to love them. Stan's mother had made sure he was well armored with faith before the badness could come out in him. Hundreds of hours they spent in the church together, while Mikolaj drew plans and laid brick and shaped his life with his dexterous hands.

Emboldened by American rationalism, Stan could depart some way from his mother's view. He could think of his mother's family as not damned but as possessing a rotten gene. And he could con-sider himself free of the gene. He knew he had a quick temper and needed to be inflexible about certain things, but he had made his way in life without attracting special attention from teachers, doc-

168

tors, or the law.

He was a disappointment to his father, that he knew. But in time Mikolaj had made him an equal partner in the business and soon after that they built a perfect house together. It was small and simple, the right investment in the right location at the right time. They made money on that house. His son was a kid then, his daughter unborn. And he remembers his father saying, just do that same thing over and over and you will be a successful businessman. And for a number of years it went well. But as Mikolaj aged and lost his energy, the business seemed to wither.

The day his five-year-old daughter had climbed the tree with the biggest rock she could carry and aimed it at her brother's head, Stan knew it was the damnation on his mother's family reaching down the generations. The priest was recruited to help her, but after a few weeks he said her ears were closed to the word of God. There was a period of years when they watched Amber with dread. But there was no further calamity. The girl grew close to her grandfather after he came to live with them. She became an outstanding student. Stan and Rosemary Zajac found their fear replaced with nervous pride. Even hopeful expectation. But then the child turned again, after her grandfather's death. All childlikeness drained out of her. When she looked at her parents her eyes were flat and sullen. Her conversation with them was the truncated testimony of a hostile witness. They hoped the switch to the new school, the academic stimulation, contact with a better class of student, would help. But it became worse.

That last night, he had been trying to find a way to reach her. A way to tell her about the strand of contamination running down through the generations of their family, how to beware of it, how to quarantine it within herself. He wanted to tell her what he had done.

"I am the evil one," he had said. "The devil is in me, not you!"

The look on her face. She wasn't his child, she was someone who looked at him and despised him. She didn't know the burdens.

"There's no devil in you, Dad," she said. "You're just a loser."

That's when he slapped her. And right away he knew there would be punishment.

From the cathedral I cross to walk on the other side of the street, which is shaded by some tawdry multi-family homes. A furious dog barks at me from behind an attic window. I hope they've left the A/C on for him.

When Tony picks me up, I say to him, "Do you remember at the autopsy? What Hemingway said about the way she was killed?"

"Not premeditated, you mean?"

"And the sudden, violent nature of it."

"Yes."

"Z-Z said Amber asked for steroids. A side effect of steroids is aggression, loss of self-control, that kind of thing. Combine that with general teenage boy stuff, maybe you've got a guy who could snap and do what was done to Amber in a moment of rage."

"Valid reasoning."

"Who abuses steroids?"

"Athletes, body builders. Those pro cyclists. Guys who have to build bulk quickly."

"Maybe high school athletes who need something extra for college scholarships?"

"Yep, also valid."

"We need a list of varsity athletes at Amber's school."

"They'll block us with the privacy story again."

"Yeah. Maybe it's time to talk to them about that. Let's take a ride out there."

Driving through the massive campus, past manicured fields and flowerbeds, it takes us something like twenty minutes just to find our way from the gate to the admin building.

"The person you need to see is on lunch. Perhaps you could come back later?"

"This is police business," I say. "Call her and tell her to come back. We'll walk around for ten minutes."

I kind of knew in my mind that private schools had pretty good facilities. But this is like some gigantic country club, only better. In the gym, there's perfect wood flooring for four basketball courts side by side. There are practice courts on the third floor. There's a coaches' room—locked, maybe it's a suite of rooms with DVD players for analyzing plays. There's a notice board next to the door with first aid instructions including an illustrated guide on how to perform the Heimlich maneuver, in case one of the students aspirates his silver spoon. In the long, long corridors, there are photos of teams going back to the 1800s so you can check what senator's son was on the tennis team. The picture framing costs alone would flatten the athletics budget of Tolland High, where I went.

"Is this where Kennedy's wife went to school?" I ask. "I remember something about that."

"I think that's the all girls' school in Farmington."

The admin person is back at her post when we return.

"I'm detective Bradley from the Webster Police Department. I think you've met my partner, Detective di Giorgio."

"Yes, I have," she says. "I'm Mrs. Gladden." By name if not by nature.

"We need a list of every male student who plays on a varsity sports team. With cell phone number and home address."

"I'm sorry, but I told your partner last week that we are bound by privacy constraints."

"Mrs.—what's your name again?"

"Mrs. Gladden."

"Mrs. Gladden, did you know they are burying your former student, Amber Zajac, this morning? I didn't see you at the funeral."

She reddens. "I couldn't be there. I had to be here."

"Was the principal there?"

"He's in Italy."

"Delightful. I love Italy in the summer. Have you ever looked at a web site called CT-Online?"

"No, I don't think so."

"Well, if you call it up," I say, pointing at the computer on her desk, "you'll find they've been following this case quite closely. What's irritated me particularly is that these web sites don't follow the same protocols as the newspapers. They pretty much print whatever they hear. They've got no money, so it's not worth suing them. If someone told that reporter Amber might still be alive if this school had provided timely information to the police, she'd have that up on line ten minutes later."

Her thin lips have gone white. Her eyes flick to Tony, who's making notes in his notebook.

"How do you spell your last name, Ma'am?" he asks.

While she's spelling it out, I hold her eyes with mine.

"So you get onto your principal in Italy," I say, "or your board of governors or whoever wags the tail here, and you ask them if they want fifty rich parents pulling their kids out of this school because the papers are saying you don't protect them from murderers, and let's see if they still feel bound by the privacy constraints." I hand her a card.

"My fax number is on there. I want that list by three this afternoon. The football varsity team, down to the lowest benchwarmer.

Soccer, wrestling, lacrosse—"

She's just staring at me. Perhaps she needs a Heimlich maneuver to help her comprehend she's just run straight into the hard side of real life.

I look at Tony. "What else?"

"Swimming, rowing, horse riding," he says.

"Horse riding, really? Who knew." I turn back to her. "And please remember, it's their cell numbers that are important. I'm sure you have those for emergency alerts, right?"

"I believe so," she says.

"Also," says Tony, "if you have a recent yearbook, that would be useful."

She goes into a back room and returns with a yearbook.

"Thank you very much, Mrs. Gladden." I look at my watch. "Italy's what, six hours ahead? He should be done with his siesta by now."

Walking back to the car, Tony says, "I'm so glad she was out to lunch. It gave you time to build up a nice case of class resentment."

"Asking her how to spell her name," I say. "That's a good one. I'm going to adopt that."

Back at the station I go first to Cynthia.

"No, I don't have your call list yet," she says as soon as she sees me in her doorway. "You'll know as soon as I know."

At 1:30 I get a call from Mrs. Gladden. The school will release the required information in response to a written request, as per their lawyers' stipulation.

"That document will be with you in ten minutes," I tell her.

"You know what might expedite things for us?" says Tony. "If we get that friend of Amber's, Jenna, down here. Because there's going to be a bunch of the names on this list, and she might be able to short-list the drug users."

173

"You're right."

The faxes start coming through, team by team. Very neat. We've really screwed up Mrs. Gladden's quiet afternoon. Tony and I look for each name in the yearbook and flag the page. Each of the seniors gets one page of the yearbook to himself, where he can dispense his philosophy of life and include a few pictures of his friends.

Jenna arrives wearing sandals and short shorts, coinciding with 3 p.m. shift change and thus causing an outbreak of testosterone in the squad room. I have removed the photos of Amber's body at the dump from the board so she doesn't see them. I have prepared the yearbook with page markers at every male athlete.

"We're going to go through all the boys from your school who play on the varsity sports teams. We're looking for those who might have bought pot or whatever from Amber. Point out any boys you saw with Amber. I also want you to point out anyone who you might know of whose personality changed in the last year or so—any boys who became more erratic, got into fights, were skipping school, that kind of thing."

"Did one of these guys kill Amber?"

"No, you mustn't think of it like that. What we're doing is casting a very wide net. You're not accusing anyone of anything by picking him out here. You're just helping us create a long list of boys who might be able to help us with the investigation."

So for an hour and a half we go through the yearbook. She's very good, Jenna, in that she takes it seriously and doesn't make any unnecessary observations. She even turns her phone off for the duration. While we do that, Tony goes through all the cell numbers on Mrs. Gladden's list, cross-referencing to the call list from Amber's personal cell phone.

And out of all that, we get a list of nine boys. Six from Jenna, three from Tony. Two of them have out of state addresses, presumably boarders, and unlikely candidates for us.

We send Jenna on her way and set out to go knocking on some expensive doors. On the way, we route past Cynthia's office. She shakes her head when she sees us.

"Didn't they promise it today?" I say. "It's after five."

"They didn't promise. I guessed wrong. You just have to accept we don't have leverage on these guys." She's snapping her purse closed, heading for the door. "My brother wants to buy me a drink, which probably means he needs me to explain to him again what women want, so I'll be just up the road at Barrington's for a while. I'll come back afterwards and check. Rest assured, I'll get it to you when I get it."

We start with the guys on Tony's list who we know have had calls or texts with Amber. Door after door through the evening and into the night, pumping some adrenaline into the parents of school kids. These are people who can go their entire lives without an interaction with a cop. A detective knocking at their door is something to them. Is your daughter home? That triggers the deep, ever-present fear that their adolescents are only a slip and slide from disaster, no matter how many Mercedes are parked in the driveway. We meet a lot of nice people. One family didn't even know that a classmate had been murdered. But none of them had anything useful to give us. And nothing from Cynthia on Amber's disposable phone. That's the way it goes sometimes. Most of the time.

DAY TEN

Thursday

My cell phone rings while I'm driving in, soon after seven a.m.

"The good news," says Cynthia, "is that we got the call list from that disposable phone."

"What's the bad news?"

"They've deleted the actual text messages."

"Jesus. Why?"

"They're not obliged to keep them more than a week. Like I said, you're dealing with a different animal here."

"But we've got a timeline and numbers of incoming and out-going?"

"Yes," she says.

Half an hour later Tony and I are in the war room with Cynthia, with a long fax of three months' worth of calls and texts.

"There's more calls on here than I expected," I say. "If these were all customers she was a busy girl."

"Maybe she didn't share Z-Z's business ethics," says Tony. "Maybe she used the phone for personal calls."

"The day she walked out of the house was Sunday, the sixth, right? Around seven?" I'm scanning down the list at the time stamps on the text messages.

"Here's three messages back and forth with the same number, between seven ten and seven forty-two," says Tony. "There's nothing else in that time. Whoever this is, picked her up that night."

I look at Cynthia. "We need this subscriber, pronto."

"I need your paperwork, as usual," she says.

An hour later, we have it. Name: Eric Tessing. Address: 136 Billings Road, Webster.

"He's not on the athlete list, but he could still be a student who just likes steroids," says Tony.

I'm scanning the display board. "Here's Catriona's list of the guys she knew with Amber. The two who picked them up the day they went to smoke pot at the reservoir. One of them was named Eric."

"The school office won't be open yet," says Tony.

I pull out my phone and dial. It takes her a while to answer.

"Jenna? It's Detective Bradley. There's another name come up. Eric Tessing?"

Silence.

"Jenna, are you with me?"

"Yeah, sorry, I just woke up. Eric used to go to Wycroft."

"When did he graduate?"

"No, he didn't. He was expelled, or asked to leave, or whatever."

"For drugs?"

"No. He was in a fight. With a sophomore. Last year. There were all sorts of stories, I don't know what actually happened."

"How well did you know him?"

"He wasn't in my year but, you know, I spoke to him sometimes. I'm sorry, I should have thought of him yesterday."

The Tessing house is in an area where you'd drive from one house to the next. Set off the road, back into the tree line of the reservoir.

"Shall we walk up?" says Tony. "Let's not get him worried about a car."

There's a bridge across a small stream, then a curve in the driveway.

"Do you notice," I say as we walk, "rich people don't like flat land. All the expensive houses in this town are built on the hills."

"You haven't been to Texas, I take it?"

The house comes into view. It's one of those glass and steel affairs, all pointy angles, three levels backing into the hill. Some architect banked a good check here. The stream runs through lush green plantings, cascading down some rocks and into a pond containing koi the size of shoeboxes. The landscaping is geometrical. There's an open top Jeep Wrangler in the driveway. We cross a small bridge over the stream. If you wanted to ride your horse through the front door, you could. I push the bell. Tony walks along the paving that runs along the glass wall, trying to look into the house.

A kid wearing only shorts opens the door. He's big and muscular but he's not a pretty boy. This is an untrimmed slab of meat and bone with a flame of acne on his cheeks and a pinched little mouth.

"Eric Tessing?"

"What's up?"

"Webster Police. I'm Detective Bradley. This is Detective di Giorgio. We need to talk to you. Can we come in?"

I can see it hit him. That little mouth twitches, and a series of expressions chase each other across his face so fast I can't read them.

"What's it about?"

"Amber Zajac—friend of yours?"

"Oh... yeah. Amber."

"You heard she was killed, right?"

178

"Yeah, I did. Sucks."

"Can we come in now?"

"Yeah. Sure. I was just busy, you know."

The entrance hall contains only a display of exotic potted plants and five cases of wine with Fedex stickers on them, pushed up against the wall. From there we pass into a massive open-plan living area. Two entire walls are glass. Eastern-looking screens create areas within the open plan. The art mounted on the stone walls looks authentic. You wouldn't want to spill any of that wine on the sofa, which is impracticably white. Maybe not for sitting on.

"So what were you busy with, Eric?" I ask.

"Working out."

"You're a friend of Amber's, right?"

"Uh, yeah, kind of, I saw her some times."

I can't take my eyes off his mouth; he talks as though the words hurt him as they come out. He sees me watching, and that makes it worse.

"You were at Wycroft with her, right, before you had to leave?"

He nods.

"We didn't see you at the funeral, though. Did you know it was yesterday?"

"She was a grade below me, I didn't see her that much. Look, shouldn't I have a lawyer here or something?"

"Why? You haven't done anything wrong, have you?"

"I should call my dad."

"Is he a lawyer?"

"No. But he'll get me one."

"He's at the office?"

"In Bermuda."

"On business?"

"No, vacation. I had to stay behind to finish my summer assignment."

"How's that going? You on top of it?"

"Yeah."

"So you've had the house to yourself, that must be fun. Made some time to have friends over in between the books, right? Break up the monotony with a bit of partying? You've certainly got enough wine there in the entrance."

"That's my dad's. He orders it specially."

Bright moment, right there. I'll remember it when I'm living in the retirement home. It comes like a sudden wave of nausea, rocks me. I momentarily wonder if I have actually physically moved. I am looking at Amber's killer. This is the guy. Looking at him, it's like I suddenly see him in additional dimensions. I can see the why, the how, and the where. I have to turn away from him.

"Well, Eric," I say with my back to him, "you should make that call to your dad. Can we put some coffee on while we wait? Where's the kitchen?"

I walk away toward where the kitchen might be. I need to put some space between me and the fire of realization.

"Can't you come back later?" he asks. I shake my head, turn my eyes back on him. "This is kind of important. Being a murder."

He doesn't want to see me; his eyes are desperate for any other contact.

"I'm going to call my dad from upstairs."

"Then I'll have to come with you. It's a normal precaution to ensure that possible evidence is not tampered with."

"What evidence? I haven't done anything!"

"People who haven't done anything don't need lawyers," says Tony.

"If you want to call from outside the house, that's okay," I say. "You can go out there on your own."

He picks up his cell phone and walks out the front door.

"You okay?" Tony asks.

"Where's the door to the basement?"

It's a basement in name only. For any normal person it would be a plush apartment. There's a pool table and a massive home cinema set-up. I keep walking and I find the workout area with a treadmill and weight machine and another TV screen. Walking deeper into the footprint of the house, into where it is backed into the hill, where the below-surface level ground temperature would be most suitable, I find what I'm looking for.

The wine cellar door is like the door to a commercial refrigeration room—clear glass and a heavy metal handle to make sure it seals, thermostat on the wall beside the door. Through the glass I can see some of the racks of wine.

"That's where he kept her," I say.

Tony's looking at me. I know he's reading not just what I'm telling him, but my state of mind. He's my wrangler.

"Why? Why not dump her right away?"

"Because he doesn't know how to even begin stuffing her in a car and dumping her safely himself. He's a privileged suburban boy. He had to wait for trash collection day so he could just wheel her out to the sidewalk and let the automated truck do the rest."

I look in through the glass. The floor of the wine cellar is brushed cement, completely clean.

"Let's get back before he comes in," says Tony.

I pull out my pocket camera and snap quickly as I back out of the basement – refrigerator, pool table, TV area. Back up the basement stairs and into the living room again. I move toward the panorama window to look outside. Eric Tessing flies by at a flat-out sprint on the other side of the glass, along the paving running down the side of the house. I spin for the door, but Tony grabs my shoulder.

"Let him go!" Holds me firmly. Outside, Eric jumps the stream, bounces into the Jeep and guns it down the driveway at racecar speed. Neither of us moves. There's our reflection in the panoramic glass with the room behind us. We look like we're in a Bond movie.

"Did you think I was going to shoot him, too?"

But Tony's eyes are serious on me. "I just want you not to get caught up in the emotion of the moment."

And I see it—he's right. That bright charge that's flooded me—that's got to subside before I can proceed as a police officer should. But it's oh, so strong. Delicious even, in its way. So standing here, looking at our shady reflections in the tinted glass, I let it run out of me.

"Thanks," I say.

"If this is the guy," he says, "let's take our time and view every step we take in the light of how it's going to look in the courtroom, in the hands of a good lawyer. Because when I look at this house I see the best lawyer in the state."

"With you on that."

"He's fled an interview, that looks bad on him. If he got in a car wreck because we're chasing him, a good lawyer can make all sorts of smoke from that. He's a kid. Sympathy starts on his side. Let's make a good faith effort to bring the parents into the discussion. We don't want to be accused of railroading him. At the same time, let's get his details out to the cars. If they find him, they request he come in for questioning. No arrest."

While I'm calling Flynn to get him started on the Jeep, Tony is looking around the kitchen.

"The only thing that's admissible is what's in plain sight in the main room," I say when I get off the phone.

"I think we can justifiably have a little look around for contact information for the parents. Besides, in my book, there's a difference between looking for evidence and looking for information."

"Well, then, what I'd like information on is how come he was running down the outside of the house."

"Let's go see."

We go out the front door and around the side of the house, back along where Eric ran from. Up some stone steps that lead to the upper level where the bedrooms are. Each bedroom has a patio outside it with French doors, and there's one standing open.

"He snuck up here to collect something," I say. "He didn't know we were in the basement, so he couldn't come through the house. As soon as he had whatever he needed, he ran. Something that's incriminating evidence. But I didn't see him carrying anything."

"Want to have quick look?" he asks.

It's definitely Eric's room. Not a tidy fellow. His mother no doubt designed it to be chic and stylish, but that's been overlaid with the preoccupations and fantasies of a teenage boy. There's a clutter of audio and computer equipment, an electric guitar, two skateboards, more sneakers than I can count, a large yellow metal sign purloined from a roadwork site. The walls are hung with posters of musicians and athletes and a vaguely familiar female celebrity in a swimsuit. The closet doors are open, routine contents. I am still struggling with my personal feelings about being in the room of the kid who killed Amber—maybe where he killed her. I'm on all fours looking under the bed when Tony calls me.

He's in Eric's personal en-suite bathroom. There's a damp towel and red boxers on the floor.

"What?" I ask.

Tony presses his foot on the pedal of the stainless steel waste canister under the sink and the lid lifts. I look inside. An unmarked plastic pill box and a disposable syringe.

Take a deep breath. "Lead me not into temptation."

Tony removes his foot and the lid drops. We turn around and walk out through the French windows into the sunshine.

She wakes in the unfamiliar room. They fell asleep in the same bed, but she woke up and felt stupid lying together like a married couple, so she moved to the sofa. The boy is still asleep across the bed. She gets up quietly and heads out into the silent, fascinating house. Her bare feet are cool on the stone tile. In her T-shirt and panties she walks through the main living room, with its two sides of glass walls. She knows the glass is artfully tinted so that she can see out but no one can see in, but she still gets a small transgressive thrill from standing nearly naked in front of the panorama window. The lush garden beyond seems to leap right into the room through the glass.

The time she came to have lunch here with his parents, Eric's stepmother had explained to her that the entire interior of the house had been designed by a Chinese expert to encourage creativity and tranquility. Every aspect of it entrances her. It is the antithesis of her father's mean world, where everything is cheap, every surface is invaded by stuff, not decorative, stuff from overwhelmed lives; where there's permanent grime on the Formica kitchen sink top where the faucets come out, and it makes Amber want to puke.

After the fight last night they drove back from the shore to Eric's house. The handsome boy had kissed her, and she knew in herself that she had drawn him in for the purpose. When Eric was jealous it was a little bit frightening but also fed something in her. Two years ago, Amber had been astonished at the power that came to her with puberty. In what seemed like one weekend, she went from being genderless to someone who had only to rest her hand on a teenage boy's arm to change his behavior. She is only mildly interested in the actual act of sex, but power of the hair-trigger weapons of sexual attraction is irresistible to her.

Eric is like a half-tamed dangerous animal. There's a fascination in being close to that, because it's also what draws them together. They're the same, her and him, both raw somewhere inside. She doesn't know what his problem is or where it came from, but she knows that he is afraid of things, despite the fact that he is often the biggest kid in the room. She knows he seeks out ways to get away from himself, and the drugs do that for him. That's the connection that first put them together, as allies. That's what they are—allies with shared problems and a shared way of dealing with them and facing the world. He is not the thing she wants, but he may be the way to find it or find out what it is. She doesn't know. What she does know is that this house has some effect on her mind and her body. Just being in it makes her feel better about everything, makes her forget her own house, makes her think that the world can be full of extraordinary things and somehow she can get there.

She stands where the sheet of tinted glass runs into the column of rough rock. Just the contrast between those two surfaces is something to her. She pulls off her T-shirt and presses her breasts against the contrast between the rock and the glass. She can feel the cool current from the air vents against her skin. She can't put words to what she's doing or feeling. She thinks about how it is possible to be different people in the same body. Like all the strands of who she might be are running along together and she can jump from one to the other and feel different, but only for a while. Somewhere down the line she would end up with just one life. It might be a life like the ones lived in this house. Or it might be her mother's frostbitten Vermont view of the world or her father's resentful, tramping life. And she has no idea how to make the right one come to be.

Googling: The house we were in earlier was designed by a firm in California and featured in an architectural magazine. I find a social-page photo of Mr. Calvin and Mrs. Elena Tessing. He looks about 60; she's either 40 or been suspended in time by Botox and surgeons.

Mrs. B puts her head in the door. Summoned to the captain's office. Just me, Tony's not invited.

"Captain?"

"Have a seat, Donna. This thing about the leak of the photos."

He stops.

"What about it, sir?"

"I've had a report that you were in the Weisz war room."

"I've been in there often, sir, I was working on that case up until Amber Zajac went missing. But I suppose you're referring to the time Detective Paterniakis came in while I was looking at the photos."

"That was after you'd been moved off the case?"

"Yes, sir, it was. But you can't possibly think— "

"What I can't do, Donna, is disregard any report made to me on this subject. You heard the chief yesterday. So I'm going to ask you a few questions."

"Okay, sir."

"You confirm that you were in the war room that day?"

"Yes, sir?"

"Why?"

"Just interested, sir. I was walking by and the door was open. The photos of the crime had been put up on the wall. I had never seen all of them before. I was in there five seconds before Bean-bag—before Detective Paterniakis walked in."

"And that was the only time?"

"Yes, sir."

"Do you know this New York Post reporter? Janine Griffiths?"

"No, sir."

"Never had anything to do with her at all?"

"No, sir."

"Okay, Donna. Thanks. We have to check everything."

"I understand, sir."

Around 6 p.m. my phone rings. Hale & DeWitt, attorneys at law. Is this the detective who visited Mr. Eric Tessing earlier today? ... Eric very much regrets his impulsive act of leaving the interview unannounced. He would like to make himself available for questioning tomorrow morning, with legal counsel present ... How about ten minutes from now instead? ... My apologies, but there's no attorney available to accompany him at such short notice ... What if he wakes up tomorrow morning and gets another case of the runs? ... The firm has represented the family in many matters and we guarantee his attendance ... Talking of the family, will his parents be in attendance? ... They are trying to get a flight back from Bermuda ... Nine o'clock tomorrow, then.

I give Tony the update and then call Angelique.

DAY ELEVEN

Friday

At around 4 a.m., a cooler breeze drifts in through the wide-open windows, so I can turn off the clicking swivel fan. Bryan is stretched out next to me in the dark, naked and asleep, my fifty-dollar mattress listing to his side. I admire and envy someone who can sleep so well in a strange place.

Yup, here I am. Like it's not enough that my ass is bouncing along the rough road of the case, now I sleep with a guy I just met? A cop. With a head like one of those things on the dock you tie a big ship to. It's making a huge dent in my pillow right now.

I am bright smack wide awake. On account of an idea that popped into my mind sometime in the night. At five o'clock, I can't wait any longer. I get up, shower and dress and make two cups of coffee. Then I shake him awake.

"Your trash can," I say to him. "If you put it on the sidewalk, it's not your property any more, right?"

Not a morning person, I'd say. He's staring at me like he doesn't speak English.

"There's some coffee," I say as I prod him awake. "We can take someone's trash off the sidewalk without a warrant, right? And whatever's in there—no expectation of privacy?"

"Yeah. What's going on?"

"I have to go. You can take your time. Just be careful of the hot water in the shower, it's really hot."

"Was it that bad?"

"No. It was fine. But I have to go."

Sitting in the car outside my apartment I text Bryan: "Better than fine."

Then I call Tony.

"You've got that furrowed brow," I say. Tony and I are cruising along the road Eric Tessing lives in, in my personal Honda, which no one would ever mistake for a police vehicle.

"It's potentially a good source," he replies. "But it worries me if it will stand up. It's way open to attack by the defense."

Trash bins are out on the sidewalk outside every home. It's one week since Eric Tessing wheeled Amber out to the curb. I have already been on the phone to the contracting company, telling them to stay off this road until we give them the all clear.

And there it is, standing on the sidewalk where the Tessing's long and winding driveway meets the road. I drift the car slowly past so I can look up the driveway. Nothing. I stop and back up so that the trunk of my car is next to the bin. Tony and I both pull on evidence gloves. I pop the trunk and we get out of the car. I flip the lid open on the bin: three black 33-gallon bags. I pull out the first one and turn to the trunk of my car.

"Hey, what are you doing?"

Across the street an elderly man is putting out his bin. He's in a bath robe and slippers. Shock of white hair. A frail-looking patrician-type.

I want to say to him, Fella, you're in no state to play neighborhood vigilante here. I start to cross the road toward him, smiling reassuringly and reaching for my shield. But in his mind I apparently look threatening, because he backs up hurriedly, catches his heel on a large decorative stone which displays his own house number, and sits smartly on his scrawny butt. I want to laugh until I see the shudder of real pain on his face. A cry escapes him as he folds up.

"Jeez!" I start running toward him.

Tony's pulling out his phone. "He might have broken his hip."

Now the old party shouts for help. I don't know whether he wants medical help or someone to defend him from me.

"Sir! It's okay." I have my shield right in front of his eyes now. "Webster Police Department. You're perfectly safe. Where's the pain?"

Elderly Man delicately throws up a tiny portion of his toast and marmalade onto his dressing gown, goes completely white, and passes out. Tony is right next to me. "The ambulance is on its way."

"No siren!"

"I told them." He's taking Elderly Man's pulse. "Go down to the house, bring someone."

I can't help glancing over my shoulder at the Tessing driveway as I go, but no curious faces are evident.

The whole thing takes another fifteen minutes. I find Elderly Man's son-in-law, who goes into a rant at his pretty wife about how he told the old man a thousand times not to futz around trying to help with the trash. Untold quantities of grandchildren emerge from the house and stream onto the road, making the whole thing the best circus in these parts for years. Still the Tessing driveway is free of all movement. Elderly Man, having quickly regained consciousness but not sanity, remains suspicious that we are raiding every house in the neighborhood for booty. The ambulance arrives and things improve rapidly as the responders strap him to a gurney and cart him away.

Pretty Wife wants to get going to the hospital but Son-in-Law wants to carry on being indignant.

"So what exactly were you doing here?" he asks me. "My father-in-law says you were interfering with the trash."

Now I've had enough.

"Sir, what you should be concerned with is how Social Services would look on this incident. Because I'm not sure your father-in-law is being adequately cared for, given his condition."

So gratifying: Pretty Wife actually grabs him by the arm and propels him away. Sundry curious neighbors melt back into their houses. The Tessing house remains unmoved. We climb into the Honda with the contents of the Tessing trash bin in the trunk and drive quietly away from the scene. The discharge of tension is like recovering from brain freeze.

"So," I say.

Tony sucks his teeth. "I think that might be the cleanest undercover operation I've ever been involved in."

"Watch and learn, my friend." I catch him a pretty good blow on the arm, even though I'm driving.

Back at the station, Flynn is staring at the three trash bags in the trunk of my car parked behind the station. I've just told him to move the tables and cabinets in the war room to create more floor space, so that he can spread out the contents of the trash bags for sorting into evidence bags.

"Every item in a separate evidence bag? That could be like a hundred bags."

"Not every item. Every personal item. You can put the kitchen waste and so on aside. But anything this kid has handled. DNA, Flynn. What's in these bags could break this case."

Tony says to him, "Gloves all the way. If they find any of your prints or DNA on the evidence you'll be on night shift till the Red Sox win the World Series again. Clear handwriting on the labels.

Don't fuck up."

Tony and I walk into the war room to find the chief scanning the items on our board, my captain and Mac standing by. Full court press.

"Good morning, sir?"

"Bradley. Have we got the right guy this time?"

"I think so, sir."

"Not one hundred percent?"

Deep breath. The chief keeps looking at me, doesn't glance at Tony.

"Ninety-nine," I say. "There's always a possibility."

"Mac is going to shadow you on media management from now on."

"My view is we should be as low profile as possible on the media, sir."

The chief looks across at Mac, who moves in smoothly. "It's not going to be like that, unfortunately. The man whose son you will interview in a few minutes is Calvin Tessing. His business is biotech, something the Governor of Connecticut is deeply in love with. He has created jobs and investment in this state and this town. His place in Bermuda is next door to the mayor of New York's. You've just taken a big fat dump on this guy's perfect life and right now a team of media assassins is being assembled for the express purpose of taking a dump on yours."

They're all looking at me. And I'm thinking I'm really glad Flynn is dragging his heels, because this would probably be a bad time to tell the chief we just stole Mr. Calvin Tessing's very exclusive trash.

"Getting this part right is as important as the police work," says the chief. "But much harder to do. So Mac holds your hand."

And then he actually smiles—a wan little smile that is quickly absorbed by the weight of fatigue on his face, but it makes me realize how much he has changed recently.

"Good luck," he says.

The chief and my captain head off, and Mac smiles that nothing-really-matters smile of his.

"I'll say what the chief wouldn't say. If this sticks, you'll take a huge weight off the department. Given what's been going on around here."

Mrs. B puts her head in the door. "You've got customers downstairs."

Interview Room 4. Outside, watching through the one-way glass is Angelique, and probably Mac, and who knows whom else taking an interest. Inside: Tony and me on one side of the table. Eric Tessing opposite us. Next to him sits the legendary Michael Duvalier, a.k.a. Little Mickey. Nothing about that nickname fits unless you know that his father, Michael Sr., a.k.a. Big Mickey, went this way before him. Father and son have been putting the fear of God into New England prosecutors for two generations. Little Mickey is not little. He's a locomotive of a human being, a bearded bear, and a study in courtesy, whatever the circumstances. His shoes are very clean.

Eric's acne is inflamed. His eyes cannot keep still, nor his foot, which is drumming on the floor intermittently.

I switch on the recorder and state the date and location, and name those present.

As planned, Tony starts. "Eric, you told us yesterday that you knew Amber Zajac. Can you tell us the last time you saw her?"

Little Mickey says, "I am going to give you Eric's testimony. Eric received a call from Amber Zajac on the Sunday afternoon before her death. She asked him to give her a ride to a party at the shore. They drove down together. The arrangement was that all the kids would stay over at the house, but Eric and Amber had an argument. Amber transferred her attention to another boy. Eric felt uncomfortable and drove home soon after midnight. He had no further contact with her after that."

"Eric," I say, "were you and Amber an item? Boyfriend and girlfriend?"

Eric's anxious little mouth twitches as he opens it to speak, but Mickey rolls smoothly over him.

"That's all Eric has to say for today."

"Yesterday," I say to Mickey, "the family lawyer called me and said Eric wanted to present himself for interview. An interview is where we ask questions and he answers."

"I'm afraid my colleague misspoke. What he should have said was that Eric was anxious to present himself if the police were searching for him. We wanted to clear up any misunderstanding there may be as to whether Eric was a fugitive."

"If Eric had nothing to do with Amber's death, his testimony could be vital in identifying the killer. I'm surprised he's so reluctant to help us."

"He's not reluctant," says Mickey. "I am. Because I think you've already made up your mind about Eric. You've already accused one innocent man of this crime, haven't you, Detective Bradley? After he gave you all the assistance he could, you rewarded him with a night in custody, a court appearance and a ruined reputation? I don't want that happening to my client."

Fuck me. Like walking into a spinning propeller. And the worst is that Eric is grinning at me like a monkey. Mickey stands up.

"Do you have probable cause to hold Eric on any charges?" he asks.

"We never said anything about holding him. What we do need is for Eric to pull out his phone and copy down for us the names and numbers of all the kids at that house on the shore."

Eric wants to protest, but Mickey is firm. "Can you do that for us, please, Eric." He turns back to me. "Then can we assume the interview is concluded?"

I don't even answer him. I check the time on my watch, pull the microphone toward me and say, "Interview terminated at ten-seventeen a.m."

I think that probably gives me the record for the shortest interview in the department.

"It would have been cheaper for them to just board up the kid's mouth with plywood," says Angelique as we walk down the corridor towards the war room. "What's your next move?"

"Hopefully, we can show you that right now."

Flynn's momma would be proud of him. He's found large sheets of plastic and laid out the potential evidence from the Tessing trash in a neat row, all bagged and tagged. Angelique gets it in a blink.

"Please tell me this came off the sidewalk."

"Friday is collection day on Eric Tessing's road. Last week, he put Amber out. Today, the evidence to hang it on him. God willing."

I scan the items and there it is—the syringe. I point it out to Angelique.

"We believe Eric has been abusing anabolic steroids. If we're really lucky, the syringe has the evidence of that, plus his DNA to match what was under Amber's fingernails."

I can see it go across her face—how come I wasn't surprised to see a syringe there? But she's smart enough not to ask. Careless of me all the same, and I'm getting an expression from Tony to confirm that, but I was distracted by an image of jamming that piece of evidence up Mickey's tight asshole. Metaphorically speaking.

Angelique looks at Flynn. "This is?"

"Patrolman Flynn. He's been coordinating things for us here."

"Was he present for the pick-up of the trash bags?"

"No."

"We're going to need his affidavit for the evidence chain of custody. It would be tidy if he also delivers the evidence to the lab."

"Flynn," I say to him, "draw a car, you're off to New Haven."

"Have him write his report as soon as he gets back," says Angelique. "Your own report on the pick-up of the trash bags also needs to be perfect. That could be something for them to attack. Would have been great to have independent verification."

Tony starts to laugh.

"Actually," I say to her, "I think we can arrange that for you."

"If he lives," says Tony.

"What are you guys laughing about?" says Angelique.

"Long story. But there was a guy who saw us collecting the trash bags off the sidewalk."

"Don't tell me. But I would like to get up to speed on your theory of the timeline of the murder and exactly what happened between these two kids that led him to kill her."

She sits at my desk and pulls out a pen to take notes. A loving and well-off admirer gave her that fancy writing implement.

"Amber has a fight with her parents Sunday night because they won't let her go to a party at the shore," I say. "So around seven p.m., she walks out the house and Eric collects her, and they head off to the shore anyway. At ten forty-six she uses her personal phone to order a delivery pizza in Old Saybrook, so that places her there. From now on, we're speculating. Eric says he returned home without her because she got friendly with another guy. But we think she came with him."

Interesting thing: Angelique doesn't take notes in prose; she draws little diagrams, with symbols and arrows and boxes on the yellow legal pad.

"The last call on her personal phone was the pizza order," Tony says, "but that doesn't mean too much because she had another phone from her dealer, and she may have had her own phone off to frustrate her parents."

"Sometime between then and Friday morning, he killed her," I say.

Angelique doesn't like that. "Sometime between Monday night and Friday morning? That's a heck of a window of uncertainty."

"They had Eric's house to themselves, there's no reason for anyone else to have seen them, so we're struggling for verifiable timeline markers here," says Tony.

"But," I say, "we're pretty sure he killed her soon after coming back to the house, and stored her until Friday, which is trash pick-up day." Then I explain to her about the conflicting time of death evidence and the wine refrigerator.

She wrinkles her nose. "I'm not keen on arguing something as soft as that with someone like Mickey."

"But if we tie him to the DNA under her fingernails?"

"Even that's not a closer. She was his girlfriend. They were having sex. You know Little Mickey will argue that she scratched him in passion, not in self-defense."

"Yes, but it would place her with him immediately prior to death."

"Maybe not immediately. Where are we on motive?"

Subject I wanted to avoid.

"Not very far," says Tony.

Angelique studies her chart for a moment. "Okay, this is what we need. We need the pizza delivery guy to ID Amber. We need as much testimony as we can get from kids that were at that house on the shore. Was she there? Was there a fight? When did they last see Amber and-or Eric? And the phones. If we could physically get hold of her two phones that would be great."

Would you like lettuce with that?

"I suspect that when Eric ran from the first interview at his house," says Tony, "it was the phones he was running with. He's tossed those in the Farmington River, I'll bet."

"I might be able to persuade a judge we have cause for Eric's Internet and cell phone activity," she says, "it's reasonable suspicion, that's a lower legal standard."

"Angelique's getting quite an opinion of herself," I say to Tony as we walk back to the war room. "Do we need her telling us our shopping list?"

"Cut her some slack," he says. "I'm sure it's not every day she gets a high-profile murder. And she's got Little Mickey to worry about."

And that's the difference between a cop and a lawyer. Maybe Angelique is as horrified by Amber's death as I am, but when she looks at the case against Eric, she does it without any moral outrage. She wasn't at the dump that day. She wasn't at the autopsy. She hasn't looked every day at the images on Amber's display board from her bedroom and the tattered piece of paper from her bag, which contained a few hand-written lines from Edgar Allan Poe.

I've been popping my head into the squad room occasionally because I'm waiting for a sizeable audience. Shift change proves to be a good time—there are a dozen detectives and uniform officers in there when I walk up to Beanbag.

"Hey, Beanbag." I have never before called him that to his face. No one does, although it's how everyone refers to him behind his back. The room falls silent.

"I'm interested to know—did you really think I was the person who leaked the photos? Or you just couldn't miss an opportunity to make trouble for me?"

Sensationally delicious moment. He's actually speechless for a second. The mustache twitches like a chipmunk, but no sound emerges.

Then he says, "Don't you speak to me like that. I made a perfectly reasonable report to the captain."

I look around the room. "Show of hands—anyone else here think it's reasonable to suggest that a fellow officer leaked photos to the press, without a shred of evidence?"

Nervous grins are breaking out.

"You were in our war room!" he spits at me.

"I was in your war room once. In broad daylight with the door standing open. You know someone who's in your war room every day? You. So perhaps you're a reasonable suspect."

I can see Beanbag's partner, Ralph Generis, heading over to break it up, so I need to get my closer in quick. "What you did was wrong. And if you thought I would say nothing about it, you were wrong again." And I turn and walk away. The rush in my blood is not dissimilar to the day I put two bullets through Z-Z's windshield.

At 4 p.m., Mac gets word that Calvin Tessing has held a press conference at his home. The first thing I do is call Amber's parents to prepare them. I'm relieved to get her and not him on the line. I can't even be sure she understands what I'm saying, her responses are so robotic.

At 6 p.m., Tony and I are with Mac in his office watching the local news. The selection criteria for local news reporters never ceases to amaze me: female, pretty, young, irony-free zone, lipgloss, can remember her own name for sign-off. The house is in the background and this reporter has clearly bought the idea that no one who existed in such a life could ever be evil.

Calvin Tessing is an impressive individual. He's good-looking, and he has a composure to him that is confident but without the smugness. He speaks calmly, but you hear him. Very believable. There's a hush as he speaks.

"All I want to do is confirm that our son, Eric, was happy to assist the police with their inquiries into the death of one of his former school friends. That was a terrible tragedy and we send our prayers and thoughts to his family. Eric did not know her well, but we understand that the police have a difficult job and have to follow all possible leads. Eric was not arrested, not charged and the police have no reason to believe he knows anything about the crime."

The lip glossed reporter returns and Mac mutes her.

"It's kind of brilliant," I say. "Every word is technically true, but the whole thing is bullshit. Are we going to counter? Tell them that actually he took the fifth and didn't give us a goddam thing? That he ran from the first interview?"

Mac gives me his crafty grin. "Confucius he say, 'dry powder.'"

"Captain, we have to drop the charges against Miller." I've caught him alone in his office and he's not happy about it.

"On the pound of marijuana? We can't do that. That's not a misdemeanor quantity."

"He didn't even know it was there."

"Maybe, maybe not."

"Come on, sir. We have screwed up this guy's life by linking him to Amber's death. We got to do right by him."

"Did you tell anyone outside the department you were investigating Miller for the missing girl?"

"No. But the media made the connection."

"Then he should sue them."

"The point is his reputation, sir. What his neighbors think. It's a very loaded subject, the whole pedophile thing. Can I make a statement saying he had no connection to Amber's death?"

"Absolutely not. That case is open until they lock the door on that kid."

"But we know it wasn't him now."

"Haven't there been a few times in this investigation when you've thought you've known something and it's turned out different?"

I don't have an answer. I do have a fleeting impulse to kick him on the side of the knee and rupture his ACL.

"Listen, Donna— "

"Detective Bradley. Sir."

Did that just come out of my mouth? It must have, because he's staring at me in a stunned kind of way, like an NFL player who's just had sand kicked in his face by a nine-year-old.

"Sorry, sir, it's just, when you and the chief call me by my first name, it always means you're going to talk to me like a girl."

He doesn't look angry, he just looks more tired. "Detective Bradley. You are going to have to learn to take your emotions out of your work. Investigations are messy. It comes with the territory. You regret rushing into Miller as a suspect. It happens. If your investigative method was imperfect, learn from it. And move on. I need to know you have that absolutely clear? Detective."

"Yes, sir. It's clear."

"Do not make any kind of statement. Do not engage Miller in any way without my knowledge. Is that clear?"

"Yes, sir."

"Good. Let's talk some housekeeping while you're here. Now that you've got a viable suspect, I need to trim your use of resources. I'm going to have to reallocate Flynn. And let's not log any more overtime on this case. Agreed?"

"Okay, sir."

"Good. Dismissed."

Fuck you and the horse you rode in on.

"Hey, Donna!"

Theresa. I'm studying the take-out menu pasted on the glass of the Mexican restaurant in Tunxis Square when I hear her happy voice behind me. She's out of uniform—her check-out-these-puppies top is obviously kept in her locker.

"What's up, Theresa?"

"You on your own tonight?"

"Not really."

"Let's get a drink. Do you like Andy's?"

"Well—"

"Oh, come on! Friday night?"

"Yeah, you know, I don't want to sit there while men try and pick you up."

And immediately regret it. A whole chapter between us plays out in the way she looks at me.

"Oh, okay," she says.

"I'm sorry, that was stupid."

"No, it's okay."

"No, come on, let's go. But not Andy's. I can't hear myself think in there."

"You know," she says, "that almost never happens. Unless I'm at a cop place."

Seedy's on South Main. Packed in here. We chose a table on the patio out back, where we can hear ourselves talk. We managed to stay off office topics all the way through the first drink.

"How's the case?" she asks, when the server brings our refills.

"Moving forward. We're not looking at your guy Miller anymore."

"Yeah, I heard. That's great. Once I met his dog, I knew he wasn't guilty."

"What?"

"Remember I looked after his dog before he got bail."

"I remember, but I still don't get it. Does the dog talk English?"

"An evil person can't have a smart dog. He can have a trained dog. He can have an obedient dog. But not a smart dog. And that is one smart dog."

"Obviously I don't know a lot about it, but I don't get the difference."

"A dog can only be smart in the space where he's loved and developed. If he lives in fear or he's ignored or he's in a world of excessive discipline, or a world of insufficient discipline, he can't develop. He's limited. Stunted. A great dog is the product of a great owner. It's just like parenting. Dysfunctional parents, dysfunctional children."

Oddly, this makes some sense to me. "It probably wouldn't stand up in court," I say, "but I wish you had given me this insight before I screwed up with him."

She shrugs. "Would you have listened?"

"Nope."

"That's why."

I don't say anything.

"People are intimidated by you, Donna."

"No, they just find me awkward."

Shakes her head. "No, you're fierce. That's just defensiveness. You underrate yourself."

"Not really," I say. "Privately, I think I should be running the place."

"I don't mean that. I mean with guys."

She looks at me. I try to look anywhere but at her. "Yeah, you know, we're not going to discuss that."

"Okay, so what did he say when you told him?"

"Miller? I haven't told him. It's not policy."

"So people still think he might be involved?"

"Yeah. That part's eating me alive. These things hang on them. People remember the accusation, the arrest, they miss the exoneration. Even if they know he's been released without charge, it's like he's marked forever."

"Somebody should tell him."

An hour later, we're still there. Girl can talk but, contrary to expectations, I really enjoy her company. She's clean of envy and manipulation and nastiness about people. When we get to our cars she steps up and wraps me in a brief, tight hug. A surprising realization dawns; she knows loneliness just like I do. Tonight, I'm sure, she's going home to nothing. And look at me. I have an actual, real boyfriend I'm meeting.

DAY TWELVE

Bryan and I have agreed to clear everything else out of our lives to spend Sunday together, so I'm running around getting a bunch of chores done when dispatch calls me.

"Detective Bradley? I've got a patrol officer trying to reach you. Patching him through."

"This is Patrolman Weldeman. Sorry to call you off duty, Detective, but I thought you might want to know. I'm at a house on Wilton Lane, called here twenty minutes ago. There was a fire. Apparently it's the house of a victim you're handling. Last name Zajac?"

"On my way. Ten minutes."

I call Tony, leave a message on his voicemail, and drive to the Zajacs' house. From the street, the house looks fine. There's a fire unit and two cruisers in the street, and a patrolman keeping curious neighbors at bay.

"In back of the house," the patrolman says. "All the action's over."

I follow the fire hose lines down the side of the house and into the backyard. Two firemen are collecting up their equipment. A third fireman and Patrolman Weldeman are standing beneath that beautiful birch. The bark on the tree's trunk is charred black around the base and up into the tree house, which is mostly burnt out. At the base, there's a portable fire pit. A soup of charred detritus is floating in several inches of water in the fire pit from the dousing by the firemen, and the ground all around has been thoroughly soaked down. Off to the side are three document storage boxes, empty. Blackened, half-burned pieces of paper are all around.

The fireman is writing up his notes.

"What happened?" I ask him.

"The husband wanted to dispose of some old documents. Very anxious about identity theft, apparently. Didn't want to throw them in the trash, too cheap to buy a shredder. So he comes out here with the Walmart fire pit and sets it up under the tree because he doesn't want to scorch the main lawn. He throws all the paper and a bunch of other stuff in, but he's worried that the documents won't be completely destroyed, so he pours some gasoline on it and throws a match. When it goes up, he realizes he's in trouble, so he goes for the garden hose. While he's doing that his wife comes out and sees the stuff he's burning and doesn't want to lose it. An argument starts. While they're arguing, the fire gets a really good hold in the tree house. He says she went to pull stuff out of the fire, and he just tried to stop her. But, while he's saying that to us, she interrupts and says 'you pushed me.' I ask her to confirm that. She says no, she fell."

"She fell? Into the fire?"

"It's not as bad as it could have been. She put her hand out as she went down, made contact with the hot metal of the fire pit. It's a bad burn, but she'll be okay. Also her wrist. She probably sprained it or broke it in the fall because it puffed up. Neighbors called the ambulance. They took her to John Dempsey."

"Did he go along?"

"Yeah. So they could carry on shouting at each other."

"Was it just documents?" I ask the fireman.

"Mostly, but there's other stuff in there." He points into the fire pit. "Maybe a stuffed toy or something, that didn't burn so good."

I turn to the patrolman. "When it's cooled down, can you collect everything, dry it out and seal in separate evidence bags."

"Is there a crime here?" he asks. "The guy's just burning his own shit. He's an idiot, but—"

"Just do it, please. Thanks."

Didn't make a lifelong friend of him. Here's Tony walking down the side of the house.

I bring him up to speed, adding, "Is there any possible way that Crazy Bird is hiding something from us?"

"I'm sure he's hiding plenty," says Tony. "Question is, is it anything to do with a crime?"

"They were fighting over it."

"Absent anything concrete, this is just a father in pain to me. The porch door is open. I'm going inside to pee, how about you?"

"I'm good. But thanks for asking."

"You should go now anyway, you never know later."

"Detective, are you encouraging me to examine this house without probable cause? That's way out of line for you."

"I'm encouraging you to practice good bladder management. Important later in life."

In the house, there's that smell again. I don't know what it is. Maybe just the dog and the dust and unhealthy people and the tang of tragedy. We separate and move quickly through the house. Zajac's computer is back on its table, surrounded by a mess of papers, several strings of used dental floss, pieces of a broken pencil, and a fresh pad of lined paper with a gouge right in the middle of the top blank page. I head upstairs to Amber's room.

Unchanged. I do use the bathroom, just to keep square with myself. It hasn't been cleaned in a while. There's a grime ring in the bath. The countertop around the sink is wet. It's impossible to wipe down because it is so crowded with prescription medicine containers. I open the bathroom cabinet and find all the shelves packed with medication.

"Zero," I say to Tony outside. "Let's go to the hospital."

We eventually find Mrs. Zajac in a treatment room in the E.R. at John Dempsey Hospital, lying on a gurney with her eyes closed, her right hand bandaged. I have a vision of her disintegrating as a person, her body breaking down into its component parts. The eyeballs are too prominent under the eyelids. Her skin seems to be carelessly draped over her skeleton, the joints looking mechanical. She's in the area between a distraught soul and a broken machine.

"Mrs. Zajac?"

She opens her eyes and looks at me.

"How are you feeling?"

"I think we left the house unlocked."

"There's a patrolman on the property. It will be safe. What happened?"

She closes her eyes.

"Mrs. Zajac, what was your husband burning?"

"Just old business records. We're trying to clean out in case we have to move."

"And you had a fight with your husband over these business records?"

"No. Just ... you know, some things she wrote."

"Things Amber wrote?"

"Yes."

"Why would he want to burn things like that?"

"You know. He's like that."

"Like what?"

She doesn't answer.

"And you tried to stop him?"

"I just wanted to save some of those things."

"NO!" It's a bellowing behind me and Stan Zajac grabs my arm, swinging me around. "You get out! You stay away from us!"

Without fuss, Tony moves in behind him and whips his arm behind his back and gives him just enough pain to quiet him down. "You need to get a hold of yourself, Mr. Zajac," he says. "We have to determine what happened here."

"No you don't. It's nothing to do with you. Is it a crime, the fire? No. Get away, you're harassing us."

I step in front of him. "It would be a crime, Mr. Zajac, if you were burning anything relevant to the investigation of the death of your daughter."

Too much. Regret it instantly. His clothes still smell of smoke and wet ash.

"What are you accusing us of?"

"We're not accusing you of anything, Mr. Zajac, we're investigating a fire."

"Why do you come to the hospital with my wife in pain like this? Go away!"

She's lying there, sucking up breath in short takes, her face gaunt and white. He's shocked himself with his aggression and is now receding into passive mode. The chances of getting a straight answer in these circumstances are zero, and we are just adding to the pain of whatever is going on.

"We'll talk to you later, Mrs. Zajac," I say to her.

Tony turns the husband around to face him. "Sir, you will not put your hands on a police officer again, do you understand me? You will be arrested and charged."

Mr. Passive-Aggressive is all hunched and eyes down now,

muttering but not daring to be confrontational.

"Are we clear?" Tony persists. "Say it so that I know you understand me."

"Yes, it's clear."

Tony's hand on my elbow is firm. "Let's get going."

Driving away from the hospital, I'm still angry with myself and yet I don't want that to cloud my judgment.

"He didn't assault his wife?" I put it to Tony.

"She's not going to support such a charge, and she was the only one there."

"And it's normal for him to be burning his dead daughter's stuff?"

"There's no normal for grief."

"So there is no way any of this concerns us?"

"Not on the facts we have now."

"You're right. Shit, I should be presenting him with the head of Eric Tessing, not getting into it with him."

"He's an easy guy to get mad at."

"Isn't he just."

Every week the envelopes come. Just the sight of one on the mat produces a squirt of dread into his gut. Within minutes, viscous liquid rises up in his throat.

Life comes at Stan Zajac through his gut. Disgusting, embarrassing symptoms, his stomach churning like a sewer. He gets a lump in his throat like a large pill that hasn't gone down. Stress, his doctor said. Globus hystericus, it even has its own diagnostic code. Last month his dentist told him that acid reflux had removed the enamel from the teeth at the back of his mouth.

The envelopes chronicle the decline and humiliation of Stan and Rosemary Zajac. In this country that his father adored for its freedom and openness, there is one bondage, one serfdom that remains—that between the sick and their healers and insurance companies. Enshrined in law, backed by the state. And all recorded in the incomprehensible language and figures contained in the envelopes. They have an entire dictionary of their own making. Deductible, pre-approval, out of network. You're in a game of bankruptcy but you haven't been told the rules. To ask for explanation is to enter a room of mirrors. To contest is useless.

It was his wife's illness that brought their world down, but Stan Zajac has processed the indignation and humiliation into his own sickness.

DAY THIRTEEN

Sunday

I've screwed up the scrambled eggs by having the heat too high—despite the fact that I can remember my mother warning me about this. Eggs are just too subtle for my cooking skills. Nevertheless, Bryan consumes them as though they are the greatest scrambled eggs he's ever encountered.

Yes, here I am on a Sunday morning doing this in my own apartment. He got up while I was still asleep and walked down the road to the store for eggs and bread and milk and coffee. And now I am watching him sitting at my only table with the newspaper open, apparently lost in the affairs of the world, in a manner that suggests this is a ritual from his childhood.

In short, I don't believe in love. I believe that people believe in it. It's one of those things we need to believe in, like honesty. I'm sure people think and feel they're in love, and there are times when they swim against reality like crazy people to keep that feeling. But it requires a suspension of disbelief that I'm just not capable of. Maybe it was watching my father do his sad little show over and over whenever he encountered an attractive woman. So in the matter of guys, I prefer the practical approach. I like the buzz of engaging with a new guy, the flash-flood of lust and that following period when you feel the fencing of inhibition fall away and you're wild in the landscape of yourself for a while. I like the friendship and camaraderie while it lasts. But love, I have no expectations.

Bryan is not the guy I would have picked out of a line-up of potential lovers. My taste usually runs more to the lean and sardonic and, frankly, seedy. Bryan is all clean and every item of clothing he owns is just slightly too tight. I have to find an unhurtful way to separate him from the cologne. But last night after dinner, we walked down the road hand in hand. I don't believe I've ever done this. My prior relationships, those of any duration, were conducted as though both of us were betraying our nations in secret. I know this comes from my lack of confidence and probably from choosing boys similarly afflicted. Co-dependency. Myself, I would have taken this thing a whole lot more slowly. In fact, left to me, most relationships just bleed out quietly. But Bryan is an irresistible force. His enthusiasm for me is intoxicating. Not just sexually. He sits and focuses on me when I talk, apparently rapt. That substantial block of body diminishes most everything else. And here's the thing: he's a naturally happy guy. Content. Glass half full. I don't think I've ever met such a person in real life. Certainly never slept with one. This is a guy with life skills I just don't have, and when I'm with him I feel better. I get a kind of giddy feeling when I snap into a vision of how we've created a relationship without even thinking about it.

As to the sex. The cops I have known intimately approached sex the same way they would a crack house raid, kick the door down, shoot first. Bryan is totally different and induces in me a response of total abandonment—something I don't think I've ever completely done before. Those arms are so powerful they're kind of awesome to watch. When we're doing it, I sometimes find myself getting a thrill out of all the moving parts of him that are so unrelenting.

No doubt I am not in control of my ship at this time. The case and the relationship are driving me along like a current. If I think about Bryan, I feel something good I've never felt before. If I think about Miller, I get hot with regret and self-hatred. And guilt. This must be what it's like to have blood glucose highs and crashes.

Miller, whose name I would like to scratch out of my memory like a furious child erasing a treacherous best friend from a diary, is the man I'm dreaming about. In my dream, a reporter asks me, How do you feel about going after the wrong man for this crime when all the time he was the guy who might have led you to the real killer?

"Hey!" says Bryan, his waving hand snaps me out of my unfocused gaze.

"What?"

"You're not here with me now."

"Sorry, I was just thinking about my guy again, Miller."

"You know what your problem is, Bradley?"

"Just the one?"

"Just the one on display right now."

"Hit me."

"Everything matters to you. You take everything like it's got to be checked against the Constitution of the United States. You'll wear out your conscience. Let the small stuff go."

"But wrongly accusing a man and ruining his reputation isn't really small stuff, is it?"

"I don't want to say that it is. Not to him, obviously. But to you, it should have a limit."

"Like you've got limits. I heard you volunteer for every SWAT assignment that's going."

"That's not true. Anyway, it's completely different," he says. "You know what's good about SWAT work? You just go there and do your job. It's not your business to weigh the factors, consider the consequences, blah, blah. You're like an athlete, complete the play. It's very liberating. Come on, let's go to the movies."

"To see what?"

"I dunno. Something funny. Just to get out and laugh and hold hands and eat a bucket of popcorn."

"You just had breakfast."

"What's your point?"

Look at that grin. Hitherto, my mother has never met any of the men I've slept with. I've maintained complete quarantine there. And I have always thought that if I ever met a boy who was a keeper, I wouldn't risk revealing my mother to him until after the ring was on my finger. But here's a stunning thing. I think Bryan meeting my mother could work. I'd like her to see that grin which has nothing to hide.

In a corner of my mind I have a thought that I know is absurd but I still can't kill it. I credit sleeping with Bryan on Thursday night with giving me the thought about Eric's trash, which gives us his DNA, which is what's going to close this case.

WEEK THREE

Monday. Tony has taken a personal day to move his mom into managed care, so I drive to Old Saybrook on my own. The smells of the sea air and the lines of boats tied in a harbor always set a part of my mind to thinking about the lives I'll never live. The pizza delivery guy confirms he was paid in cash by a guy matching Eric's photo. I get the delivery address and drive around there, a large bungalow on South Cove. The parents know exactly why I'm there the moment they see my shield and are achingly aware of their bit part in the death of a young girl. A son is summoned from the depths of the house and he has clearly been briefed. Parents were in New York, had friends to sleep over. Yes, Amber and Eric were here that night. Yes, he heard there was an argument, but there was a lot going on. There was a bonfire out on the sand and some people were down there, some up at the house, some driving around looking for stuff, you know. Anyone who was out of sight was out of mind. Some kids slept over here, some at a house in Stonington. He really has no idea where Amber was, but she was not here in the morning when they were all woken by the local police following up a complaint about the litter on the beach. I get a list of names and numbers from him. Follow-ups on those produce pretty much the same story. The news is spreading faster than I can move—the cautious statements are ready for me when I call.

Cynthia calls to tell me Angelique succeeded in getting a warrant for Eric's cellphone and internet activity, but the intern can't find anything about Eric on the Internet.

"I'll tell you what's happened," says Cynthia, "the father has hired a team of digital erasure experts. There are companies who specialize in this, if you have the bucks for it. We may get something with perseverance, but it's not a high probability.

Tuesday morning.   Hubbub at the station. The *Hartford Courant* reports that the investigation of the Weisz case has been removed from the Webster P.D. and taken over by the state police, following the leak of the crime scene photos. The paper says two state officers are traveling to Mexico to follow leads on the suspected yard worker. This is a day to give the brass a very wide berth.

I call the lab. They haven't got to Eric's syringe yet. So here I am at my desk with like fifty pages of Eric's cell phone activity in front of me. All I can do is start dialing numbers at random, trying to find some kid willing to confirm that his buddy, the zillionaire's son, is a killer.

My cell rings. Cynthia. "Got something for you," she says. I can hear the smile. "Want to come down to the coffee shop outside the gym? Bring the handsome guy."

Cynthia is just one of those people who is capable with life. I've never been able to get even a chair in this place, but she has annexed a table meant for four, and spread paperwork on it.

"Tough luck," I say, "Tony's out."

"That's a bitch, because I really wanted to show off how smart I am."

"Why are we down here? You prefer paying double for your coffee?"

217

"There's a lot of information zinging around in my office right now. I needed to get somewhere and be with this alone. Are you going to get something?"

I shake my head and she shifts her laptop so I can see the screen.

"I got the phone company to send me Eric's phone activity for the last year as a digital file so I could play with the data. First I sorted the phone numbers by quantity and frequency and graphed them. See these subscribers where the activity is fairly consistent in frequency? Those are his friends that he talks to regularly. Green is outgoing, blue is incoming. Notice they're about the same. That's a normal friendship."

I should have got coffee.

"So then I started to look for outliers, which I did with a standard deviation run." She brings up another chart on the screen. "Look at this one. There's intense activity for a short while and then it tapers off. That's someone he had dealings with for a period, like someone he was doing a school project with. Now look at this one. What do you see?"

"There's a lot of activity over a concentrated period."

"And?"

"Green is outgoing?"

"Yes."

"So he was continuing to phone, or text, that person, without getting any activity in response."

"Which would indicate what?"

And suddenly I get it. "It was a girl who dumped him. He kept texting her, she didn't want to know."

She pats me on the shoulder like an eleven-year-old. And this, ladies and gentlemen, is why people who can do math are going to be farming the rest of us like sheep.

"Speaking now as a fellow woman," Cynthia continues, "I

would think that if you chat to that girl, you might get some insight into young Eric."

"As a fellow woman, I'm impressed."

"Not at all, I'm enjoying your case, Donna. It's fun isn't it?" she says, and thumbs the last of a half pound bran muffin into her mouth. "I'll request that subscriber name as part of the existing warrant. They'll buy that. For all the other numbers on Eric's call list, I've got my intern working on a simple program to automatically run them through the reverse look-up for you. A lot of them will be unlisted, of course, but it's a start."

"How come you're here with us and not making a fortune with some hedge fund or something?"

"I have a husband to do that. Best of both worlds."

"You got kids, Cynthia?"

She shakes her head. "Too noisy."

"Jenna, it's Detective Bradley."

"Oh hi."

"Where are you?"

"It's difficult for me to talk now."

"Get out of it, call me back in ten."

"I can't."

"You had some phone calls with Eric Tessing you didn't tell me about. You lied to me. Call me back or we come get you."

Now the silly child is walking toward my car in some sort of Spy vs. Spy get up, wearing large sunglasses and a cap pulled down low over her face. We're meeting in the old Blockbuster parking lot off Route 44. Once she's in the car she doesn't want to meet my eyes.

"So what's deal with you and Eric?"

"How do you even know about that?"

Jesus. She's arrived here with the idea of being fresh. It's taking a long time for this girl to realize that the shield of wealth doesn't go this far. I just look at her.

"I was getting stuff from him," she says, sullen.

"Stuff. Drugs?"

"Just weed."

"When I interviewed you at your house—"

"I couldn't talk about it in front of my mom!"

"And then when I called you and asked you who Eric was, you acted like there was nothing between you."

"I never lied," she insists.

Like I said, teenagers lie. The rich ones, the poor ones, the plain ones and the glossy girls whose mothers watch them like hawks. And when they do, they have a mechanism for convincing themselves it's not a lie.

"Jenna, I don't care what you tell yourself or your mother about this. But I get the truth, and the whole truth from you right here and now, or I will not protect you. Do you understand?"

Sulky face but she nods.

"What's the background with Eric?"

"Sophomore year, Eric was the first person I knew who could get anything. But I only tried it a couple of times. Then, last year, there was a lot more stuff around. Dope and coke. And Eric was the guy I could get it from."

"But, you did know where he got it. You told me you knew that he was getting it from Amber."

"Yeah."

"So why didn't you get it straight from her?"

"Because, you know..."

"I don't know."

"Eric has always been trying to get with me. So that just made it easy."

"You slept with him for drugs?"

"No! He's not my type. I was just … nice to him. And he would always be okay with getting stuff for me, and delivering it. Like that."

"Give me a picture of who uses drugs at that school. Is it everyone?"

"I don't know. I guess there are some kids who have nothing to do with it, and then there are most of them, like me, who just party sometimes. The potted plants, it's basically their whole lives."

I keep looking at her, hoping something more might slip out.

"Weed should be legalized," she says, "It's less harmful than alcohol. I've seen kids do stupid stuff drunk."

"That your senior essay topic?"

She rearranges some of her hair under the cap. It doesn't all fit.

"Did you ever see Eric violent?"

"No."

"Get angry, got a temper?"

"I didn't see it. I heard about it. He broke that kid's arm or shoulder or something."

"But it was just that once?"

"No, he was like a bit of a bully, but it wasn't violent like that. It was more cool cruelty."

"Who's Riley Hartegan?"

"Dunno."

"No one by that name at the school?"

"I mean, I don't know everyone. Maybe a freshman, but not my grade."

"Okay, we're done."

"You going to tell my mother?"

"No."

"Thanks."

She gives me the big smile that usually gets her whatever she wants. Get out of my car and carry on with your life.

It's taken me half a day to track Riley down and I end up finding her walking distance from the station. At the bottom of the stairs behind the library, the architects of Tunxis Square left a shadowy nook where the buildings meet at a sharp angle, and this has become something of a burrow for kids hanging out here, smoking and talking shit while the parade of comfortable Webster goes by.

Funny how you associate some names with a certain type. In my mind, Riley is a cute perky kid, like Geena Davis's little sister in League of Their Own. Not this one. Riley Hartegan's hair, eye make-up, lipstick, nails and clothes are black. Her flesh is pale; the belly button is gruesomely pierced.

I knew Goths when I was young. They were peaceful folk who made their own clothes. I'm not exactly clear on the precise classification of species in this area but Riley and her tribe look to me more like wannabe rebels who bought their costumes from Hot Topic with their parents' credit cards.

"Riley?"

She scowls at me like a badger pretending to be willing to fight to the death. I detach her from the pack and sit her down at one of the steel tables on the plaza.

"What you want with me?"

"You're not in trouble."

She shrugs, looks past me, scratches her exposed midriff. Some of them do severe goth, some do grubby goth. Riley does sexy goth, riding her jeans low, a tattoo writhing up from the cleft of her butt.

"Eric Tessing," I say.

Amazing. It's like I actually raised my hand to strike her. Just for a microsecond, she braces herself.

"What about him?"

"You were his girlfriend?"

"Fuck no."

"Save the curse words for your brethren." I take my time unfolding Cynthia's chart from my pocket. I show it to her.

"Between January tenth and March fourteenth you exchanged eighty-three phone calls and texts with him."

"What the fuck! You tapping my phone!" She takes a good glance over at her friends as she says this, to make sure they're watching.

I let some time go by, then I talk to her quietly. "Riley, I have no interest in you personally. But if you make me interested in you with this disrespectful behavior, then you're going to bring unnecessary shit down on yourself and your friends."

"It's illegal for you to tap my phone. I know that."

"These are not your phone records, these are Eric's."

"What's he done?"

"That's what we're trying to find out. Your calls to him stopped very suddenly. He kept texting and calling you for a few weeks afterward. You dump him?"

"Yeah, I dumped him."

"Why?"

She's going to say something and then she stops.

"Did he hit you?"

The pale skin flushes with color. "That's none of your business! I shouldn't have to talk with you!"

I stand up and put my hand on the cuffs on my belt. I'm not really planning to cuff her, I just want to nudge her, but she now gets it into her head to run. The goth footwear, with its thick, chunky soles, is not designed for a speedy getaway and I'm on her in two strides. I don't take her down to the ground, I just hold her by the shoulder of her shirt, like a fussing nine-year-old.

"Get a grip, kid! You live in the suburbs, for fuck's sake. You think you're going to light out for Mexico or something?"

Her tribe is shuffling around close to each other and raising their voices, trying to get a response going; seriously, it could be some wild planet thing on TV.

"Come on, this can be over in ten minutes, if you just tell me. It's not about you."

I let her shirt go, and she adjusts her costume.

"Isn't the station just around the corner?" she asks.

"Yeah."

"Take me in. We'll talk there."

"Okay, good, let's go."

"In handcuffs," she says. "Take me in the handcuffs."

I want to laugh, but this could be serious territory. I'm ninety percent sure she just wants to create an awesome legend for herself. But she might be cunning enough to be laying a trap for a police complaint.

"You're not a suspect, Riley. I can't handcuff you."

"You were just going to."

"No, the cuffs were sticking me in the side. I was adjusting them. But let's do this—"

And I grab her by the shirt again and turn her around and walk her quickly in the direction of the station, and that seems to satisfy all parties.

I put her in an interview room.

"What can you tell us about Eric?"

"I met him, we hooked up for a while, I got sick of him. He's a rich boy."

"Did he give you drugs?"

"I don't take drugs."

224

"Riley, nothing you say in this room today can be used against you. There's no recorder running. That's a promise."

She hesitates, then nods.

"Where did you meet him?"

"At school. He only came last year. He was expelled from his old school."

"So you had a relationship. You went for ice cream, you did algebra together, he came to your house, you went to his, all lovey-dovey?"

"He would only take me to his house when his parents weren't there. And once when they were there, but he hid me in the basement. I stayed the whole night there. They didn't even know."

"Are they often not there?"

"They're rich, they travel all the time. You should see his house."

"What kind of guy is he?"

"At first, I thought he would be too straight for me, you know, he had like a straight look at school, and his clean Jeep and all that. But he asked me to go smoke with him one day. It started off okay. It was fun because he had money for anything, you know, if we wanted music or a movie or whatever he would just buy it on Amazon. He got alcohol from his house, no one seemed to care."

"Sounds like the perfect boyfriend. What went wrong?"

She looks away to answer. "I just started to get scared of him."

Let her take her time.

"He doesn't like hanging out with other kids. He has some wrestling buddies and stuff like that, but mostly he prefers to be on his own. He never wanted to go out in a group—or really go out much at all. He likes to be at home in the basement with the lights off, the big TV screen on, and drugs. Like some kind of underground animal."

"Pretty weird, but not really scary."

"Am I going to have to say this to anyone else?"

"No."

Straight up lie. If we get Eric to a trial, we're almost certainly going to want Riley's testimony. But I need to know what's in her head right now and I'll fix the rest later.

"There's a whole gym in his house. There's a mirror on the wall and he watches himself in that while he works out."

"Most gyms have mirrors. It's so you can see you're doing the exercises right."

"It's so you can get off on your own abs or tight butt or whatever. The way Eric watches himself, it's sick. He watches porn. Like all the time. Rough stuff. It's like he doesn't have normal ideas about sex."

She's dancing around it. I need to push her in.

"Porn, gym, drugs. I don't know, Riley, he sounds like the typical high school jock to me. You sure he didn't just get tired of you?"

"He wanted me to do this thing..."

"What?"

"This sex thing."

Long silence. "Riley. I've heard it all before. You can't shock me."

"Where you cut off the blood supply, you know, like suffocating?"

"Erotic asphyxia."

"Whatever. He's like it's a higher high. He told me the French word for coming is little death. Like he was an expert on it or something. We got high and I said I would try it but he was getting scary because he was, you know, too excited. Eric is usually all about being cool, but that night he was sort of shaky and edgy. He told me he knew from wrestling just how to hold my neck for it, it would be safe, but when he had me down ... down on the sofa

226

in the basement and his thumbs were here on the side of my neck..."

"Just hold on. I'm sorry, Riley, but I need to understand this. This was while you were having sex? You were both naked, he was on top of you?"

A hand she's forgotten about is rubbing at that pierced belly button. There's an incipient infection there. I can see the irritation. She can't meet my eyes.

"So, with Eric, he sometimes had a problem. You know? Getting hard. Or keeping it. He would have it and then it would go away and he would get mad with himself. I think that's why he needed the porn. If we watched porn while we had sex, then it was usually okay. It was like a distraction."

"But that night specifically?"

"He was having a problem. And that made him more edgy. And when he had his hands on my neck. He's really strong, you know, he just does weights all day basically. I suddenly got terrified. It was like there was evil in him that night. Like the devil. I thought he was going to kill me."

"What did you do?"

"I pretended. I pretended to faint. Then I really did choke a bit. And I coughed, and then I just made myself cough and cough, into his face, like I couldn't control it, until he got sick of it. He made a joint and we sat in front of the TV and then I said I was going to the bathroom. I got my clothes and I ran out of the house. I walked the whole way home in the dark."

"Riley, where are your parents when you're running around like this?"

"My dad's been gone for years. My mom's got her own problems. She has to be at work all day, and you know, she drinks at night."

"But she doesn't know when you're not in your room?"

"I guess she knows sometimes. But if she asks me what I'm doing then she would have to ask herself what she's doing. So we have a kind of agreement, I guess. I never miss school."

When I've sent Riley on her way, I say a few silent words of apology to my parents.

Thursday morning, the admin at the prosecutor's office tells me Angelique has a full slate at the courthouse and will be there all morning. We get in the gallery and watch her for a while. Amazing woman. She has a pile of maybe twenty different case dockets on her desk, yet she's able to joust with the defendant's counsel on any one of them without opening the file. And when she sees us she intuits exactly why we're there.

"Eric Tessing's DNA?" she asks.

"Is a match."

"Excellent."

"So? Can you get us an arrest warrant?"

"Can we meet this afternoon? To review?"

Oh, come on.

Four long hours later the three of us are in her office. She seems to have all the time in the world.

"Let's imagine," she says to me, "all the witnesses for both sides have been heard. The accused has not testified. He's just sitting there in a good suit, butter wouldn't melt. You're giving the jury your summation. Let's hear you tell the jury exactly what went down that night in the basement. Sell it to me."

"Why are we doing this?" I ask.

"I sometimes get the feeling you think I'm obstructing you or making your life difficult or just being a general smart-ass," Angelique says. "To do my job, I need to have two things. I need to believe in my heart the guy is guilty, and I have to understand why he did it. And then I have to believe I can sell that to a jury against a guy as brilliant as Mickey is. You need to help me with that. So now you show me how you would deal with some of the doubts I have about our case, maybe we can both see each other's point of view."

"Okay. Eric had the house to himself. His family was in the Bahamas. Amber was staying with him because she'd had a fight with her father."

"The father is a solid witness?"

"The mother would be better. She saw it."

"Why do we care why she was staying there? How's it relevant to Eric's actions?"

"Well, she wasn't signed on as his live-in girlfriend. She was only there because, in her mind, she didn't have a choice at that time."

Angelique frowns. "Is that important for the jury? We have to work in clear, uncomplicated steps. We won't worry about why she was there. Go on."

"We know from Riley Hartegan that Eric has kinky sex ideas."

"Specific."

"He watches a lot of porn, took drugs before and during sex. On the last occasion they were together, he tried to force her to cooperate in erotic asphyxia, a form of sexual behavior that is known to be dangerously attractive to risk-taking teenagers."

"I thought the autopsy showed Amber died from a sleeper hold?"

"Is the jury allowed to butt in like this?"

"Sorry, you're right. Carry on."

"The syringe found in the defendant's bathroom contained anabolic steroids. It's well established that abuse of steroids causes erratic mood swings and potentially violent outbursts of anger. Lack of impulse control. We heard testimony earlier from a boy who said Eric broke his arm, basically over nothing. Eric was expelled from his elite private school for that. They knew what he was like, and they weren't prepared to risk having him there any more, even though his father must be a valued donor."

"Just the facts, counselor," says Angelique.

"Even though," I continue, "Eric was number one on their unbeaten wrestling team. The state medical officer has told you that Amber Zajac died of cerebral ischemia. Lack of oxygen to the brain caused by compression of the veins in the neck. This never happens by accident. You have to intend to kill someone. And you have to know how to do it. It's a skill known to some police and military specialists, professional killers, judo experts. And wrestlers.

"So what happened during Amber Zajac's last minutes alive? The accused has already admitted under oath that he and the victim were sexually active together. We know she was a drug procurer for him, we know he used pornography and tried to get his sexual partners to play dangerous sex games—"

"Don't call it a game," Tony chips in. "Makes it sound okay."

"Practices. Specifically a practice that involves partially cutting off the blood supply to the brain to induce a state of semi-consciousness. Is it possible that Amber's death arose from sex getting out of control? That's what the marks at the front of Amber's throat indicate. Amber may have been persuaded to submit to that. But something changed. She got scared. She saw something in Eric's sexual needs that she felt put her in real danger. So she tried to get him to stop. Maybe she pleaded, maybe she threatened to expose him. We'll never know. But we do know that at some point Eric took a different hold on her. A killer's hold, known only to the kind of person who needs to know. And he knowingly, purposefully, with intent, kept that hold on her for the minimum of two minutes that it took for Amber's sixteen-year-old brain to die. She died in his hands. Somewhere in that night, the defendant lost all sight of Amber as a human being. She became an object of sexual gratification to him, and he wanted to push that until he got to the ultimate boundary."

I stop to catch my breath.

"Bravo, counselor," says Angelique.

"Not finished," I say. "Members of the jury, you heard testimony from Riley Hartegan earlier that Eric wanted her to do this with him. He tried to make it sound sophisticated by telling her what the French call an orgasm. `La Petit Mort' ... the little death. Ask yourselves now what the boundary was for the defendant that night."

Angelique's eyes light up. "She said that?"

"I just remembered it. She couldn't remember the actual French phrase, but I looked it up on Wikipedia after our interview."

"What's she like?"

"Riley? She's a goth."

Angelique gets that little frown. "Does Mickey know that?"

"I doubt it. Not from us."

"But he will."

"We can probably clean her up a bit."

"I'll have to talk to her."

"Okay."

"Also the assault that got him kicked out of the previous school? Can we get the victim of that?"

"On it. There's also a very credible girl Eric supplied drugs to."

"By credible you mean...?"

"Good family, big money, well presented."

"I need to see her. Other girlfriends, too, if possible. And you know what would be really good? A wrestler from Eric's team, someone who will testify that wrestlers have interest in, and are

231

competent at, all kinds of holds. I'm sure the jocks sit around the locker room talking about how they'd like to strangle the math teacher who failed them. Find a homicidal-looking individual."

When Angelique paces a room, her calves look fantastic.

"And you want all this before you'll go for an arrest on Eric?" I say.

She stops pacing. "Hell, no. I'm going for the warrant first thing tomorrow morning."

On the long, loping lawns of the Tessing estate, a landscaping crew, all Latino, is at work with mowers and blowers. I can see a burst of exchanged glances flash through them as our vehicle passes. And surely our little caravan is designed to alarm anyone whose immigrant status might be less than pristine. Tony and I are up front, followed by a state forensics truck, our crime scene vehicle, and a patrol car bringing up the rear. Calling in State forensics was my captain's idea, and a good one; gives us a partner with added authority on the witness stand.

Eric's Jeep is parked at the bottom of the steps to the house. Tony blocks it in with our car so we won't have a repeat of last time. A woman opens the door.

"Webster Police, ma'am," I say.

"What's going on?" she asks, looking past me to the driveway crowded with vehicles. The forensics guys already have the back of the truck open and are pulling out their coveralls.

"We're here to execute an arrest warrant on Eric Tessing and search warrant for the house." I hold out the two warrants for her, but she ignores them.

"Are you Eric Tessing's mother?"

"Stepmother," she says.

Of course. Too young, too unmarked to be the mother of a six foot, one-hundred-eighty pound, needle-pushing wrestler. Trophy wife. Calvin Tessing has deployed his wealth so predictably.

"Is Eric home?"

"Yes," she says and turns and walks across the immaculate stonework of the foyer. Did not have this scene in mind when she signed on as curator here.

Eric comes quietly from his lair. Tony hands him over to the patrolmen to watch in the car. First step is a 360-degree photo of Eric's room and the basement for the record. Then we walk the forensics team leader through where they should look. They'll start in Eric's room so that our crime scene guys can go in after them and haul everything of use back to the station. Trophy Wife is standing in the middle of the feng shui living room, hips canted, iPhone to ear, watching us go back and forth, and presumably reporting up the chain of command.

Interview Room 3. Me, Tony, Angelique, Eric, Little Mickey. And, no doubt, Mac and my captain watching through the glass. Eric has decided that for this event in his life, he should wear the hood of his Abercrombie & Fitch sweatshirt up around his face, bless him.

"I really don't think we need to do this here," Mickey is saying. "My client is not going to say anything. We could discuss any charges without him."

"Even if he chooses to remain silent," says Angelique, squaring up the file on the desk in front of her with her slim fingers, "we need to know he's heard what's going on. Because, in the end, it's his head on the block, right?"

Mickey shrugs without emotion. Angelique v. Little Mickey is going to be a good contest. "Eric, we now have your DNA from the syringe found in your trash," Angelique says.

"Which will be contested," Mickey butts in, "both the admissibility of the search and the quality of the DNA sample."

"Which matches the DNA found under Amber's fingernails," Angelique continues.

I swing a chair around and sit on it backwards, where I'm in Eric's face, but he keeps it turned away from me anyway.

"She scratched you while you were strangling her, Eric," I say.

"Pure fantasy," says Mickey. "They were lovers. It would be surprising if there wasn't some of his DNA on her."

"What's your theory of the crime, then?" I say to Mickey. "She was sleeping over at his place, she ends up dead in the trash, but he doesn't know anything about it?"

"We don't have to have a theory of the crime, Detective." Mickey smiles lazily at me. This is tennis with a five-year-old to him. "Do you have a witness placing the deceased with my client at the time of death? No. Do you have motive? No. Do you even have a crime scene?"

Some silent seconds go by.

"Riley Hartegan," I say to Eric.

Eric switches his eyes to Mickey, flickers of panic.

"Who?" says Mickey.

"Riley Hartegan. Sixteen. Same school as Eric. She also slept over at the house," I say. "Back in January she and Eric were a hot item, doing drugs together. Right, Eric?"

He's twitching and full of color.

"What's the relevance, if any?" asks Mickey.

Angelique draws breath but I ride straight over her.

"Riley was easy, right, Eric? Impressed with everything you had. And because she dressed weird you thought she would be weird about sex like you are. At your trial, Eric—when you're on trial for murder, in front of a jury—Riley will tell them how you tried to strangle her during a sex act—"

He comes up out of his chair in one explosive movement. Tony pounces on him, but he's not really coming for me. He just physically cannot sit still any longer.

"That's bullshit!"

Tony sits him down in his chair.

I look at Mickey. "So you were asking about motive. Eric likes to play rough. Some of them, like Riley, are too scared to complain, and just run away afterward. But maybe Amber fought back."

Angelique pushes the sheet containing the lab results along the desk to Mickey. "Report on the syringe from Eric's house."

"The DNA match is not going to stand up in court, counselor."

"If you look at the whole report," she says, "you'll find that the substance in the syringe was HGH. Human growth hormone. Does your client have a doctor's prescription for this? He doesn't appear to have symptoms of stunted growth."

"Are you charging him with drug possession?"

"I wouldn't waste your time. The abuse of HGH by athletes, body-builders and nightclub bouncers is strongly correlated with severe mood swings and outburst of rage. Especially in adolescents." She looks across at Eric. "It also affects the skin. In adults, HGH can be an effective treatment for acne. But in adolescent boys, it can cause outbreaks."

Eric is drowning in pent-up emotion and his face is glowing but he obeys Mickey's hand signal for silence.

"So," says Angelique. "Last chance. Does Eric want to tell us anything more than could assist our investigation?"

"He does not," says Mickey.

"Then I'm going to charge him and hold him."

After we get rid of the lawyer and parents, we process and feed Eric. Then it's time to go home, but I find I can't leave the station. I want to be near him. I go for a walk around Tunxis Square and watch the people coming out of the restaurants. I sit in the war room and do paperwork till after midnight. I wander through to the back and make small talk with the officer on duty in the holding cells. Then I drift down the corridor to the four cells.

Eric's the only occupant tonight. I shuffle as close as I can without getting into his line of sight. I've never had a murderer of my own before. There's sound. Coming from his cell. Closer. Peep in. He's lying fetal, swinging his leg off the edge of the cot and kicking the wall with the heel of his bare foot in a perpetual motion. His hoodie is pulled down around his head and face. He's keening. Almost like a song. Or a prayer, except the word fuck is a big component. Feel sorry for him? No. Because I saw Amber at the dump. Feel something for him? Yes. In the end, for all his blundering strength and pitilessness, he is just a kid—a head full of curdled emotion and fucked-upness attached to a much too strong body. Maybe he was born evil like Riley thinks. But he wasn't born with that twitchy mouth. I am not a psychiatrist but I am qualified to judge that twisted mouth because I was a fucked up kid myself. That's parent-inflicted or peer-inflicted, and maybe everything he does comes from a reaction to pain and confusion and the drugs and an absence of the ability to cope. Maybe with a little parenting and attention this kid could have made it.

The foot has stopped moving. He's seen me. I've drifted into view because I was trying to catch sight of his face in the half-light. Eye contact. He doesn't move or speak.

"I've got one question for you, Eric," I say. My voice is a low monotone. "Why did you dress her before you put her in the trash bag? You put her shorts and T-shirt back on. There was no need. She could have gone in the trash naked just as well. What were you feeling?"

Not a move.

"The person who felt that, Eric, might have the balls to admit

236

what you did."

I turn away and go home.

Shock and awe. We have just witnessed why people pay Little Mickey a thousand dollars an hour or whatever and Angelique, in particular, is smarting from it.

We're standing at the back of the courtroom where Eric had his bail hearing twenty minutes ago. It was a media circus. Angelique requested two million in bail, stressing that Eric's parents have the resources to send him far away and hide him there in comfort for the rest of his life. Mickey was on it instantly, calm and conversational as can be.

"I am a little concerned, your honor, that the Webster Police Department might be feeling some pressure, owing to another high profile murder case which is unresolved. It would be egregious if that had led to a hasty charge here."

In the back of the courtroom, Angelique is still seething. "Do you see what he did? I have just been screwed by that smooth fucker in front of a live audience."

An audience that you arranged, I'm thinking. The media was here in force because Angelique and Mac decided to issue a press release about the charges against Eric. They thought the kid might be pressured to confess if he got a taste of what it was going to be like for him.

"Go easy on yourself," Tony says to Angelique. "The judge didn't buy it."

"He wasn't talking to Judge Baring! He was talking to the reporters. He was encouraging them to equate the two cases. He was transferring the failings of that case to this one. He was inviting them to be skeptical about the evidence against Eric. It's brilliant. He starts contaminating the jury pool at the first arraignment. Hofman's going to flay me."

Hofman being Connecticut's famously media-sensitive Chief State's Attorney and Angelique's ultimate boss. His staff is known to joke that he starts a review of every case with the question "how will this improve my run for Congress?"

Back at the station, the reception is unusually crowded so I don't see her until she is upon me.

"Detective Bradley?"

Mrs. Zajac. Like a wraith, visited upon me unexpectedly for examination of my shortcomings. She still wears a small bandage on her left hand from the fire. That dry, flaky transparent skin of hers.

"Can I have my photos of Amber? Have you finished with them?"

"Of course, Mrs. Zajac. I should have brought them sooner. Can you sit here for a few minutes, I'll go get them."

When I get back with the photos, she asks the real question that brought her here.

"Is it him?"

"We can never be one hundred percent sure—"

"Please just tell me."

"It was him."

"Why?"

Keep it simple, Bradley. "He's a substance abuser. Including anabolic steroids, which are sometimes used by people who want to build muscle. All those baseball players you read about a few years ago? It can make you very aggressive, short-tempered."

"He killed Amber because he lost his temper?"

"There may have been something between them that we'll never know. Even if he confesses and elocutes—if the judge makes him give an account—it won't be what really happened. It'll be his twisted justification."

238

"I just can't imagine how anything can be so bad between kids."

"I know how you feel."

She's fallen into one of her contemplative dozes.

"How's Mr. Zajac doing?"

"He blames himself."

"Because of how Amber left that night?"

She nods, eyes down.

"All kids fight with their parents. It's just bad luck that it led to her going to stay with this creep."

Rosemary Zajac is not a crier, as far as I can tell. To her, it's more like being a resigned witness to the mercilessness that life has for some people. But her mouth becomes a lipless slit in her face as she bites down on her place in the universe. I need to come up with something to say.

"Your business with her, as parents—I'll bet it's the same as anyone else's. But because something terrible happened to her, you look for reasons, and you come up with the things that in any other life would be normal."

She shakes her head. "It was a terrible fight."

I feel like if I touch it, it will go off in my face, but I can't leave it. "About what?"

She looks up at me. "Thank you," she says. And then she hugs me. The feeling of her weightless, slightly noxious body makes me want to wriggle away.

"Are you okay to get home, Mrs. Zajac?"

"I'll catch the bus. We sold my car and Stan's got some work today, which is a blessing."

"Come on, I'll give you a ride home."

In the car she stares out front, apparently prepared to pass the whole trip in silence.

"How's the hand?"

"It's nothing," she says. "I've got a high threshold of pain."

"I heard you've been ill," I say. "Are you doing better now?"

"Yes," she says.

"I hate being sick," I say.

"I had surgery in January. There was a post-operative infection. They treated me, discharged me. A week later I was in intensive care."

"That's terrible."

Jesus. She's in intensive care and that's when it starts getting bad. This is why I never want to grow old.

"You have to hit sixteen when the dealer has a ten."

"That's crazy," I say. "I might bust, then I'm out."

"Just do what I tell you. The other people at the table can't wait while you make amateur mistakes."

"Kick your ass you talk to me like that."

I tap my fingers on the green baize and the dealer serves me up a nine.

"I told you!" I elbow him.

"It's still the right strategy," Bryan says with that grin. He has his hand on my shoulder while I sit at the table, and it feels wonderful. I feel like I can do a whole lot of things I've never done before.

Saturday night, Mohegan Sun casino. An hour ago, I was at the Dave Matthews concert, six rows from the front. I told Bryan I was disappointed tickets for this concert were sold out online by the time I heard about it. But Bryan knows a guy. Of course. And came up with this as a surprise for me.

We rode down on his motorcycle. He's not a Harley guy. He's a track bike guy. As we prepared to go, he handed me a helmet.

"Where's yours?" I said.

"I don't like them," he said.

"Then why am I wearing one?"

"Because people get killed without them."

Then he opened the gas and conversation was eliminated for an hour.

Much of the way to the casino, the highway goes through pure forest, a tunnel of green that we cut open like a missile. Leaning into the turns at speed I felt the naked thrill of fear at being smeared on the road like guacamole. The suddenness with which we came up on cars and then flicked by them with a tilt of the hips. Stepping off the bike at the end was like stepping off a boat, the sensation of the bike stayed with me for a few moments, the vibration still tingling and the ground feeling clumpy and odd.

At midnight we're on the balcony of our room with a candle and a bottle of champagne on the table.

"Tomorrow," he says, "my family's having a big lunch. You want to come?"

Terror. Right there.

You date another cop, it's either a secret or it's everywhere, there's no in-between—and that would be okay with me. I've prepared myself for that. But the whole meet-the-family thing, that drops me like a sucker punch. I have never been the girl they take home to Mama. And vice versa—I wouldn't risk exposing any boy I was keen on to the unpredictable experience of my mother.

I have communicated all this to Bryan in an instant without opening my mouth. I can read in his eyes that he's read it in mine, even though his all-purpose smile remains firmly in place.

"It's okay," he says. "Was just an idea. No big deal."

It's not okay. Everything is changed. Every single thing. We'll never be again the way we were talking a moment ago. We've left that way station. We're on our way further down the trail.

"Bryan, you know I really care about you, right?"

"But it's wonderful to hear it out loud for the first time," he says.

I reach across the table and squeeze his hand. "I'm just scared. Especially all at once. Can't we start on your family one by one, like with the second cousins, and then work our way to your parents?"

"We can do anything you like."

"Thank you. Oh, shit, and anyway, I wouldn't have been able to do tomorrow. I have to be down at the state police in Waterbury, logging every piece of crap from my suspect's bedroom."

"And you know what I love about you?"

Tell me. Tell me all night long.

"You didn't use work as an excuse to get out of tomorrow, which you could have done."

Dear diary, the sex was great that night. I am someone different.

WEEK FOUR

Forensically, we drew a blank on the Tessing house. The wine cellar floor had no DNA from Amber or anyone else, only multiple traces of chlorine bleach. That in itself is an indicator of guilt, but not one you can take to court.

We spend Saturday on the physical product of the search. We need more space than is available at the station, so we're working at a state police facility. Eight tables in a large room. Laid out and labeled in neat rows on those tables is every single item not nailed down in Eric's room. On several boards are photographs of the room as it was before the search started so that we can map the items on the floor to their location in the room. The same for his car.

No drugs, no steroids, no alcohol. Not a cigarette. No lady's underwear, or anything else that might be Amber's. Eric did a very thorough job of cleaning the crime scene. But, you know, there seems to be one thing that boys just cannot give up and that's the porn. Maybe they get a sentimental attachment to it. Or they just never know when they might need it urgently. Or they hide it so well for so long they can't remember where all of it is—like a dog with a lifetime's worth of bones buried in a yard. I've got a feeling that last one probably applies to the two DVD discs we find slid into a large brown radiographer's envelope, next to X-rays of Eric's wrist, dating from 2003. First wrestling injury.

Porn is not illegal. It's not an indicator of criminal tendencies. Porn has become so mainstream it's a subject for sitcom jokes on network television. But I'm pretty confident that these two discs will play their part in building for the jury a picture of Eric as a guy who is dangerously maladjusted to society.

But maybe that's wishful thinking, because by Sunday afternoon, I have to accept there is nothing of evidentiary value from the search. Everything laid out on the tables here could come from any person's house. Or any person with a lot of money.

Little Mickey is going to enjoy that.

There's the chase and there's the case. The chase is why most detectives get up in the morning, that visceral drive of pursuit. But the slog work of building the case is what makes them want to take early retirement and go into security consulting in Florida. Tony and I split up the load. He goes looking for the kid who got his arm broken by Eric. Surprise, surprise, the kid isn't keen on standing up in court to tell the story of how he got his ass kicked. I handle Jenna and it turns out that her father actually knows Calvin Tessing—same golf club—so they aren't that willing either. Everybody wants justice done by someone else. We have to utter the magic word—subpoena—more than once.

First thing Wednesday I have a cleaning with the hygienist—always get the first appointment, before they start running late. When I get out, there's a gusty wind that suggests change. It's the hard end of summer now. The lawns of Webster have lost their lushness and are lying flat and bleached and tired of summer.

"Hey, Bradley." Tony on my cell.

"What's up?"

"Where are you?"

"On my way in. Be there in ten."

"Okay, we can talk when you get here."

He's standing in the parking lot behind the station when I turn in, and walks across to my car.

"Stay in the car," he says as I start to get out. He gets in the passenger side, sitting sideways so he can face me. And then he reaches over and takes my hand in his—and for a crazy moment I think he's going to awkwardly admit falling in love with me and he can't hide it any longer and there's going to be an absurdly embarrassing scene.

His eyes are cradling mine as he says, "Bryan Zellinger was killed this morning."

There's something about how everything converges on that moment before you pull the trigger. People have different methods. Mine is to start with the gun sight slightly off line, then I let it drift onto the target, as if it's being drawn to the exact right spot by a force outside of me. A moment from then I reach the top of a breath cycle and I squeeze the trigger. It's given me one of the highest range scores in the department.

We're at the range out in Simsbury that backs up against the base of the ridge. Me, Tony and Theresa. Yesterday, after Tony told me the news I just went home and sat there. I didn't know what else to do. My mother was at work, but anyway, I haven't even told her about my relationship with Bryan yet. Then I cleaned my apartment. That's what I did. At two o'clock, Tony knocked on my door. We went to his place and watched half a movie. He made no recommendations to me.

This morning, Theresa showed up at my door. We had breakfast, and then I drove around with her in the Animal Control vehicle for an hour. We responded to a call about skunks. After lunch we came here.

"Did you shoot when you were a kid?" Theresa asks me as we swap weapons.

"Never picked up a gun until I was at the academy."

They don't ask me how I'm feeling. What I feel is a growing fear of how I'm going to feel when it hits me. I don't know anything about myself under these circumstances, how I will react, how I will manage myself under shock.

Theresa makes me sleep over at her house. An actual house she owns, not large, but more than she could carry on a cop salary so I assume she has parental help. Thelma and Louise is on the TV and we stare at it for an hour, eating chocolate. She has two cats and nice furniture.

Somewhere in that long night I am lying on my back in the dark, staring at my last exchange of text messages with Bryan. We have been in the habit of texting each other something at the end of every day.

HIM: 20 PAGES. DONE!

The first time he came to my apartment and saw my bookshelf, he announced, with some pride, that he hadn't read a fiction book since high school. The first time I went to his place, I took three books with me, told him I wasn't coming again until he had read them. That was later amended to read one.

ME: WHICH ONE?

HIM: THINNEST ONE.

ME: HAHA. TEST TOMORROW. MY OFFICE.

HIM: SPANK ME?

ME: IF U GOOD.

HIM: CANT WAIT. SLEEP TIGHT.

ME: U TOO

Seven hours later he was dead.

We eventually find parking in a Walgreens lot two hundred yards down the street from the church. The heavy downpour is over and the rain is just a light mist now, so Tony and I walk up the street without an umbrella. The road is strangled with police vehicles from all the neighboring towns—Wethersfield, Newington, Windsor, as well as Connecticut State police, even vans from UConn. There's a yellow school bus which must have been hired to bring in mourners.

In the road directly in front of the church there's a long row of police motorcycles, maybe thirty of them. They're all parked at the exact same angle to the curb, their handlebars tilted likewise so that they form a kind of banner of honor across the front of the whole church, chrome shimmering with rain drops. That gets me, but I manage to keep it to myself. The riders are grouped under the large tree in front of the church, their yellow reflective jackets sharp in the dull light rain.

Inside the church we find an inconspicuous spot. I feel like an interloper. Who am I here? Just another officer in a throng who all knew Bryan to one degree or another. Some must have trained with him, served next to him for years. There must be officers here who saw him die. Bryan and I were secret lovers for a couple of weeks. We didn't mean to be secret, but we were just too involved in finding out about each other to include anyone else yet. We had not been out with friends; never done introductions to the family. As far as I'm aware, Tony and Theresa are the only people who know about us. And Sy, the insurance guy.

I can only see the backs of the people in the front row. I know he had two sisters and I think I can pick them out. I feel guilty for even expecting a piece of the grief over this.

On the way out, I keep my head down, aided by the fact that the rain is coming down again. I prod Tony when he starts looking around as though he's going to talk to someone, and we're at our car before we hear the first motorcycles start.

Labor Day weekend I drive with my mom to Massachusetts, north of Boston, where her brother is hosting an extended family barbecue. He's the one who's had enough success for us all to feel a dose of resentment while enjoying his hospitality. Two days immersed in familial soup. A bunch of cousins, none of whom is quite comfortable with me because of the cop thing. Everyone is asking what's going on, and every time I say nothing. What would I tell them? I loved this guy you never heard of, knew him less than a month, then he was shot and buried on a rainy day? It doesn't make sense. So I just roll with the usual program, the inquiries about whether I have a boyfriend, always suffixed with the unspoken "yet." There's an aunt who wants to ask me if I'm gay—she keeps clipping me with glancing blows around the subject, primed to spring on the confession with a liberal-minded understanding. On the last night I seek oblivion in alcohol and find it, confirming a wide range of suspicions.

Now a week of compassionate leave. If compassion were their aim they would load me up with work until I couldn't stay awake. Tony talked to the Captain. I am ordered not to go into the station, not to work on the case. They have boxes to tick in the HR manual. At first I was angry with Tony for talking, but it seems to be confined to my captain and the chief.

Tony has appointed himself my guardian. He or Theresa check in with me daily, breezy little conversations that make no reference to Bryan, invitations to do time-wasting things. The three of us go bowling on Berlin Turnpike like docile civilians. Afterward we go to a restaurant, pursuant to Theresa's mission to get me to eat.

At a table with a greasy surface and no napkins, Tony says to me, "There's a lot of noise going around about the op that Bryan was on when he got killed."

It's the first time either of them has made direct reference to him for a week.

"I'd rather you hear it from me," he continues.

We all know exactly what he's doing. By the book: how to manage information flow to victims. In an information vacuum, victims assume the worst. Victims latch on to rumors and exaggerate them. The best treatment is to give them news as soon as possible, reduced to the simplest interpretation.

"People are saying it was poorly planned, but that's not on Bryan. It wasn't his case, he just went along as back-up. There's a bad guy with multiple outstanding warrants who's been evading them for a while. Eight o'clock the night before, they got a tip off that he was going to be spending the night at a girlfriend's house in north Hartford. That short notice, they didn't put together a proper SWAT team, just who was available. Went in at 4 a.m. In retrospect it looks like a set-up. The outside of the house was rigged with concealed motion detectors. There was a heck of a fire fight. Sixty two rounds fired by the officers. That's all the real information I have at present."

I don't know what to say, so I say "Thanks."

"It's just a mess," says Theresa, squeezing my hand on the table.

"You know," Tony says, "we all have access to counseling at any time—"

"I am not going for any fucking counseling. You start with that shit, we won't be friends."

They both invite me to stay over at theirs, but I go home. The heating in my apartment has kicked in for the first time this fall. It's only half past nine but I get into bed and turn off the light. In the dark I go back to where I always go—that last texting with him. Did he know, then, that he was going on the op? Or did they call him after that?

I need to start living again.

This was the explanation that Helen, Leonard Miller's wife, had offered for her abrupt decision to return to England. That she would go without him didn't seem to need to be discussed. The unspooling of the journey of grief had been different for them. He had no regret from her leaving. She needed to be with her family again and to rebuild herself. He needed nothing of the kind. He had no intention of setting foot again on the soil that contained his child.

"You should try and get some help," she said. "And some friends. If I'm not here you're going to need friends other than the dog."

Over the following months, Miller came to think the opposite. Bella's suitability as a companion derived from the fact that it was impossible for Bella to know that Miller's daughter was dead. She couldn't overhear it, read it, ask about it, suspect it. She couldn't offer him sympathy, avoid the subject, treat him differently or normally, give him his space, recommend treatment, or be patient with him. Together they pass the days in the house on Wilton Lane.

It is into this house that the detective steps on a cold Wednesday evening.

His first look on seeing me standing there is not anger. I don't know what it is. His eyes are sunken and weary. I did that. Or some of it, at least.

"What do you want?"

"Can I come in?"

After a moment, without inviting me in or sending me away, he steps away from the door, leaving it open. I follow him to the living room. To buy some time, I kneel down to get eye level with the dog. Her hair is very short, evenly gray across her whole body. She lets me stroke her briefly then takes a step back—can't have me getting the idea I've been accepted.

"I came to try and tell you how sorry I am."

I get nothing back. He just looks at me.

"I screwed up."

"And so predictably." He drops his eyes and shakes his head briefly. Then he gets out of his chair and walks through an archway to the kitchen, returning with a whisky bottle, two glasses and a plastic tray of ice cubes from the freezer. He pushes a glass at me to help myself. That is not my forgiveness, but the acknowledgment of my apology.

"You know we got him?" I say. "The guy who killed her."

"I read about it. But I'm still sitting here with a drug charge hanging over me and an expensive loan for the bail."

"I know, and I'm sorry about that, too. It's not in my power to drop those charges, but I'm working on it."

He goes again to the kitchen and returns with crackers for the dog. "Why did he do it?"

"I'm sorry, but we're still building a case, so I can't talk about it."

"So that's when you figured it wasn't me?"

"No. I dropped you as a suspect when we got a police report on you from England, and I learned about your daughter."

He looks at me for a long time. "What's Gracie got to do with Amber?"

I'm fearful, but it has to be done. Otherwise, what am I doing here? "It explained everything about you that looked off in the first place."

"You mean I suddenly didn't look like a pedophile anymore?"

I could give him a hundred versions of how police investigations, like water, take the path of least resistance. But I'm here for redemption, not justification.

"Yes. I'm sorry, but that's pretty much it. Like I said, I really screwed up. You were just a perfect fit."

He looks at the back of his hands for a while. "I can see that my situation isn't typical," he says. "My wife and I came to this country when she was offered a position at Wesleyan University. European history, that's her field. But really we came to get away from England. There were just too many reminders of Gracie. It helped, being in a new country, being away from all that. After a few years my wife missed her family, she didn't like it here. But I still couldn't face going back. And our marriage was not surviving. So I stayed. When I engaged Amber, it was just about having a dog walker—Bella spends a lot of time alone during the day, it was useful to have someone come by.

"But then I started to look forward to seeing Amber. Hearing her talk about school, hearing the odd bit of teenage gossip. It gave me something. Gracie would have been about Amber's age now—a little younger. Just that spark of adolescent life that Amber would bring into this house. Do you understand?"

"I guess so."

"I came here to get away from memories of my daughter, but then I found that I wanted these little episodes of what her life might have been like. Amber was so full of life. Gracie was like that. So I paid her to walk Bella more than was strictly necessary. Just to see her for ten minutes once in a while, hear her stories, her teenage outlook on life, everything I missed because of what happened. Obviously, she needed to have a key to get access to the house. I never thought there would be a problem about it. I truly never thought about it. I gave her so much freedom here that she could hide drugs in my basement and I didn't even know. Maybe I am at fault on some level."

"I don't think you should blame yourself for that. Teenagers can be devious. Amber was a big risk-taker, reckless even. She put herself in a dangerous situation, you didn't have anything to do with putting her there."

He pours himself another whisky. I shake my head at the offer. I can't get into a drinking game with the former suspect. Or with myself, these days.

I see his eyes rest on me for a long moment in that way, like he's going to ask me what's wrong with me, why do I look like I haven't eaten for two weeks? And, I discover, I have a compulsion to sit here and tell him. Drink whisky with him, talk for hours. Because this is a house where you could do that. Because somewhere inside me I feel an affinity for this guy. Maybe this is some kind of reverse Stockholm syndrome. No, it isn't. It's because we're both outsiders. Because I could tell him the worst fears in my heart. Because we're both lonely.

I stand up abruptly. "I must get going."

He gets up to walk me to the door. "What are you working on now?"

"I'm between cases."

"Any progress on the guy who killed Nathan Weisz?'

"That case has been taken over by the state police."

"Because of the leaked photos?"

"Not officially."

"Are they looking for a ConCare customer?"

"I think the suspect is an undocumented immigrant who did casual work at their home."

"Looking at those photos, Nathan Weisz was killed by a customer. I'll guarantee you."

"They get that mad?"

"You're in your thirties, right? You've probably never been really sick. What happens between people unlucky enough to need serious medical care and their insurance companies is a war. Nothing less."

I'm on the porch, he's in the doorway. The dog slides her nose up next to his knee, studies me.

"Again," I say. "I am so sorry. We're not supposed to say that. But I felt this was a special case."

"I appreciate your coming by," he says.

Monday morning. For the first time ever, I have a reluctance, a dread, of walking into my place of work. But it has to be done. I watch myself walking down the corridor like a radioactive beacon, there she goes. I keep my eyes down. Officers greet me, but nothing more. As it should be? How bewildering it is to be dislodged from one's routine perch in the world.

In my absence Tony has completed Angelique's task list, we're now waiting for her to come back for anything further. My captain says he has nothing for me right at this moment, and suggests I ride along with Tony while he does legwork for a team on another case. We're driving back to the station after an unproductive interview when Tony suggests we stop for something to eat.

I shake my head. "Not for me, but get something for yourself."

"You okay?"

"Yeah, just tired. Not sleeping well."

He says nothing.

"We have to find a way to change this," I say.

"Change what?"

"You glancing over at me to check I'm not slashing my wrists. You've been doing it ever since."

254

He says nothing.

"I'm sorry," I say. "I just feel like everyone's looking at me, like, when's she going to freak out?"

Still nothing.

"Does everyone know? About me and Bryan?"

"I have not broadcast it to anyone. But when people have asked me, I have answered honestly."

"But how did people even know to ask?"

"Maybe Bryan was less reticent about your relationship. Maybe he told his friends he was in love. I don't know."

We don't say anything for a few minutes. We're now going west on Farmington, heading out of town.

"I've been having bad dreams," I say. "They wake me up, then I don't want go back in my head again for a while, so I get up and a few hours go by. So I'm tired."

"I thought you got some sleeping pills from the doctor?"

"Don't like how they make me feel. Bit scared of them actually."

"Not to state the obvious, but you've been through a hell of a lot," he says. "Maybe you should take some more time off."

"I hate time off. I just wish I didn't have to go in to the station for a while."

On our right is one of the town reservoirs. Behind that, extending up the ridge is the protected watershed area for the reservoirs, which includes a few hundred acres of trees and trails. Canada geese are feeding on the bank next to the road. They're well known for frequently crossing on foot here, in large families. Most of the time cars stop for them, sometimes not.

"Years ago when I was a patrol," I say, "I got dispatched here about five o'clock one summer morning. Dead deer on the road. The car was gone. We never got a report from the driver. This deer was lying right on the road. Perfect specimen—the side I could see, it was basically unmarked. The impact must have been on the side that was on the ground. I had to drag the body—carcass—off the road. Thing was still warm. That wide black eye, I felt it was watching me all the time I was dragging it by its feet."

Tony takes a right onto a road that winds up the ridge. The tree screen is thick here. He's still silent.

"It's the flies," I say.

He lets a beat go by and then he says, "Just tell it to me."

"The flies on Amber's body at the dump. Do you remember?"

"Yes," he says.

"I wasn't even particularly aware of them at the time. But I dream about them now. I can be having a dream about anything, and there will be flies in it. And the sound of them, always there, like ringing in my ears. The rest of the dream carries on, all different things happening, but the flies are driving me nuts. Sometimes after I wake up, it's like they're in my apartment with me. I thought it would stop at the end of summer, but it hasn't."

The tears are coming out of my eyes now. Although I'm not making a sound, I have to wipe my face with my sleeve. Part of me is thinking about Tony managing me like any of the civilians he's had to take through a trauma. And part of me is shit-faced embarrassed and another part is glad it's happening here with him alone in a car and not anywhere else.

Near the bridge over the Farmington River, he pulls into a small shopping area with a Starbucks. He parks way back, away from other cars.

"Is there any more news about what happened?" I ask. "On that operation?"

He takes time to pick his words. "It looks like it originated in a turf battle. The snitch was set up to get the officers to raid the house. The fire that came from the house was sustained, like from an assault weapon. When the squad eventually got control of the house, there were two men inside. One of them was wounded. There were three handguns in the house. None of them matched the bullet that killed Bryan. Under further interrogation, the wounded guy admitted that the original target of the operation had been in the house but had escaped. That would explain why the weapon could not be found. So at the moment, they think the guy who killed Bryan is still at large."

"It sounds like a monumental fuck-up by someone in Hartford P.D."

"Yeah. The word is they're bringing in people from outside to review the operation. Neutrality. You want anything? Pepsi? Coffee?"

"Large cappuccino. One sugar, one sweetener. Thanks."

I watch him amble across the lot. Two soccer moms gossiping between their SUVs turn their heads as he goes by. I wonder what a bad day is in their lives.

I know Bryan is dead. The flesh, in the ground. Inert. But the swirl of being that was Bryan, the impish grin, the love of life, the pure strength of the man... that feels like it's still out there somewhere. And suddenly I'm scared of the heartbreak I still have to go through. This is the moment I think I just don't know what to do with myself.

FALL

September's gone and most of October. Eric Tessing remains out on bail, confined to the state of Connecticut, has to report to a police station Mondays and Thursdays. The media tried a few times to keep the story alive, but Calvin Tessing's had good advice and made his family disappear. The police station Eric is reporting to is way up in the northeast corner of Connecticut, presumably they've acquired a place there for him to lay low in for a while.

"Come in, Bradley."

Captain Donald closes the door behind me, points to the chair.

"How are you doing?"

"Good, sir, thank you."

"You been seeing Dr. Jarro?"

"Yes, sir. Twice a week."

"Making progress?"

"Definitely. He's excellent. Given me a lot of perspective."

"Your case is with the prosecutor, right?"

He knows exactly where the case is. He's just making nice with me.

"Yes, sir. The trial is slated for January."

"Your first big court testimony?"

"Yes, sir."

He nods. Then he waits for me. I prepared. I rehearsed. It's all gone.

"The reason I wanted to see you, sir, is to thank you."

"What for?"

"Well, sir, you were very supportive of me. And sometimes, I was ungrateful."

"I didn't notice," he says stiffly, "so don't worry about it."

He's no better at this than I am.

"For a long time I felt that I didn't get what I deserved. And then I was pissed—excuse me, sir—when you teamed me with Tony because I thought he was babysitting me."

"He was."

"Yes. But it worked out. He has experience I don't have." Now I want to get out of here as fast as possible. "And I know you've made it easy for me these past weeks, work-load-wise, and I appreciate that. I'm back in the game now." I stand up.

"Bradley, you know we try very hard not to treat officers differently based on gender. We may not always get it right."

"I understand."

"So what I'm going to say to you now, it's not about being female."

I wait.

"Your aerial's too sensitive, you take too much on board personally. That same thing, it's what makes you a good detective. So your particular challenge is to try to get a balance."

"I agree. Thank you, sir."

"Good. Thanks for coming in."

That's that ticked off the list.

"Oh, Bradley."

I stop at the door.

"Pengelli says you started the SWAT training?"

"Yes, sir. I'm already into the first module."

"It's a tough course. Tougher than when I did it, years ago."

"Yeah, it's great."

"But when you've got your certification, I don't want you volunteering for every operation in the state. You're a detective in this department, I need you here."

"Thank you, sir. That's a way off."

Yeah, I gave in about seeing the counselor. I went and sat down and talked about myself, twice a week. First the words had to be hauled out of me like rocks, but I got used to it. I took the medication. The nights were bad for a while. I would be reading stuff on the phone in the dark in bed at 2 a.m. I would get out of bed and do sit-ups to try and tire myself out. Pulled an ab doing that, could hardly move for a week. I started having chest pains. I found a lump in my breast that wasn't there. I couldn't shake the obsession that everyone knew about Bryan and me and was treating me sympathetically because of it.

"Those that know, they probably are treating you differently," Dr. Jarro said. "You had a personal loss, that's what people do. Some of them are clumsy about it, maybe, but it's well meant."

"I don't want them to know. It's got nothing to do with them."

"Sure it has. It's information in their world they can't avoid. They feel bad for you. They can't change that."

"I don't tell people my problems. It just makes me look weak. Especially in the squad room."

"I'm going to guess you've been self-isolating your whole life," he said. And as soon as I had a word for it, I realized I had been. So we felt our way along like that, Dr. Jarro and I.

These days I go to those things I used to avoid. The bar meet-ups, barbecues and keggers. I can be seen playing pool at the American Legion bar.

I'm happy to allow that Dr. Jarro did something for me, but the thing that got me out of the death spiral was the SWAT training. I went because I thought it would take me out of the station and I would be around people who don't know my story. Because it would fully occupy my mind and make me hurt and sweat and tire me out so I could sleep. And yes, maybe I went because of Bryan. To understand what he liked about it, to be closer to him, I don't know. Anyway, I liked it. I liked that the training is made up of lots of little apparently mindless components you need to perfect. I got hooked on trying to beat my own time on basic drills like reloads and cover-to-cover movement. Then we started to learn how putting these components of skills together in different combinations is what gives a SWAT team its ability to react to any situation. All the small parts become a superior machine. So it makes me feel part of something exceptional. I'm skinny and my five-mile time is the best it's ever been. I don't keep alcohol in the apartment. I don't drink alone. That was a problem for a while. At night at home I read. What was that old song called? Comfortably numb.

Snow before Thanksgiving Day. Not a good sign. But a good time to be on inside work. I've been desk-bound, helping another team on a cyber-crime case that involves a lot of paper-trail checking. I haven't seen Tony for about a week—he's been helping on another case—so we arrive at the restaurant separately. We're meeting with Angelique at her request. She's offered to buy lunch if we come downtown to a place across from her office behind the courthouse in Hartford.

Watching Angelique swing her hips through the tables toward us, snatching a last glimpse at her blackberry, I realize I have come to know her well. I can deduce things about her mood from the way she moves. She has an overflowing leather binder that she carries which says, I am much busier than you. This will be easier if you simply do what I want.

She orders a salad and a glass of tap water. Her blackberry vibrates annoyingly on the table, but with a superhuman display of willpower she ignores it.

"Thanks for coming," she says. "I wanted to tell you guys in person."

"Tell us what?" I say. Tony is looking at his plate, carefully removing the radishes from his salad.

"Mickey came with an offer."

A stab of adrenaline, missing from my life these past several weeks. Her hands are moving too much. She's anxious.

"Accidental homicide. Occurring in the course of a dangerous sex game."

"Right," I say. "He put her in a sleeper hold for their mutual pleasure."

Angelique purses her lips briefly, and I get a flood of feeling that she's heard stuff about me, that I'm emotionally loose, that I need managing.

"What did you say?" I ask.

"I talked it through with my boss and the others in the office. There was a strong consensus." She always brushes a hand against her hair when she wants time to compose some legalese. "We told them we wouldn't accept accidental. He has to plead to negligent homicide."

"What's the sentence on that?" I say.

"Donna, remember we had to take into consideration that he's under eighteen. He's a juvenile in the eyes of the law in this state. The view on adolescent criminals these days is that they can't be held responsible to the same degree as an adult. Mickey made a strong case of that in his brief."

"What's the sentence on that?" I repeat. We all hear the tension in my voice.

"He'll do three years. A bit less with good behavior."

"So it's done?"

"Yes."

I look at Tony, but he's decided to write a doctorate on his salad. Neither of them says anything for several moments.

"Are you fucking kidding me?" People at the next table take a sidelong peek at me. "He strangled his girlfriend! That's not negligent."

"There's no one to testify to that."

"He tried to strangle a girl who will testify."

"A teenage girl who Mickey would tear to pieces on the stand."

What I want to do is smash the table in front of me to shreds. Instead I just whack it with a flat hand. All the cutlery jumps. "Why do we even fucking bother?" Again the peek from the guy at the next table. "Will you fuck off!" I say to him. That solves it.

"Donna, I'd like to eat here again, if you don't mind." Angelique's hands flutter across the blackberry, the binder, as if she needs the reassurance of touching the symbols of her place in the scheme of things. Tony's finally looked up from his salad, watching me, deciding whether he's going to have to intervene.

"Can I ask you your plain personal opinion?" I say to Angelique. "Without dressing it up in consensuses and considerations, whether you think this is right?"

"Three years is still going to effectively destroy the life of a guy like Eric. The life he expected to have."

"Yippee."

Tony's chair scrapes back and he stands quickly, puts his hand on my shoulder. "Come on, partner, we should go tell the parents."

I catch the grateful look Angelique shoots him.

The Zajac's driveway hasn't been plowed, the snow on the steps to their door has been trodden down hard and slippery. I told Tony I would handle telling them on my own, and he didn't argue. I called and got Mrs. Zajac, she said come at three. Inside, I think the house looks much tidier until I realize that most of the small stuff has been moved into packing boxes, three of which are in the middle of the living room. I take off my coat and hang it on the back of a chair. She wanders off into the kitchen and starts making coffee without asking me if I want any.

"Is your husband home, Mrs. Zajac?"

"No. He went to the town hall."

"I've got news about the case," I say, when she's got her back to me. She doesn't turn around. "You know, technically, he's a juvenile. Eric Tessing." Listen to me, straight out of Angelique's playbook. Still she says nothing. She has a Band-Aid on the inside of her forearm, over the vein used for blood draws or drips.

"Do you take milk?" she asks.

"Sure. Thanks."

She passes a mug to me. We sit at the table.

"You, know, Mrs. Zajac, the majority of cases never go to trial. The prosecutor and the attorney for the accused work out a deal."

"I understand."

"We heard today that they have done a deal—a plea bargain— with him."

"With who?"

"With Eric Tessing. The boy who killed Amber."

"Oh, yes."

"He'll plead guilty to a negligent homicide. That means he admits killing Amber. He's going to do three years in jail."

She nods vacantly at me. "That's good."

And she just keeps looking at me. My turn to speak. The surrealness of the situation. She doesn't seem to grasp at all what I'm talking about. But I have told her. I've discharged that responsibility. Is it up to me to make her understand what an outrage this is? Now I wish I'd brought Tony.

She sips her coffee and makes a face. "Oh, I'm sorry, the milk's off. We're trying to run down our perishable supplies." My coffee is untouched.

"I'm very sorry it turned out this way," I say. "It's just really hard to get conclusive evidence in a case like this. No witnesses."

She pours her coffee away down the sink. "When Amber was young, she did something very strange. Something inexplicable. We took her to the priest, and he talked to her several times. He said she had no fear of God."

I mark time by sipping the awful coffee. Standing on the kitchen counter is a large plastic container packed full of medication vials. I remember the cluster of medications in the bathroom cabinet upstairs, the day of the fire.

"This boy was the rock she broke herself on," Mrs. Zajac says to me.

Now I can't sit here any longer. I stand up with my coffee cup and walk over to the sink and rinse it out, slowly and thoroughly.

"So you're moving home, Mrs. Zajac?"

"Yes."

"I'm sure it's hard. Good to get away from the memories."

"It's not that. We needed to sell before the bank foreclosed on us."

"Oh. I'm sorry to hear that."

"Actually the bank has been pretty decent. They gave us five months grace on the payments, but even after that we couldn't make it. My medical costs wiped us out. Truly, if I had known, I would have chosen to die."

This woman, who has had all vanity and artifice scraped off her, is not being dramatic when she says she'd rather have died. From where she is now, she means it.

"It's terrible. You must be very angry."

She shrugs. "When I was still sick, my husband hid the costs from me, he thought knowing about it would make me worse. He did all the fighting with the insurance company. He protected me from it. But it didn't help in the end."

"Where are you moving to?" I ask her.

"Northern Vermont. That's where I come from."

"So you'll have family around you?"

"My uncle has an unused cottage on his farm. It's pretty run down, but we'll have to make do."

"It could turn out to be a fresh start."

"I hated it there when I was growing up. I hitched a ride down here on a farmer's truck when I was twenty-two. I thought I was finished with it, never going back to the long winters and the black flies."

I walk over to the chair and collect my coat.

"Do you have a snow shovel, Mrs. Zajac? I'll clean off your steps."

Cynthia's desk is heaped with paperwork and she barely looks up when I walk in.

"Anything less than grievous bodily harm, you go in the queue."

"This is two minutes," I say.

"Speak."

"When Amber Zajac first went missing, we brought in the family computer. I think you said you would mirror the hard drive so we could give them back the computer."

She nods. "Sure."

"Can I have a look through it? I'm just looking for stray information that might help build our case against the kid."

"I heard that was a done deal?"

"Not quite. You never know."

"The mirror of his computer will be on a portable hard drive. I'll get Simon to find it and hook it up to a terminal for you."

Stan Zajac has preserved the records of his misery in a neat cascade of folders and sub-folders. He kept a log of every contact he made with the hospitals, the doctors, and his insurance company, Concare. Date, time, person, what happened on the call. He recorded his requests and their responses. No doubt he thought that he would build a cast-iron case of interlocking detail, a picture of a fair man asking for a fair shake. He tried hard to make sense of what was happening to him. The notes are all of neutral tone, quite different from the volatile man who wrote them. It takes me three hours to get a picture of what he went through.

When I'm finished doing that, I go on the internet and read some more about the late Nathan Weisz, CEO of Concare. The pictures of him are mostly corporate headshots, posed and professionally taken. He had a lot of white hair and full, soft lips like a girl. I can see that a certain kind of woman might have found him attractive, but my father would have said that he looked like he needed a slap. I watch a video of his presentation to Congress, opposing Obamacare.

I arrive at the reservoir ten minutes early. Susan Conover was at pains to make it clear that she wants her walk to begin at 4.30, not 4.35.

There are a lot of cars—a warmer front has melted the snow and brought out the exercise enthusiasts—runners using the fence rails for their warm-ups; cyclists fussing with mountain bikes, the usual plethora of Webster dogs.

"Mrs. Conover?"

"Hi, you're Detective Bradley? Call me Susan."

"Donna," I say, shaking her hand. She's a biggish girl but sturdy and vital. She needs to be; the dog is a powerful beast.

"Robert!" She tugs sharply on the leash. "He'll calm down once we're moving. Let's go."

"What kind of dog is that?"

"Ridgeback. They were bred in Africa for lion hunting, apparently."

"I can believe it."

The walk is a two mile circuit around the two reservoirs, and starts with a decent climb. I have to open my stride to keep up with her.

"I'm intrigued," she says. "You guys actually arrested Leonard Miller in connection with that girl's death, right?"

"Briefly, yes."

"Yet he's recommending to me that I talk to you? I would have thought he'd be mad at you."

"I guess we've come to understand each other better."

"This is definitely off the record, right?"

"Yes," I say. "When did you leave ConCare?"

"Just under a year ago."

"What was your job?"

"Claims. That's how I know Leonard. He's a freelance claims adjuster."

"And Mr. Miller said you'd become disillusioned?"

"Disillusioned. Yes, that's one way of putting it." Her smile is grim. "I was there twelve years. My father worked there. Some other members of my family, too. Nathan Weisz came five years ago. In that time, he's basically gutted everything the company was about."

"Businesses have to adapt, though?"

"Sure. It's become very short-term. Shareholder value, quarterly performance, blah, blah. But Nathan turned it into a company that exists purely to gouge its customers. Insurance can be good business for everyone if you just do it right. Everything he did was about how to get another few cents out of customers, how to confuse them, trick them, how to stop them claiming, how to collect premiums from the healthy ones and reject the ones who might actually need insurance."

She's walking faster and faster as she gets angry.

"I was actually in a meeting where the PR department had written a description of a new product and Nathan said to them, 'This document is too clear. You're making the limitations of cover too obvious.' He made them go back and write it with more complications and terms that no one understands so that people would just stop reading."

"Mr. Miller thinks it's possible that a disgruntled customer could have killed Weisz."

"By using the word disgruntled you're telling me you still don't get it. Some of these folks are not 'disgruntled'—their lives are destroyed."

"So you think it's possible?"

She shrugs. "People in that situation aren't rational any more. I've dealt with some of them myself. If you ask me what my first reaction was when I heard about him being killed? What goes around comes around. Seriously. Obviously, it's not justified or anything, but we need a change in this country." She laughs at herself. "Yeah, here I am, a suburban housewife walking her dog and talking revolution. It's not a contradiction. I'm not against making money. I'm against certain ways of making it. I'm against corporate conduct that destroys human values. I'm going to pull over here and let this other dog go past, because if this guy gets wound up there's a problem."

A soft rain has started to filter down, creating a patina on the surface of the reservoir.

"Do you know what Nathan Weisz paid himself last year?" Susan Conover says to me.

I shake my head.

"Sixty-two million. Now, he's not the only one, for sure, but if you were a customer who'd lost everything to your medical expenses, you might dwell on a figure like that."

"He used to give a heck of a lot to charity."

She wipes rain off her eyebrows and looks at me as if I'm a sweet but dense child.

"If a man who has a hundred dollars in the whole world gives away twenty dollars, that is an act of remarkable charity. When a man who has fifty million gives one million for a library, that is a calculated investment in his social and business network and his legacy. And an opportunity for his wife to wear a ten thousand dollar gown."

The rain is getting harder.

"Come on," she says. "We're going to run."

"What's going on?" asks my mother. I've turned up on her doorstep with a bag of groceries and a bottle of wine. Outside, gaunt trees besiege the house and the ground is thickly bedded with frozen piles leaves. I could not live here.

"Ma, you need to call Dad and tell him to get his ass up here and fix that roof leak. The stain on that wall has spread like six inches since I was last here. You can't let the place go."

"Yes, dear," she says.

Onion, bacon, capers, mushrooms, garlic, a can of pasta sauce. Penne.

"This is what you used to love when you were a kid," my mother says, as she watches me cook.

"When I was a fat kid."

"Well, now you're too skinny, so it's okay."

After dinner I wash up and she makes coffee. Then my mother curls her feet up on a sofa that hasn't been re-covered since I was born, and starts to crochet. She's become caught up in the crochet revival; her den is full of it. The pipes are noisy when the heating kicks in.

"I must bleed the radiators for you, Mom, remind me."

Some time goes by.

"There's something I want to tell you, Mom."

She doesn't look up from the crochet work. "You haven't been yourself recently."

"An officer I was dating was killed. Line of duty."

"When?"

"Back in August."

She purses her lips but passes it off as a response to a misstep in the crochet.

"Just dating? Or in love with?"

I can't answer. I have to squeeze my eyes. She wants to jump up and hug me, but we haven't been that way for many years.

"That's hard. I'm sorry. What was his name?"

"Bryan. I was going to tell you, I was planning to get you two together."

"I understand. You couldn't have known him very long."

"That's what's so weird. How did I put so much into that relationship in so little time? In many ways, we barely knew each other, but it's like I can't remember what I was without him. Was I walking around so lonely?"

"Well, I'm glad you came tonight."

For a few minutes the crochet work progresses in silence.

"Things are so screwed up, Mom."

"Well, naturally. That's a terrible thing to happen."

"Not just Bryan. I have ruined the life of a guy who wasn't guilty of anything. I made such a mess of an investigation that the kid who killed Amber, that teenage girl, is basically not going to pay for it. The girl's mother is being slowly eaten by some disease and her daughter's dead and her husband is crazy. This avalanche of shit comes down on her and she's the only person in the whole saga who hasn't complained about anything."

"The husband is mentally ill?"

"I don't know what a shrink would say. Can you go mad from guilt and humiliation? People go through so much pain and chaos and do things they can't control in the moment. It's ridiculous for us to judge them, but we have to. There isn't a single possible outcome in this case that you would call just. It makes me want to go do something completely different."

"No you don't. You love it. But you sound like you're exhausted, dear."

I get up, walk over the sofa she's sitting on, plunk down next to her and put my arm around her. She's getting smaller. She used to have very good posture, now she's showing the first signs of crumpling a bit. We sit like that for a while.

"I wish you'd move out of the woods and into town, Mom. Be closer to other people."

"I'm happy here," she says. "You should sleep over tonight. You've had quite a lot of wine."

"Too much hassle."

"Your bed's made up," she says. "I'll make hot chocolate." She extracts herself from under my arm and heads for the kitchen.

My old bedroom feels smaller. Same curtains, same lampshade, yellow marks on the walls where I used scotch tape for my posters. I remember looking out of this window onto these leafless tree limbs, trying to see down the road to the house by the pond, where they took the kids away from the parents. The mental image I have is of the kids being led away through the trees, as if they were being kidnapped by characters from fairy stories.

I'm in a deep sleep when my cell phone rings. 6.20 a.m. Still dark.

"Can you come?" Her voice is raspy.

"Mrs. Zajac? Is that you?"

"Can you come to the hospital? He wants to see you."

Turning left off Farmington onto the grounds of the UConn Health Center. I have been here three times in my life, all in the past two months, and all in connection with the Zajac family.

"Are you a visitor?" the psych ward receptionist asks me in a tone which suggests the preferred answer is no.

I show her my shield. "You have a patient named Stanislaw Zajac. He asked to see me. I investigated the death of his daughter recently. I'd like a brief on his condition before I see him."

The resident who briefs me is a pocket-sized Asian who looks about twelve. She reads rapidly from the chart. "The EMTs responded to a nine-one-one call at around nine-forty last night. Patient was semi-comatose on arrival. His wife had been out, she came home and found him. He was in the shower stall, but the water was not running. There was vomit in the stall."

"He took something?"

She nods. "The empty medicine containers included Lexapro and Welbutrin. Quantities consumed could not be determined so the protocol for massive overdose was followed. He was treated in emergency overnight and was stable this morning, so they transferred him here. He was evaluated by Dr. Wickham and is under observation for twelve hours."

She closes the file and looks up at me. I feel like a giraffe next to her.

"Observation?" I say. "For medical reasons or psychologically? Is he still considered a risk to himself?"

"Not medically, although he is still on IV fluids. Observation means that we can't determine the psychological risk yet. You should talk to Dr. Wickham, he'll be on rounds at eleven."

"But there's not someone sitting in the room with him the whole time?"

"No. Staff rotate through the room regularly. Also," she points at a row of monitor screens in the nurses' station, "there's a camera covering every bed. He's in room three," she says, to encourage me to get moving.

Stan Zajac is in bed, hooked up to an IV drip stand. Sheen of Vaseline around his mouth, which is red and swollen. The skin on his bony-beak face is tight and pale. It's his eyes that are changed—the crazy bird wildness has been replaced by the slack look of a man who's taken a beating.

Rosemary Zajac is in a chair next to the bed, slumped forward with her head on the raised mattress of the hospital bed. She jerks upright when she hears me enter. Neither of them say anything.

"The doctor told me you're going to be okay," I say to him.

That goes by him without any indication that he heard or understood me.

She stands, carefully, legs a little apart as if anticipating a dizzy spell. She rummages in her purse on the bedside unit for a hairbrush. She drags it harshly across her scalp a few times and her sparse white hair stands up with the static. Then she picks up the purse, turns away from the bed.

"I'll be in the visitors' lounge," she says, and pads toward the door. Her shoulders are like a wire hanger. The door closes behind her. Half a minute goes by while I stand next to the bed waiting for him to say something.

"What's going on, Mr. Zajac?"

"What's going on?" he says back at me, like he's trying English for the first time. I'm not convinced there's no medical consequences from the drug overdose; maybe he's got some sort of brain damage from the coma or something. He's conscious, but not fully with me. I remember Tony saying that Stan Zajac's war with God could only have one outcome.

"Your wife called me, she said you wanted to speak to me."

He's picking at the adhesive bandage taped over the IV tube on his forearm. Maybe I shouldn't crowd him. I walk away from the bed, over to the window. From here I can see all the way to the Connecticut River. I imagine there's quite a few property developers who think this is an expensive view to squander on people who can't get out of bed to see it.

"I only went there to talk to him." I think that's what he says. At least, that's what my body responds to. I do have several conscious reactions, but it's the visceral one that controls me. I swing around and take one long stride to the bed.

"Stop talking."

"I want to be free of this," he says.

I have to suppress a reflex to put my hand over his mouth.

"Shut up, Mr. Zajac."

He starts coughing violently. A few bright spots of blood fleck onto the white hospital linen. The door swings openly and a nurse walks in.

"Are you okay Mr. Zajac?" The camera.

She administers water from a cup with a straw.

"Did you excite him?" she says accusingly to me.

"No."

"Mr. Zajac? You must stay relaxed," she says with that enunciated clarity nurses use for people who are only half in this world. "Your throat is raw from the tube they used to pump your stomach. Do you understand?"

"Fine," he says.

She watches him for a moment, then checks his IV.

"Will you be long?" she says to me.

"Just a few minutes."

She gives me a look that starts the timer on that and walks out, leaving the door ajar. I go across and close it and then sit in the chair next to the bed.

"Mr. Zajac. Listen to me. Are you listening?"

He nods.

"You're not clear in your mind right now. I'm not taking any statement from you. Do you understand? Say yes."

"Yes."

"I want you to think about one thing only. Your wife needs you. She needs you with her now. She doesn't deserve any more pain. Do you understand?"

His mouth is starting to tremble.

"You get yourself straight, you take her up to Vermont and look after her, you forget everything else."

For a period we just look at each other. During which I wonder what else I can do with my life if they throw me out of the department.

I stand up. "I'm going now. I don't want to see you again."

Walking rapidly past the nurses' station, I hear Mrs. Zajac's voice calling me from down the corridor, but I keep moving. Driving down the hill from the hospital, I can see the Chief Medical Officer's building, where I watched Amber Zajac's autopsy.

When he drove there, it wasn't clear where the town road ended and the private driveway began. At the fork, he took the long loop to the right toward what looked like the main entrance. Then he thought he must have the address wrong, this looked like a small hotel or a convention center. What private home would have parking for ten cars, a half basketball court and a pool?

He parked his car neatly between the lines. The house towered over him as he approached the door. He pressed the doorbell and heard a melodious tones ripple through the interior. Nothing stirred. He turned and retraced his steps to the car. Then he remembered the satellite picture of the house on the internet. There was a large garden to the north of the house in a symmetrical pattern, so large he had thought it could only really be appreciated from that point of view, from high above. He wondered if Nathan Weisz went on the internet to look at his own garden.

He walked around the large house, along stepping stones through the flower beds. Weisz looked up as he approached. His face was red with effort and the heat. Sweat bloomed on his pink golfer's shirt.

As their eyes met, they seemed to know each other instantly.

"Who are you?" said Nathan Weisz.

"I want to tell you about my wife," Stan said.

JANUARY

"People who are up against it cross the line," says the fireman. He's absurdly handsome, like a recruiting poster. "That's what's happened here, I'll guarantee it. We just have to find the traces of the accelerant."

Tony and I are tramping around the blackened remains of a warehouse in the bottom southwestern corner of Webster, where the rail line from New York comes through. A low-rent commercial area with more than a few shuttered premises. Two inches of snow fell last night and it's a couple of degrees above freezing.

"So while you do that, we'll start looking at the owners," says Tony.

This will be our job for the next several weeks, trying to pin arson and insurance fraud on the owner of a company that hires out party equipment. We're walking back to the car when my phone rings.

"Bradley?" It's Pengelli. "Got a slot for you on a team tonight."

"Tonight? You know I've only done the basic, right? The secondary course is not till March."

"I know, this will be more like a watch-and-learn thing for you."

"Okay, I'm in."

"It wasn't optional," he says. "Dress warm. Twenty-two degrees tonight. You might be outdoors for a while."

When I tell Tony, he says, "So, basically you're going to become an action hero and I'm going to be left with the neat and tidy casework?"

"You love that stuff, don't you, old man?"

At 8 p.m., in the armory at the station, Pengelli issues me an automatic rifle and three clips, which I load myself. Night-vision goggles. Bulletproof vest. Then we drive south in his personal car.

"There'll be a briefing there," says Pengelli. "I'm going to give you some background. There are two pimps who run girls out of a motel on the Berlin Turnpike. Some girls are local runaways, some are imports. It's been going on for years. They do a suppression, it goes away, a year later it's on again."

"So this is a state op?"

"Combined, I think. Personnel from a couple of departments. I know the leader and I see an opportunity to blood you. I've stipulated that you're in a non line of fire role, you probably won't even see the targets until it's all over. But you'll get the feel of a live operation, feel of the team, the adrenaline, it's like a practice run."

The staging point is a Thai fast food place on the turnpike with the blinds pulled all the way down. Owner must owe someone a favor. There are twelve of us, one other female. I recognize two of the guys vaguely, must be from PDs around us. There's one guy who could be taken for a pimp himself, a Latino with a massive tattoo writhing up from under his hoodie, threatening to consume one side of his head. The op leader, guy with a lot of beard, hands out state police ID vests. I'm wearing thermal tights under loose cargo pants and a thermal top under two layers and I am sweating in the heated room. We pull chairs around a table for the brief.

The leader places two arrest photos on the table.

"These are your targets for tonight."

One white, one Latino.

"I'm going to hand over to Henry, who's been under cover with them." The leader points to Tattoo guy, the most unlikely Henry you'll ever see. Frankly, he's not that different than the targets.

Henry's voice is as modulated as a librarian's is. It's like a polite ventriloquist is tossing his voice into this guy who looks like a killer. "I think you all know we're going after some pimps. This area's been that way for years. But these two sweetie-pies moved here about a year ago from New Jersey and upped the stakes. We're talking about complete animals. They terrorize and drug girls of thirteen, fourteen and make them work every night. Their specialty is tattooing their own names on the back of their girls' necks—like a stock-keeping record. You're my product forever until you're dead. I've seen a photo of one of their girls with a dollar sign carved in here, right above her fanny. Not a tattoo, a scar from a knife. That photo was taken on the autopsy table.

"I've been getting tight with these guys for a few months by bringing them stolen cars they can rotate. Cars they think are clean but are actually carrying GPS locators. That's enabled us to get to know a lot more about them. I'm pretty confident that both of them are going to be on site tonight. I'm delivering them a Mercedes two-seater they've been licking their lips for."

"You draw from petty cash to buy that?" asks Pengelli.

"Product of a raid on a container warehouse in Boston. Was on its way to Brazil."

The leader puts a diagram plan of the motel grounds on the table.

"The way they work," says Henry, "they have four or five rooms here at the end of the block. The owner doesn't ask any questions. Whether he ever gets an actual, real motel guest is doubtful, but some cons know it as a place you can get a bed when you first come out. Our pimps operate from their cars in the parking lot. That's their escape route. If there's a raid they can get to their cars quickly and onto the turnpike for a run. The johns come to the cars, they pay, they get sent along to the rooms. One of the pimps runs the money in the car. The other one keeps discipline over the rooms."

"We're going to drive from here to this lot in front of the dollar store next door," says the leader. "It'll be mostly empty. From then on, synchronization is of the essence. You'll park, get out quietly and move to your positions, which I'll assign in a minute. When we're in place, Henry's going to drive in through the front entrance of the motel lot here and proceed on toward the back where their cars should be. That's our time to move, because the headlights of the Merc will temporarily blind anyone in that area in front of the rooms. Meanwhile, a town services truck is going to be staged just here, ready to drive across the gate and block any escape by vehicle. Riding behind the truck will be four vehicles with uniforms to help us process.

"Henry's going to park with the front of the white Mercedes sports pointing to the car they're using as home base. That's a focal point to be aware of. One of the targets will be in or near the car. Or they might both come over to the new Merc to check it out. When he's sure that both the pimps are on the premises, Henry will signal me electronically, and I dispatch the strike team. Okay, now I'm going to brief you separately by team."

The other female taps me on the shoulder and takes me aside.

"I'm Genevieve, state special services."

Big girl. No-shit eyes.

"Donna, Hi."

"You're going to be with me. We have two jobs. We're going to be the stopper group outside the motel, in case the targets get by the strike group and out into the road on foot. Our main job, as soon as we get the all clear is to get in there fast and secure the girls. We are not arresting them. We are securing them for their own safety and to give evidence later. But they won't know that. They're going to be terrified—of us, of the johns, of the pimps. They're probably going to be high. Some of these girls are pretty

281

disturbed individuals. So basically anything can happen. Now, Donna, you have to look after yourself in this situation. You do not want to be bitten or scratched by one of these girls, you get what I'm saying?"

"Sure."

"When we're done with the weapons, gloves on, keep them on while you're handling the girls. Watch your face. Talk to them all the time. Inform them you're police. Tell them you're safe, you're okay, relax, police, we're here to help you, say it over and over calmly and clearly. Be a calm but irresistible force." She looks me over. "Take your headgear off so they can see you're a female right away."

"How many will there be?"

"Henry's guessing not more than five. Some off duty girls might be in a spare room, sleeping or whatever. The uniform support will be coming in right behind us. As we secure each girl, we hand her off. We have to go room to room. Every room in the place. Okay?"

I nod. The adrenaline is starting to pulse. That beautiful, terrifying feeling.

The leader beckons us over to the map. "Donna. You and Gen are going to be out here, on the median between the two lanes of the turnpike, where you've got a clear view of the exit from the motel. The moment we go in, a patrol car is going to block this side of the turnpike so you don't have to think about any civilian car coming across you. Your line of sight is unobstructed and you've got no civilians beyond the target to worry about. It's a beautiful shooter set-up. I checked it myself this morning." He grabs my eyes with his and studies me. "I know this is your first assignment."

"Yes, sir."

"If one of those pimps comes out, it's shoot to kill. These savages are not escaping my operation. You ready for this?"

"I am, sir. Just one thing. How do we tell the pimps from the johns that might be running?"

"The pimps will have clothes on." He lets a beat go by. "I'm kidding you. It's not going to happen that way. The pimps will be out within thirty seconds of us going in, or they're not coming. We'll have them cuffed before the first john can get to the window."

"Okay."

"I saw your range scores. Out here, it's different, but the same. You'll be fine."

And off he goes to light the fire under the next team.

"Just so you know," says Genevieve, "I can't shoot for shit. So that part's on you."

Cool. Thanks for that.

We're in Genevieve's car directly across the turnpike from the motel. I'm going without the night glasses because they're a distraction and the entrance to the motel is sufficiently illuminated by the street lighting. With my thumb I check that the spring on the magazine clip is smooth before locking it into the rifle. I'm not bothering with the spare clips; if I fire at all it'll be five rounds max. I don't want to be weighed down when we're dealing with the girls. I remember what Bryan said about SWAT operations— just do your part like an athlete. Then the leader's voice is in my earpiece, "Ready." The metal of the rifle is cold. I can't have a glove on my trigger finger. I look at Genevieve. She smiles.

"Positions."

The whole machine goes into action at once. The white Mercedes comes almost soundlessly into view, swings into the lot entrance, its lights sweeping across the scene beyond, showing us a few cars and the doors of the rooms for an illuminated moment. As Genevieve and I cross the turnpike to the median, we see the strike team get out of their cars in the lot next to the motel and start moving. To my right I can see the town truck heading toward us, and the patrol car's roof lights come on as it blocks the road.

I'm bright with anticipation. Slip the safety. The throb of the town truck.

"Go!"

Eyes wide. Breathe normally. The strike team goes in at a run. As the shouting starts, the truck blocks our view of the scene. I bring the rifle to my shoulder. The team is shouting to confuse and intimidate. One loud shot. Definitely a rifle. Keep the gate in focus. Two quick shots. Silence.

"It's done." Leader's voice in my earpiece.

"Let's go," says Genevieve.

Running through the entrance, swing left toward the line of rooms. Sidestep the front desk clerk who's been roughly shepherded out by one of the strike team.

The door to the first room is unlocked, but the room is empty. The second door is standing ajar. Inside there's a white man pulling on his shoes. There's a heavy smell of disinfectant.

"Where is she?" Genevieve snaps.

He's trembling with shock. He points to the empty bed.

Genevieve steps across, kneels next to the bed, puts her head down under it. "It's okay," she says, "Police. We're here to help you." She looks back at me and gestures to the door. "Go on."

As I run to the next room I glance across the courtyard. In the swirl of activity I can see two men are down.

The door is locked. I beat my fist on it. "Open up! Police."

Nothing.

"Open up. We're not going to hurt you!"

At the next door down, a small face pops out and then ducks back. I get there before she can lock it again. My shoulder bursts the door back, knocking her down.

"It's okay, don't be frightened."

Two girls in the room, eyeing me like feral animals. One white, standing across the room by the window, ten ounces of assorted metalwork in her face. The one I knocked to the floor is Asian, the size of a ten-year-old. A rank odor in the room I've never known before.

"Take it easy, okay, we're here for your protection. You're not in trouble."

A female uniformed officer comes in behind me.

"You take the blond," I say.

I step slowly toward the Asian girl. Her eyes follow me but nothing else about her moves. I'm awash in adrenaline and it's hard to gear down. I put my hand on her arm.

"Come on, get up. You're okay."

I wrap my other hand around her wrist and hoist her to her feet. Her wrist is pencil thin, the weight of her no more than a cheap folding chair. In that absence of substance to her I find my outrage start to rise and I have to bite down on it.

"I'll take her," says an officer behind me.

"Come on, let's clear the second floor," says Genevieve.

Fifteen minutes later, Genevieve and I have accounted for all the rooms. Just four girls. Looking down onto the courtyard, now lit by the blaze of crime scene lighting, I can see the techs are already at work on the forensics. Loud voices and laughter from near the entrance where the SWAT team is standing—the release of tension in the team.

"Bradley." For a man his size, Pengelli moves like a ghost. "Come with me for a minute."

I follow him along the corridor and down the stairs onto the courtyard. He leads me through the working techs and the evidence markers toward the body of one of the men on the ground. The bullet hole in him is dead center of the sternum. His cell phone is next to him on the ground. He's wearing expensive boots.

I see Pengelli watching me. Quietly he says, "This is the guy that shot Bryan Zellinger."

We drive forty minutes back to the station in complete silence. Pengelli can be comfortable like that. When we get out of the car, all he says is, "Give me your stuff, I'll check it back in for you. You go home."

Sunday. It's freezing on the river. Everything is dirty blue and gray. Looking downstream I can't even tell where water ends and the dull sky begins. From the time we set out, my fingers wouldn't work properly. I struggled for ten minutes with the sticky zipper on my parka. I can't say I'm enjoying myself but Tony is invigorated by it. I can see him and his father doing this, years ago.

We traveled south toward Long Island Sound, but when we got onto the exposed water near the Middletown Bridge, the wind was just too cold. So we turned back and anchored in the shelter of a bluff. I'm stuffing the leftovers of the packed lunch I brought into a plastic bag. I can't wait to get my gloves back on.

"It wouldn't have gone down like that if he wasn't a cop killer," I say.

"He got his due process. In Kentucky we had a phrase for that kind of situation. Exterminating circumstances."

He wipes his fingers on his pants and stands up.

"We should get going before the weather gets worse. You want to drive back?"

"Sure."

The wind and water sting my face but I like feeling the power of the boat in my hands.

Acknowledgements

I would like to thank Detective Thomas J. Martin, Retired, South Windsor Police Services for reading many, many pages and guiding me to a better understanding of police procedure. Any remaining errors are all mine. Additional valuable insight was kindly provided by Brian W. Kelly, Lieutenant, Retired, Hartford, CT Police Dept., and by H. Wayne Carver II, M.D.

Eileen Albrizio helped me see my storyline and my characters and also edited the manuscript. Her contribution was invaluable.

My thanks to the friends who read and commented on drafts of the manuscript and contributed to its growth. My brother Robin was the one who stopped me abandoning this after 30 pages. And I want to make special mention of the Fiction Writers' Group at the West Hartford Library, where parts of this project were dissected and improved.

Finally, nothing would be possible without Sandi.

- P. J. Lee.